D1498650

DOM CASMURRO

DOM CASMURRO

A Novel

Joaquim Maria Machado de Assis

Translated by
Margaret Jull Costa and Robin Patterson

Liveright Publishing Corporation

*A Division of W. W. Norton & Company
Celebrating a Century of Independent Publishing*

For information about permission to reproduce selections from this book,
write to Permissions, Liveright Publishing Corporation, a division of
W. W. Norton & Company, Inc., 500 Fifth Avenue, New York, NY 10110

For information about special discounts for bulk purchases, please contact
W. W. Norton Special Sales at specialsales@wwnorton.com or 800-233-4830

Manufacturing by Lake Book Manufacturing
Book design by Brooke Koven
Production manager: Julia Druskin

ISBN 978-1-324-09070-0

Liveright Publishing Corporation, 500 Fifth Avenue, New York, N.Y. 10110
www.wwnorton.com

W. W. Norton & Company Ltd., 15 Carlisle Street, London W1D 3BS

1 2 3 4 5 6 7 8 9 0

Introduction

Bento (or Bentinho) Santiago, the narrator of the elusive, enigmatic *Dom Casmurro*, is writing his account at some point during the 1890s, and the novel itself was published in 1899. However, as so often in Machado de Assis's work, the main events being described take place several decades earlier, starting in 1857 when Bento was fifteen, and extending to the breakdown of his marriage in 1872.

The action of the novel takes place entirely within the city of Rio de Janeiro and its immediate environs. Rio itself had changed markedly in those intervening years from a city that was still essentially colonial in nature to a vibrant and increasingly self-confident metropolis, abuzz with theater, opera, salons, and social life. The quiet, somewhat isolated childhood that Bento is trying to recall is, then, a lost world, and seems to bear no resemblance to that bustling age.

Despite being perhaps Rio's greatest chronicler, Machado rarely describes the city overtly, and he writes, first and foremost, for a reader who knows the city as intimately as he does. Place names are used sparingly, often to tell us about the characters and their social status. Hence Rua de Matacavalos, Bento's childhood home, was, in the 1850s, one of the most desirable addresses in the city, but was soon to be eclipsed by the newer, more fashionable neighborhoods of Glória, Catete, and Flamengo, curling southward along the shoreline of the bay, where the focus of Bento's life shifts following his marriage. Engenho Novo, where Bento lives in later years, was a respectable but much less prestigious inland suburb that developed following the building of the railways.

Bento's use of old street names also marks the passing of time, emphasizing the sense of a city that no longer existed when the narrator is telling his story, and exists even less today: Rua de Matacavalos was renamed Rua do Riachuelo in 1865, and Rua dos Barbonos (Bento's walk home from the seminary in Chapter LXVII) became Rua Evaristo da Veiga in 1870. Indeed the São José seminary itself, one of the oldest in the Americas, was gone by the time Bento was describing it—the seminary had moved to the outskirts of the city, its former buildings had been abandoned, and the entire hill that it stood on, the Morro do Castelo (Castle Hill), which had been the very nucleus of the colonial city, would eventually be razed to the ground in a series of grandiose urban improvements. Even the newer neighborhoods of Glória and Flamengo were on the cusp of dramatic urbanization, with their respective beaches, so central to the novel, soon to be buried beneath the first of a series of sweeping coastal esplanades that so define modern Rio.

Politically, too, Bento was looking back over a period of fundamental change. The ending of slavery had begun, painfully slowly, in 1871, and abolition was finally achieved in 1888. Within a year the monarchy had gone, too, and Brazil soon became a republic, although most of the old elite remained very much in charge. All of this is alluded to in the novel, but, as always with Machado, you need to look carefully.

Machado is equally circumspect in advancing any kind of

explicit social critique: his own position depended almost entirely on government patronage (see the Biographical Note at the end of the book), and his readers were mostly from the social class we might expect him, the mixed-race grandson of a freed slave, to criticize. And yet it is there in the various references to the slaves owned by Bento's mother, perhaps most clearly in Escobar and Bento's offhand conversation about the slaves' names—each beginning with a different letter of the alphabet and differentiated by offensive nicknames for the convenience of their masters. Machado leaves it to readers to draw their own conclusions.

So, while Machado did move away from naturalism and realism, largely eschewing physical descriptions, as well as any neat beginning-middle-and-end plot, he still tells us much about the society of the day. And in getting rid of the omniscient third-person narrator, he frees up his narrator to go off on tangents, to address the reader directly, and to be completely partial in his account of events. Indeed, he proves to be a most unreliable narrator. In the very first chapter, and in the first of many obfuscations, he tells the reader not to bother looking in dictionaries for the meaning of his nickname, *casmurro*, saying: "You won't find the sense in which the common folk use it, for they use the word to mean someone silent and self-absorbed." Now, this is guaranteed to send any reader, and certainly any translator, scurrying to the dictionary to find out if this is true. Well, modern dictionaries give two senses, one of which is pretty much the one Bento gives, which clearly fits his older, solitary lifestyle: glum and withdrawn. (Some say that Machado himself invented this definition, which then made its way into the dictionaries—life imitating art indeed.) The other, more established definition (the one that Bento is forlornly trying to hide from us, but which every reader would have known) is used to describe someone who is stubborn and tends to fixate on one idea. And here, perhaps, is revealed the true Bento, his fatal flaw, for one of the first things he tells us is that he now lives alone in a house that he has had built as an exact replica of his childhood home, his aim being "to connect those two points in my life and restore adolescence to my old age." His memoir is also an attempt to do just that. Alas:

> If all I was missing were other people, fine, a man can more or less console himself for such losses, but I myself am missing, and that lacuna is everything. What's left, if I can put it like this, resembles the dye one applies to beard and hair, and which merely preserves the habitus exterior, as they say in autopsies; the interior remains impervious to dye.

So Bento is withdrawn *and* obsessive. He is also, in a sense, the child of an obsession: his mother is determined to keep the vow she made to God when Bento was conceived, namely, to have him ordained a priest. Later, he becomes obsessed with marrying Capitu, the girl-next-door. And when he does marry her, he becomes convinced that she has been unfaithful. So, yes, self-absorbed, reclusive, stubborn, and obsessive. The thin-skinned young man on the bus was quite right when he chose that nickname, adding further irony with that "Dom," a title usually only used by royalty and the most elevated ranks of the clergy.

And having been misled by our narrator in the first chapter, can we ever trust him again? Everything and everyone are presented to us through his eyes. There are, as usual, many literary references, everything from Goethe to Dante, from Montaigne to Camões, from the Bible to Homer. And, of course, Shakespeare. Since this is a book about jealousy and obsession, it is inevitable that Othello will get a mention, and he does. Bento's Desdemona, Capitu, is intelligent, savvy, and eager to learn, be it Latin or drawing or music, and those qualities are initially deemed admirable, but later come to be seen as potentially dangerous and perfidious—her eyes are described by family friend José Dias (in his anti-Capitu phase) as being "like a gypsy's eyes, oblique and sly," and later by Bento himself as "eyes with an undertow."

Shakespeare's play is a tragedy because Othello, a military commander and hero, is brought low by the vengeful connivings of Iago, but also by his own credulity and insecurity. But Bento is no hero, and he needs no Iago to stoke his suspicions;* his credulity and insecurity are more than enough to ruin his marriage and his own happiness. He is all too easily swayed, be it by an overheard conversation or by two names scrawled on a plaster wall. The mixture of dark and light, humor and cruelty, is very Shakespearean, but Bento's life is more bourgeois farce than tragedy. Or perhaps, as the disgruntled Italian tenor put it in Chapter IX, an opera with words by God and music by Satan.

Machado slyly draws us into Bento's story, leaving us full of uncertainties, convinced only of the shifting, unpindownable nature of human beings. When exactly, and where, did Capitu and Escobar meet to discuss exchanging the money she had saved from household expenses? And what is Escobar doing at the front door when Bento returns early from the theater, having gone there alone because Capitu is, supposedly, ill? And what is the meaning of Sancha's ardent gaze when the two young couples gather at her and Escobar's house one evening? And what do we make of Bento and Escobar's intimate and at times ambiguous friendship? And

---

*   As Helen Caldwell (1904–1987), the noted American scholar, translator, and author of several groundbreaking critical works on Machado de Assis, points out, the narrator's name, Bento Santiago, contains words meaning "blessed" and "saintly," as well, of course, as the name "Iago."

why does Dona Glória suddenly start behaving so coldly toward Capitu, who has previously been such a favorite? And, of course, the big question: Did Capitu have an affair with Escobar or did she not? Machado's aim, it seems, is to raise all these questions but to provide no answers. He plays with us much like the cat that has caught the mouse in Chapter CX. Like everyone else, we watch the mouse's flailing legs, then Machado chases cat and mouse away. Like Ezequiel we cry:

"Oh, Papa!"
"What's wrong? It'll have eaten the mouse by now."
"Exactly, but I wanted to watch."

Yes, we want to watch. Machado turns us all into jealous husbands, and we, too, begin to suspect everything and everyone.

Not surprisingly, generations of readers and critics have come to wildly different interpretations of the novel, and each generation's differing reactions have perhaps told us as much about ourselves and our own times as about Bento and his world. Is Capitu a wronged woman, falsely accused and cruelly punished by her deluded husband? Or is she cunning and manipulative, giving as good as she gets? Or was there something else that went wrong in their marriage, indeed was it doomed from the very start?

One of the tantalizingly few pieces of information we have on Machado's own personal life is that he expressed a dim view of first loves, writing to his fiancée Carolina (his third love, and the love of his life), and citing Madame de Staël's *Corinne*, that "first loves are not the strongest because they are born simply out of the need to love." Still more tantalizing, or perhaps simply salacious, are the rumors that have surfaced from time to time that Machado had an affair with the wife of his close friend and fellow novelist

José de Alencar (who is mentioned in Chapter LXXIII), and that he was the real father of Alencar's son Mário, who, apparently, bore an uncanny physical resemblance to Machado. The truth of those rumors will, of course, never be known—something which, in itself, finds echoes in the plot of this novel. Perhaps it is simply one more puzzle in this, Machado's most perplexing novel.

—*Margaret Jull Costa and Robin Patterson*

DOM CASMURRO

Chapter I / *About the title*

ONE NIGHT, on the train back from the city to Engenho Novo, I happened to meet a young man from around these parts, with whom I had a nodding acquaintance. He greeted me, sat down next to me, spoke about this and that, everything from the moon to politics, and ended up reciting a few poems he had written. The journey was a short one, and the poems may not have been entirely bad; since, however, I was rather tired, I did occasionally nod off, and that was enough for him to stop reading and put his poems back in his pocket.

"Oh, please, do go on," I said, opening my eyes.

"No, I'd finished anyway," he murmured.

"Charming poems."

He made as if to take them out of his pocket again, but stopped; he was clearly most offended. The next day, he started making rude comments about me, and ended up giving me the nickname *Dom Casmurro*. The people around here, who dislike my gloomy, reclusive, silent habits, embraced the nickname and, eventually, it stuck. Even this did not upset me. I told my friends in the city about it, and they, as a joke, also began calling me by that nickname, some even addressed letters to me under that name: "Dom Casmurro, I'll be dining with you on Sunday." "I'm off to Petrópolis, Dom Casmurro, staying at that same house in Renânia. How about leaving that cave of yours in Engenho Novo and spending a couple of weeks with me up there?" "My dear Dom Casmurro, don't go thinking you can wriggle out of coming to the theater tomorrow; you can spend the night here; I'll provide a box at the theater, tea, and a bed; the only thing I won't provide is the girl."

Don't go looking up *"casmurro"* in any dictionaries. You won't find the sense in which the common folk use it, for they use the word to mean someone silent and self-absorbed. The *"Dom"* is ironic, as if I were giving myself airs and graces. And all because I fell asleep! Anyway, I couldn't come up with a better title for my story; if I fail to find another by the end of the book, *Dom Casmurro* will have to do. The poet on the train will know then that I bear him no ill will. And given that the title is his, he can, with a small leap of the imagination, consider that the book is also his. There are books that owe little more than that to their authors, some not even that much.

Chapter II / *About the book*

NOW THAT I'VE EXPLAINED the title, I will set about writing the book. First, though, let me explain what it was that prompted me to take up my pen.

I live alone, with one servant. The house I live in is my own; I had it custom-made, on a whim so bizarre that it rather embarrasses me to set it down in print, but here goes. One day, some years ago now, I decided to re-create in Engenho Novo the house where I grew up—in what was then Rua de Matacavalos—reproducing the exact appearance, both internal and external, of that other, now-vanished house. Both builder and decorator carried out my instructions to the letter: it's the same two-story house, three windows at the front, veranda at the back, the same bedrooms and reception rooms. In the main room, the decoration on the ceiling and the walls is also more or less the same: here and there a few garlands of tiny flowers being borne along in the beaks of some large birds. In each of the four corners of the ceiling, there are figures representing the seasons, and in the center of each wall, plaster roundels of Caesar, Augustus, Nero, and Masinissa, with their names underneath . . . Why those particular figures, I have no idea. They were already there when we moved to the house in Rua de Matacavalos and dated from the previous decade. It was obviously fashionable then to add a classical touch with figures from ancient times painted in bright colors. Everything else is pretty much the same too. I have a small backyard, some flower beds, a vegetable plot, a casuarina tree, a well, and a washtub. I use old crockery and old furniture. Now, as then, there is the same contrast between life inside, which is peaceful, and life outside, which is noisy.

My obvious aim was to connect those two points in my life and restore adolescence to my old age. Well, sir, I failed to restore what once was and what I once was. As in everything, the face might be the same, but the physiognomy is different. If all I was missing were other people, fine, a man can more or less console himself for such losses, but I myself am missing, and that lacuna is everything. What's left, if I can put it like this, resembles the dye one applies to beard and hair, and which merely preserves the habitus exterior, as they say in autopsies; the interior remains impervious to dye. A certificate declaring I was twenty years old might, like all forged documents, deceive strangers, but it could not deceive me. My remaining friends are of recent date; the old ones have all gone off to study the geology of graveyards. As for women friends, some

I've known for fifteen years, others less, and almost all of them firmly believe in their continuing youth. A few of them would have others believe this, too, but the language they speak often requires one to consult the dictionary, which can become wearisome.

Besides, a different life does not necessarily mean a worse life; it's simply different. In certain respects, my former life does now appear to me as being devoid of the many charms I thought it had; it's also true to say that it has lost many of the thorns that made it so painful, and I do retain a few sweet, enchanting memories. Anyway, the fact is that I go out very little and speak even less. Few distractions. Most of my time is spent gardening and reading; I eat well and sleep fairly well too.

However, since everything eventually grows tiresome, the monotony of this life did finally wear me down. I needed a change, and it occurred to me that I could write a book. Jurisprudence, philosophy, and politics occurred to me as possible subjects, but I simply could not summon up the energy. Then I considered writing a *History of the Suburbs*, nothing as dry as Father Luís Gonçalves dos Santos's memoir of the city; it would be a modest work, but would initially require documents and dates, all very long and arid. It was then that the painted busts on the walls began to speak and tell me that, since they were unable to bring back those past times, I should pick up my pen and write about them. Perhaps the act of writing would give me the illusion of retrieving my lost youth, and the shades of the past would brush lightly past me, as they did the poet, not the one on the train, but the author of *Faust*: Ah, do you come again, you restless shades?

I was so enthused by this idea that, even now, the pen trembles in my hand. Yes, Nero, Augustus, Masinissa, and you, great Caesar, thank you for encouraging me to set down my thoughts. I am most grateful for your advice, and will write whatever memories come to me. In this way, I will relive what I have lived, and will thus prepare my hand for some work of greater note. Yes, let us begin by evoking a famous November afternoon, one I will never forget. I have known many other afternoons, some better, some worse, but that particular afternoon has never faded from my mind. As you will see.

Chapter III / *The revelation*

I WAS ABOUT TO ENTER the room when I heard my name mentioned, and so I hid behind the door. The house was that original house in Rua de Matacavalos, the month was November, the year, well, yes, it was quite some time ago, but I refuse to change the dates of my life simply to please people who dislike old stories; the year was 1857.

"Dona Glória, are you still determined to send our Bentinho to the seminary? If so, it's high time you did, especially since there might well be a problem."

"A problem?"

"Yes, a major problem."

My mother asked what that problem could be. After thinking for a few moments, José Dias went to see if there was anyone listening in the hallway, and, since he did not spot me in my hiding place behind the door, he returned and, lowering his voice, explained that the problem lay in the house next door, with the Pádua family.

"The Pádua family?"

"I've been meaning to say something about this for some time, but didn't dare. It doesn't seem right to me that our Bentinho should spend his time huddled in corners with *Tartaruga's* daughter; *that* is the problem. If they should fall in love, you'll have a very hard time separating them."

"I really don't think so . . . What do you mean by 'huddled in corners'?"

"That's just a manner of speaking. I mean whispering to each other, always together. Bentinho barely leaves her house. The girl's a flibbertigibbet, and her father, of course, turns a blind eye; well, he'd be perfectly happy if things did go that way . . . Now, I can tell from your face what you're thinking, senhora. You don't believe in such scheming, you think everyone is as pure of heart as you."

"But, Senhor José Dias, I've seen the two of them playing together, and I've certainly never seen anything to arouse such suspicions. Besides, they're still so young. Bentinho is barely fifteen, and Capitu turned fourteen last week; they're just children. Don't forget, they were brought up together, after that great flood ten years ago, when the Pádua family lost almost everything; that's how we first got to know them. And you want me to believe . . . Cosme, what do you think?"

Uncle Cosme responded with a "Huh!" which, translated, meant: "It's all in José Dias's imagination; the children are enjoying themselves, I'm enjoying myself. Now, where's the backgammon?"

"I agree. I think you're mistaken, Senhor José Dias."

"Possibly, senhora. I very much hope you're right, but believe me, I have only spoken now after giving the matter a great deal of thought—"

"You're right, though, it really is high time," said my mother, interrupting him. "I'll try to get him into the seminary as soon as possible."

"As long as you haven't given up on the idea of making him a priest, that's the main thing. Bentinho must do as his mother wishes. A man can rise very high in the Brazilian church. Let's not forget that a bishop presided over the Constituent Assembly, and Father Feijó was Regent of the Empire—"

"Regent, my eye!" said Uncle Cosme, succumbing to old political resentments.

"I'm sorry, sir, I'm not defending anyone, I'm merely stating facts. All I'm saying is that the clergy still have an important role to play in Brazil."

"What you need is a good thrashing at backgammon. Go and fetch the board. As for the boy, if he's destined to be a priest, then it's certainly best that he doesn't start saying mass to himself behind doors. But, sister, does he really need to be a priest?"

"I made a promise, and promises must be kept."

"I know you made a promise . . . But a promise like that . . . I don't know . . . When it comes down to it . . . What do *you* think, Cousin Justina?"

"Me?"

"The truth is, everyone knows what's best for themselves," Uncle Cosme went on. "Only God knows what's best for everyone. But a promise made all those years ago . . . Now what's wrong, Glória? Are you crying? Is this really something worth shedding tears over?"

My mother blew her nose and did not respond. I seem to recall that Cousin Justina stood up and went over to her. A long silence fell, during which I was on the verge of stepping into the room, but something stronger than me, some other emotion, stopped me . . . I couldn't hear what Uncle Cosme said next. Cousin Justina was saying: "Come, now, Cousin Glória!" José Dias was apologizing: "If I'd known how you'd react, I would never have spoken, but I did so out of respect, esteem, and affection, to fulfill a very painful duty, the *most* painful of duties . . ."

Chapter IV / *The most painful of duties!*

JOSÉ DIAS LOVED superlatives. It was his way of giving ideas a monumental feel; in the absence of any ideas, they served as a way of prolonging a sentence. He got up and went to fetch the backgammon, which was in another room. I pressed still closer to the wall and watched him pass by in his starched white trousers, trouser straps, jacket, and stiff cravat. He was one of the last men in Rio, and possibly the world, to wear trouser straps. He wore his trousers slightly short, so they were always stretched tight. The black satin cravat, with its steel stiffener inside, immobilized his neck; such was the fashion at the time. On him, the cotton jacket, the light, homely vest, looked like formal attire. He was thin and gaunt, his hairline just beginning to recede; he would have been about fifty-five. He moved at his usual slow pace, not the laggardly pace of the lazy, but a logical, measured slowness, a complete syllogism, the premise before the consequence, the consequence before the conclusion. The most painful of duties indeed!

Chapter V / *The retainer*

HE DID NOT ALWAYS walk in that slow, stiff manner. He could also be quite brisk in his movements, was often quick and nimble, and appeared equally at home in both modes. Then again, he could laugh loudly if necessary, a humorless, but infectious guffaw, so much so that cheeks, teeth, eyes, his whole face, his whole being, the whole world seemed to be laughing. At moments of great seriousness, however, he was very, very serious.

He had lived with us as a kind of retainer for many years; my father was still living on the old family plantation in Itaguaí, and I had just been born. One day, José Dias turned up claiming to be a homeopathic doctor; he carried with him a manual and a medicine chest. There was a terrible outbreak of fever at the time; José Dias cured the plantation overseer and one of the female slaves, and refused any remuneration. My father then proposed that he should stay on and be paid a small wage. José Dias declined, saying it was only right that he should instead go minister to the poor in their straw huts.

"There's nothing to stop you from traveling farther afield. Go where you like, but live here with us."

"I'll come back in three months' time."

He was back two weeks later, and, while he accepted food and lodging, he refused any form of payment, apart from any gifts he might be given on high days and holidays. When my father was elected deputy and moved to Rio with our family, José Dias went, too, and was given a room in one of the outbuildings. One day, there was another outbreak of fever in Itaguaí, and my father asked him to go back to the estate and tend to our slaves. José Dias said nothing at first, then he sighed and finally admitted that he was not a doctor. He had taken that title in order to advertise the new science of homeopathy, and had only done so after studying long and hard; his conscience, however, would not allow him to take on more patients.

"But you have cured people before."

"Yes, I think I did, but it would be truer to say that the remedies in the books did the healing. Yes, *they* did it, with God's help. Yes, that's the honest truth, as God is my witness. I was a mere charlatan . . . No, don't deny it. My motives may have been, and indeed were, honorable. Homeopathy is the truth, and in order to serve that truth, I lied; but it's time now to set the record straight."

My father did not dismiss him then, as José Dias asked him to, for my father could no longer do without him. José Dias had the gift of making himself welcome and indispensable; his absence was felt as much as if he were a member of the family. When my father died, he was plunged into grief, or so I was told. I can't remember. My mother was very grateful to him, and would not allow him to abandon his room in the outbuilding; after the seventh-day mass, he went to bid her farewell.

"No, stay, José Dias."

"If that is your wish, senhora."

My father left him a small legacy in his will: a few investments and some words of praise. He copied out those words, framed them, and hung them in his room above his bed. "This is the best possible investment," he would often say. Over time, he acquired a certain authority within the family, or at least a degree of influence. Not that he abused this, and he knew how to offer his opinions deferentially. He was, after all, a friend, not the best of friends, perhaps, but then not everything is for the best in this world. And don't imagine that he had the soul of a subaltern; when he bowed, he did so in a calculated manner, not because it came naturally to him. His clothes lasted him for ages; unlike some people who can ruin a brand-new suit in a matter of days, he wore his old suit carefully brushed and with not a crease in sight, painstakingly mended and buttoned up, revealing a poor but modest elegance. He read books, albeit rather hastily, but was sufficiently well read to enliven an evening at home or an after-dinner conversation, or to explain some phenomenon, to speak of the effects of heat and cold, of the poles—North and South—and of Robespierre. He frequently described a journey he had made to Europe and confessed that, were it not for us, he would willingly return there; he had friends in Lisbon, but, as he always said, our family was everything to him, next to God.

"Next to or below?" Uncle Cosme asked him one day.

"Oh, below, of course," said José Dias in reverent tones. And my mother, who was very devout, smiled approvingly, pleased to see him set God in his rightful place. José Dias nodded gratefully. My mother would give him a little money now and then, and Uncle Cosme, who was a lawyer, entrusted him with copying out various legal papers.

Chapter VI / *Uncle Cosme*

UNCLE COSME had lived with his sister, my mother, since she was widowed. By then, he, too, had been widowed, as had their cousin Justina; it was a household of the widowed.

Fortune often plays tricks on nature. Brought up to lead the tranquil life of a capitalist, Uncle Cosme did not grow rich as a lawyer: he merely got by. He had his chambers in what used to be Rua das Violas, near the courthouse, where the old prison, the Aljube, once stood. He was a criminal lawyer, and José Dias never missed one of Uncle Cosme's closing speeches for the defense. He would help him off with his robes, always heaping him with fulsome praise. At home, he would give an account of the arguments on both sides, and Uncle Cosme, despite a pretense of modesty, would nod and smile proudly.

He was a plump, heavily built man, always short of breath and with very sleepy eyes. One of my earliest memories is of watching him, every morning, mounting the mule that my mother had given him and which carried him to the office. The slave who had fetched the creature from the stable would hold the reins, while my uncle placed one foot in the stirrup; this was followed by a minute of rest and reflection. Then he would give an upward push, the first, and his body would seem about to lift off the ground, but then didn't; a second push, again to no avail. Finally, after a few long seconds, Uncle Cosme would gather up all his strength, mental and physical, and give one last upward thrust, and this time would land on the saddle. It was rare for the mule not to give some sign that it had just received the weight of the world on its back. Uncle Cosme would then settle his ample posterior on the saddle, and the mule would set off at a trot.

The other thing I will never forget is what he did to me one afternoon. Although I had been born in the countryside (which I left when I was two), and despite the customs of the time, I did not know how to ride, and was afraid of horses. So Uncle Cosme picked me up and plonked me down on the back of the mule. Finding myself so high up (I was nine at the time), alone and helpless, with the ground far below, I started screaming desperately: "Mama! Mama!" Pale and trembling, she rushed to my aid, convinced that I was being murdered, and immediately pulled me down from the mule, hugged and comforted me, while her brother asked:

"Surely a great big boy like him isn't afraid of a tame mule!"

"He's not used to it."

"Well, he'll have to get used to it. If he becomes a priest and ends up as a country padre, he'll certainly need to know how to ride; and for as long as he's still here in town and not yet a priest, if he wants to cut a dash like the other young men and still doesn't know how to ride, well, he'll have you to blame for that, sister."

"Let him blame me, then. I'm just afraid for him, that's all."

"Oh, really! Afraid!"

The fact is that I only learned how to ride much later on, not because I wanted to but because I didn't want to admit that I couldn't. "Ah, now he'll start chasing after the girls," they said when I started taking lessons. The same could not be said of Uncle Cosme. Riding for him was an old habit and a necessity. He no longer chased after anyone. They say that, when he was a young man, he caught the eye of many a lady, as well as being quite the political hothead. However, the years had carried off most of his ardor, both sexual and political, and his portliness put paid to any other aspirations, both public and private. Now he simply did his job, although with little enthusiasm. He spent his leisure hours either staring into space or playing backgammon, and, occasionally, telling jokes.

Chapter VII / *Dona Glória*

MY MOTHER was a kindly woman. She was just thirty-one when her husband, Pedro de Albuquerque Santiago, died, and she could have gone back to Itaguaí. She chose not to, however, preferring to stay close to the church where my father was buried. She sold the family plantation and the slaves, bought a few more whom she sent out to work or else put out for hire, purchased a dozen or so properties and some government bonds, then withdrew to the house in Rua de Matacavalos, where she had spent her last two years as a married woman. She was the daughter of a lady from Minas Gerais, who was herself descended from a lady from São Paulo, the Fernandes family.

Now, in the year of our Lord 1857, Dona Maria da Glória Fernandes Santiago was forty-two years old. She was still young and pretty, but insisted on concealing what remained of her youth, however hard nature tried to preserve it from the ravages of time. She always wore the same plain dark dress, with a black shawl folded into a triangle and pinned with a cameo. She wore her hair parted in the middle and caught back with an old tortoiseshell comb, and she occasionally donned a frilly white cap. She would bustle quietly about in her flat leather shoes, overseeing all the household tasks from morning to night.

Over there on the wall I have a portrait of her hanging beside a matching portrait of my father, just as in the other house. The paint has darkened over time, but it still gives a fair impression of them both. I don't remember him at all, apart from a vague recollection that he was tall and had long hair; in the painting he has round eyes that follow me everywhere, an effect that astonished me as a child. He is wearing a black ruffled cravat, he's clean-shaven, apart from a small section just beside his ears. My mother's portrait shows how very pretty she was. She was twenty then, and is clasping a flower between her fingers. In the painting, she appears to be offering the flower to her husband. If conjugal happiness can be compared to the lottery, then what you can read in their faces is that they won their happiness with a joint ticket.

I conclude that lotteries should not, therefore, be abolished. No winner has yet accused lotteries of being immoral, just as no one has yet dubbed Pandora's box evil, because hope was left inside, and hope must be somewhere. Here they are, the happily married couple of yesteryear, the fortunate, loving couple who left this life for the next, doubtless to continue their dream. When I grow weary of the lottery and Pandora, I look up at them and forget about wasted tickets and that fateful box. The portraits are as good as the originals. My mother, shown offering a flower to her husband, seems to be saying: "I am all yours, my handsome chevalier!" My father, looking straight at the viewer, is saying: "See how much this young lady loves me . . ." I do not know if they suffered illnesses or anxieties, just as I do not know if they met with any sorrows: I was a child and, before that, had not even been born. After he died, I do remember that she cried a lot, but here are their two portraits, their young faces unsullied by time. They are like photographs of happiness.

Chapter VIII / *It's time*

BUT IT'S TIME TO RETURN to that November afternoon, a clear, cool afternoon, as tranquil as our house and the part of the street in which we lived. It really did mark the beginning of my life; everything that had happened before was like the actors putting on their makeup and their costumes before coming onstage, the lights being lit, the violins tuning up, the whole orchestra . . . I was about to begin my own opera. "Life is an opera," an old tenor used to say to me; he was Italian, but he lived and died in Rio . . . And one day, he explained this definition so convincingly that I believed it. Perhaps I should give it here; it will only take up a chapter.

=== Chapter IX / *The opera*

BY THEN, HE HAD NO VOICE, although he insisted that he did. "I'm simply out of practice, that's all," he would say. Whenever a new company arrived from Europe, he would go and see the impresario and lay before him all the injustices of heaven and earth; the impresario would then commit a further injustice, and the singer would leave, railing against the iniquities of life. He still sported the mustache he had worn in his various roles. And despite his age, whenever he walked he looked as if he were off to pay court to a Babylonian princess. He would sometimes hum an aria that was even older than him, or almost; and when someone sings softly like that, it feels as if all voices have their possibilities. He sometimes came here to dine with me. One night, after drinking a great deal of Chianti, he trotted out his usual definition of life, and when I said that life could as easily be an opera as a sea voyage or a battle, he shook his head and replied:

"No, life is an opera, and a grand opera. The tenor and the baritone compete for the favors of the soprano, in the presence of the bass and the other members of the company, apart from when it's the soprano and the contralto competing for the tenor, in the presence of the same bass and the same members of the company. There are numerous choruses, plenty of dancing, and the orchestration is excellent . . ."

"But, my dear Marcolini . . ."

"What?"

And after taking a sip of liqueur, he put down his glass and told me the story of creation, which I summarize below.

God is the poet. The music is by Satan, a young maestro with a great future, who trained in the conservatoire of heaven. He could not stand his rivals, Michael, Raphael, and Gabriel, winning all the prizes. It may be, too, that the overly sweet, mystical music of his fellow students was abhorrent to his essentially tragic genius. He plotted a rebellion, which was foiled just in time, and he was expelled from the conservatoire. Things would have gone no further had God not written an opera libretto, which he then discarded, feeling that such passing entertainments were unsuited to his eternal nature. Satan took the libretto with him down into hell. Intending to show that he was better than the others—and possibly as a way of being reconciled with heaven—he wrote the score, and as soon as it was finished, he took it up to the Eternal Father.

"Lord, I have not forgotten the lessons I was given," he said. "Here is the score, listen to it, correct it, have it performed, and if you find it worthy of these heavenly heights, then allow me to return and sit at your feet . . ."

"No," said the Lord, "I do not wish to hear a single note."

"But Lord—"

"No, not a note!"

Satan continued to plead with him, but with no success, until God, grown weary and filled with pity, agreed that the opera could be performed, but outside heaven. He created a special theater, this planet, and invented a whole company, with a full cast, soloists and supporting roles, as well as the chorus and the dancers.

"Do come to some of the rehearsals!"

"No, I want nothing to do with the rehearsals. It's enough for me to have written the libretto, and I'm happy to share any royalties with you."

This refusal was perhaps a mistake, for it resulted in a few rather confused passages that could have been avoided if God had agreed to attend a rehearsal or offered a little friendly collaboration. Indeed, there are places where the words go to the right and the music to the left. Some say that therein lies the beauty of the composition, thus avoiding monotony, which is how they explain the trio in Eden, Abel's aria, and the choruses about the guillotine and slavery. The same scenes often recur for no apparent reason. Certain motifs grow tedious because they are merely repetitious. There are also some very obscure sections; the maestro overdoes the choral parts, often blurring and muddying the meaning. The orchestral parts, however, are very skillfully done. Or so think certain unbiased listeners.

The maestro's friends believe it would be hard to find a more accomplished work. A few do admit that it is not without its flaws, and there are a few lacunae, but as the opera progresses, these are filled in or explained, and any flaws disappear completely, with the maestro open to emendations wherever the music does not entirely correspond with the sublime thoughts of the poet. The poet's friends are of a different opinion. They swear blind that the libretto has been sacrificed, that the score has entirely corrupted the meaning of the words, and while it is very pretty in some parts and adroitly composed, in other parts it runs completely counter to the drama. There is, for example, no grotesquerie in the poet's libretto; that is a mere excrescence added in imitation of *The Merry Wives of Windsor*. This point is hotly contested by the Satanists, and not without reason. They say that, at the time young Satan composed his great opera, neither the farce nor Shakespeare had been born. They even go so far as to state that the English poet's sole genius lay in transcribing the libretto with such skill and fidelity that he appears to be the real author, whereas he is clearly a plagiarist.

"That opera," concluded the old tenor, "will last as long as the theater lasts, although who can know when astronomical expediency will demand that the theater be abolished. Meanwhile, its success continues to grow. Poet and composer receive their regular royalty payments, although not in the same way, because the money is shared out in accordance with the words of the Scriptures: "Many are called, but few are chosen." God is paid in gold, Satan in notes.

"Very witty," I said.

"Witty?" the furious tenor roared, although he soon regained his composure and said: "My dear Santiago, I am not *witty*, I have a horror of wit. What I'm telling you is the truth, pure and simple. One day, when all the books have been burned as useless, there will be someone, possibly a tenor, maybe an Italian, who will teach this truth to mankind. Everything is music, my friend. In the beginning was the *do*, and out of the *do* came the *re*, and so on. This glass [which he refilled], this glass is a brief refrain. Can't you hear it? Then again, you can't hear a piece of wood or a stone, but they all have a part in the same opera . . ."

≡ Chapter X / *I accept the theory*

THIS IS CLEARLY much too metaphysical for just one tenor; but it may be explained by the loss of his singing voice, and, besides, there are philosophers who are basically out-of-work tenors.

I, dear reader, accept my old friend Marcolini's theory, not just because it's plausible, which is often all one can say of the truth, but because my life fits his definition perfectly. I sang a very tender duet, then a trio, and finally a quartet . . . But let's not get ahead of ourselves; let us go back to the beginning, when I realized that I was already a singer, because José Dias's revelation, dear reader, was aimed principally at me. He revealed myself to me.

≡ Chapter XI / *The promise*

AS SOON AS I SAW José Dias disappear down the hallway, I left my hiding place and ran to the veranda at the back of the house. I wasn't concerned about my mother's tears or what had provoked them. Their cause doubtless lay in her ecclesiastical ambitions, and that is what I'm going to tell you about now, because, by then, they were already ancient history, going back sixteen years.

Those ambitions dated from the time of my conception. When her first child was stillborn, my mother pleaded with God to let her next child live, promising that, if it was a boy, he would enter the priesthood. Perhaps she was hoping for a girl. She said nothing to my father, neither before nor after giving birth to me; she would, she thought, tell him when I went to school, but she was widowed before that. As a widow, she became terrified of being apart from me, but she was so devout, so God-fearing, that she sought witnesses to her promise, telling relatives and close family friends. Except that, in order to postpone our separation for as long as possible, she had me educated at home to begin with, and I was taught reading and writing, as well as Latin and Church doctrine, by an old friend of Uncle Cosme's, Father Cabral, who came to the house each evening to play backgammon.

It is so easy to postpone things; in the imagination, such postponements become infinite. My mother waited for the years to pass. Meanwhile, I was getting to like the idea of the Church; childish games, religious books, images of saints, conversations at home, all pointed the way to the altar. When we went to mass, I always told myself that this was so that I could learn how to be a priest, and that I must pay close attention to the priest, and not take my eyes off him. At home, I used to play at holding mass—although I kept this to myself, because my mother was always saying that mass was not a game. Capitu and I would make an altar. She would be the sacristan, and we would change the ritual slightly, in the sense that we would share the host between us, the host being a piece of candy. On the days when we played like that, she would often say: "Is there a mass today?" I knew what this meant, and would rush home to ask for a host by another name. Then I would come back, and we would make our altar, mumble some garbled Latin, and rush through the service. I was supposed to say, *Dominus, non sum dignus*, three times, but I think I only used to say it once, because both priest and sacristan were greedy for the host. We drank neither wine nor water; we had no wine, and the water would have ruined the taste of the sacrifice.

Lately, no one had mentioned the seminary, so I'd assumed the matter had been forgotten. Since I had no vocation, my fifteen years were crying out for the seminary of the world, not the seminary of São José. My mother would often sit gazing at me like a lost soul, or clasp my hand for no reason, and squeeze it tightly.

Chapter XII / *On the veranda*

I STOOD ON THE VERANDA; I felt dizzy, stunned, my legs trembling, my heart beating so hard it felt as if it might leap out of my mouth. I did not dare to go down the steps and into the neighboring backyard. I began pacing back and forth, now and then coming to an abrupt halt to steady myself, then I would begin pacing again, and stopping again. A jumble of voices kept repeating José Dias's words.

"Always together . . ."

"Whispering . . ."

"If they should fall in love . . ."

Ah, you, the paving stones that I trod and retrod that afternoon, ah, you, the yellowing pillars that passed me on the left, and then on the right, as I paced back and forth, yes, you bear the imprint of much of that whole crisis, the sense of a new pleasure that wrapped about me only to release me, disperse me, send shivers down my spine, and fill me with a kind of inner balm. Sometimes I found myself smiling, a smug grin on my face, which gave the lie to the abominable nature of my sin. And still the jumbled voices repeated over and over:

"Whispering . . ."

"Always together . . ."

"If they should fall in love . . ."

Seeing me so restless and guessing the cause, a coconut palm murmured from above that there was nothing wrong with fifteen-year-old boys hiding in corners with fourteen-year-old girls; on the contrary, adolescents of that age had no other purpose in life and corners no other role. It was an old coconut palm, and I believed in old coconut palms, more than I did in old books. Birds, butterflies, a grasshopper rehearsing for the summer—all the living creatures of the air were of the same opinion.

So, I loved Capitu and Capitu loved me? It was true that I was virtually tied to her petticoats, but I couldn't think of anything that happened between us that was really secret. Before she went off to boarding school, it was simply a matter of us getting up to the usual childish mischief; when she left the school, it's true that we didn't immediately recapture our former intimacy, but this had gradually returned, and in the last year it had been just as it used to be. And the things we talked about remained exactly the same. Capitu sometimes said I was cute or a real sweetie; she sometimes grabbed my hands and counted my fingers. And I began to recall those and other gestures and words; the pleasure I felt when she ran her hand over my hair, saying how lovely it was. I didn't ever reciprocate, except to say that her hair was far lovelier than mine. Then Capitu would respond with a terribly disappointed, melancholy shake of her head, which was all the more surprising because her hair really was gorgeous; and then I would tell her off, saying she was crazy. When she asked me if I had dreamed about her the previous night, and I said I hadn't, she would always tell me that she had dreamed about me, and that we'd had some amazing adventures together: flying through the air up to the top of Corcovado, dancing on the moon, or being visited by angels who wanted to know our names so that they could give them to other angels who had just been born. And in all these dreams, we were inseparable. The dreams I had about her were quite different, they merely reproduced our normal daily life together, and were often mere repetitions of what had happened during the day, some word or gesture. I would tell her about those too. One day, Capitu commented on this difference, saying that her dreams were prettier than mine; after a moment's hesitation, I said that was because they resembled the person having the dreams . . . She blushed scarlet.

Frankly, it was only now that I understood the thrill I felt when she confided in me like that. It was a sweet, new emotion, but just why I was feeling it had until then escaped me, and I had never pondered the reason or even suspected what it might be. I now felt that her silences of the last few days, which had meant nothing to me before, were like signs, as were certain half-spoken hints, certain curious questions, vague responses, kind gestures, the delight she took in recalling our childhood days. I also registered another new phenomenon: I woke up thinking of Capitu, remembering things she had said, and I trembled when I heard her footsteps. If anyone mentioned her at home, I would immediately prick up my ears and, depending on whether she was praised or criticized, any pleasure or displeasure I felt was more intense than when we had simply been playmates. I had even started to think about her during the masses I attended that month; not all the time, it's true, but I never thought of anyone else, only her.

All these things had been shown to me now in the words of José Dias, who had revealed me to myself and whom I forgave everything, the evil he had spoken, the evil he had done, and whatever might arise from either of those two things. At that moment, he was worth more to me than Eternal Truth, Eternal Kindness, and all the other Eternal Virtues. I loved Capitu! Capitu loved me! And my legs kept pacing up and down, then stopping short, trembling, and feeling as if they could bestride the world. I've never forgotten that first rising of the sap, that first experience of self-consciousness, and I've never found it even remotely comparable to any other similar feeling. Obviously, because *I* was feeling it. And obviously, too, because it was the first time.

⟹ Chapter XIII / *Capitu*

SUDDENLY I HEARD a loud voice coming from next door:
"Capitu!"
And in the backyard:
"Yes, Mama!"

Again the voice from the house:

"Come here!"

I could not resist. My legs took me down the three steps that led into our backyard and headed straight for the yard next door. This is what they usually did in the afternoon, and in the morning too. Because legs are people too, barely inferior to arms, and they have a mind of their own when the head is not overruling them with ideas. My legs arrived at the wall between our two backyards. My mother had had a door installed there when Capitu and I were little. The door had neither key nor latch; you opened it by pushing from one side or the other, and a stone attached to a piece of rope ensured that it closed by itself. It was almost exclusively ours. As children, we would gain entrance by knocking on one side and would be received on the other with many bows and curtsies. When any of Capitu's dolls fell ill, I was the doctor. I would stride into her backyard with a stick under my arm, in imitation of Dr. João da Costa's heavy cane; I would check the patient's pulse and ask her to show me her tongue. "The poor thing is deaf!" Capitu would cry. Then I would scratch my chin, as the doctor used to do, and end up ordering her to apply some leeches or give her an emetic: this was the real doctor's usual recommendation.

"Capitu!"

"Yes, Mama!"

"Stop making holes in the wall and come here."

Her mother's voice sounded closer now, as if it were coming from their back door. I wanted to go through into their backyard, but my legs, so sprightly before, now seemed as if nailed to the ground. Finally, though, I pulled myself together, pushed open the door, and went in. Capitu was standing by the wall opposite, with her back to me, scraping away with a nail. The sound of the door opening made her turn around; when she saw me, she leaned against the wall as if to hide something. I went over to her, and I clearly had a strange expression on my face, because she rushed to meet me and asked anxiously:

"What's wrong?"

"Wrong? Nothing. Why?"

"No, there's something the matter."

I tried to protest, but couldn't speak. I was all eyes and heart, a heart that, this time, would definitely leap out of my mouth. I couldn't take my eyes off that fourteen-year-old girl, that tall, strong, sturdily built girl, wearing a close-fitting, rather faded cotton dress. Her thick hair hung down her back in two braids, with the ends tied together, as was fashionable at the time. She was dark-complexioned, with large, pale eyes, a long, straight nose, a delicate mouth and a strong chin. Her hands, despite being accustomed to doing various household chores, were well cared for; they didn't smell of expensive soap or eau de toilette, but were kept spotless with water from the well and ordinary soap. She was wearing a pair of rather battered flat cloth shoes, which she herself had patched up.

"What's wrong?" she asked again.

"Nothing," I finally managed to stammer out, then immediately corrected myself. "It's just some news I heard."

"What news?"

I considered telling her that I was about to go to the seminary, just to see her reaction. If she looked upset, then she really did care for me; if not, then she didn't. However, I thought this in only a very vague, cursory way. I felt I could not speak clearly, that my eyes might betray me . . .

"What news?"

"You know . . ."

I then happened to glance over at the wall, at the spot she had been scratching away at with the nail, writing or making holes, as her mother said. I saw a few marks and remembered how anxious she had been to cover them up. I immediately wanted a closer look and took a step forward. Capitu grabbed hold of me, but, either because she was afraid I might escape her grasp or hoping to find some other way to stop me, she ran back to the wall and tried to erase what she had written. This only inflamed my desire to read what was there.

Chapter XIV / *The writing on the wall*

EVERYTHING I DESCRIBED at the end of the previous chapter took a matter of seconds. What followed took even less. I leaped forward and, before she could erase the marks she had made, I saw these two names scratched on the wall with the nail, and arranged like this:

BENTO
CAPITOLINA

I turned to her; Capitu was staring down at the ground. Then, very slowly, she looked up, and we stood there gazing at each other . . . Ah, such childhood declarations of love could easily merit a page or two of prose, but I prefer to keep things brief. In fact, we said nothing; the wall spoke for us. We did not move, or, rather, our hands did, very gradually reaching out, all four of them, clasping, squeezing, merging into one. I did not note down the exact moment of that gesture. I should have; I feel the lack of some note written that very night, one I would include here, complete with any spelling mistakes, but there would have been no errors, for therein lies the difference between schoolboy and adolescent. I knew all the spelling rules, but had no inkling of the rules of love; I had known whole orgies of Latin, but, as regards women, was a virgin.

We did not let go of each other's hands, and whether out of weariness or indifference, our hands did not let go either. Our eyes gazed and ungazed, and then, after wandering about nearby, they once more fixed upon each other . . . I, a future priest, stood there as if before an altar, with one of her cheeks as the Epistle and the other as the Gospel. Her mouth could be the chalice, her lips the paten. All that was missing was for me to say the new mass, in a Latin that no one learns and yet is the universal language of mankind. Don't think I'm being sacrilegious, dear, devout reader; the pristine nature of the intention behind my words washes clean anything less than curial about my style. There we were, and we had heaven inside us. Our hands, nerve endings touching nerve endings, made of us not just a single being, but a single seraphic being. Our eyes continued to say infinite things, while no words even attempted to leave our lips, returning to the heart as silently as they had come.

Chapter XV / *Another sudden voice*

ANOTHER SUDDEN VOICE, this time a man's voice:

"Are you two having a staring contest?"

It was Capitu's father, who was standing at the back door, next to his wife. We immediately let go of each other's hands and stood there, feeling very awkward indeed. Capitu went over to the wall, picked up the nail, and began discreetly scratching out our names.

"Capitu!"

"Yes, Papa!"

"You're ruining the stucco!"

Capitu was scraping away at the marks she had made, doing her best to erase them. Her father came out into the yard to see what she was up to, but Capitu had already started drawing something else, a profile, which she said was a picture of him, but which could just as easily have been of her mother; more importantly, she made him laugh. Not that he was angry; rather, he gazed at her very fondly, despite the equivocal, or entirely unequivocal, position in which he had found us. He was a stout, stocky man, with short arms and legs, and hunched shoulders, hence the nickname José Dias had given him: *Tartaruga*, or *Turtle*. No one else called him that at home, only José Dias.

"So you were trying to see who could stare the longest, were you?" he asked.

I looked very hard at a nearby elder tree. Capitu answered for us both.

"Yes, we were, but Bentinho always gets the giggles, he just can't do it."

"He wasn't laughing when I saw you."

"But he was before. He can't keep a straight face. Just watch."

And she solemnly fixed her eyes on mine, inviting me to play. Fear, however, is naturally solemn, and I was still recovering from the alarm caused by her father's arrival on the scene, and was incapable of laughing, even though I really should have, to back up Capitu's explanation. Eventually, grown tired of waiting, she looked away, saying that the only reason I wasn't laughing now was because her father was watching. Even then, I didn't laugh. Some things you only learn how to do later in life: You have to be born with that ability if you're to do them early on. And naturally early is always better than artificially late. Capitu, after two more failed attempts, went over to her mother, who was still standing in the doorway, leaving me and her father both feeling utterly charmed; her father looked over at her and then at me, saying tenderly:

"Who would think that little creature was just fourteen, eh? More like seventeen. Anyway, how's your mother?" he went on, turning to face me.

"She's fine."

"It's been some days since I've seen her. It's high time I beat your uncle at backgammon again, but I haven't had a chance, what with having to bring work home in the evenings; I spend every night writing furiously, for a report I have to do. Have you seen my pet tanager, by the way? It's down at the bottom of the yard. I was just going to fetch its cage; come and have a look."

As you can easily imagine—and I hardly need swear this by heaven, or indeed by earth—I had absolutely no desire to see his pet tanager. My one desire was to run after Capitu and talk to her right then about the difficult times that lay ahead for us; but a father is a father, and he really did love his birds. He had various species of different colors and sizes. There were canaries in cages lining the courtyard around which the house was built, and they made a devil of a racket with their singing. He swapped birds with fellow bird-lovers, others he bought or caught with traps right there in the backyard. And if they fell sick, he cared for them as if they were people.

≡ Chapter XVI / *The interim administrator*

PÁDUA WORKED in a department of the Ministry of War. He didn't earn a great deal, but since his wife did not spend much, either, they made do. Also, he owned the house they lived in, a two-story house like ours, although slightly smaller. He had bought it with the big lottery prize he won, ten *contos*. His first thought, when he got the prize, was to buy a thoroughbred horse, some diamond jewelry for his wife, a family burial plot, a few birds from Europe, and so on, but his wife—the same Dona Fortunata standing there at the back door of the house talking to Capitu, and as tall and strong and well-built as her daughter, the same head, the same pale eyes—she told him that it would be far better to buy a house and set aside any money left over for possible future emergencies. Pádua thought long and hard, but, in the end, he had to take heed of my mother's advice, for Dona Fortunata had turned to her for help. And this wasn't the only occasion on which my mother helped them out; one day, she even saved Pádua's life. Listen: it won't take long to tell you the story.

The administrator of the department in which Pádua worked was sent up north on a special mission. Pádua, either by special appointment or because it was simply his turn, stood in for him and received the statutory increase in salary. The change of fortunes rather went to his head; this was before the lottery win. Not content with buying new clothes and crockery, he made all kinds of extravagant purchases, bought jewels for his wife, celebrated certain church festivals by dining on suckling pig, was seen at the theater, and even went so far as to buy himself some patent leather shoes. He lived like this for twenty-two months, imagining that his interim appointment would last forever. Then, one afternoon, he came to our house in a terrible state, almost crazy, saying that he was about to lose his job, because the real administrator had arrived back in the office that very morning. He begged my mother to watch over his family, the poor unfortunates he would be leaving behind; he could not bear the disgrace and was determined to kill himself. My mother spoke to him kindly, but he wouldn't listen.

"No, I cannot bear the humiliation! Bringing my family down in the world like that, being forced to take such a retrograde step . . . No, I've decided. I'm going to kill myself! I can't possibly tell my family this shameful news. Not to mention other people. What will the neighbors say? And our friends? And the public?"

"What *public*, Senhor Pádua? Stop all this nonsense now and be a man. Your wife, remember, has no other means of support . . . And what would she do then? For a man to . . . No, come, now, be a man."

Pádua dried his eyes and went home, and for a few more days, he remained silent and plunged in gloom, either shut up in his bedroom or else hiding in the backyard, next to the well, as if thoughts of death still lingered. Dona Fortunata told him off:

"Joãozinho, don't be such a child!"

But when he continued to speak of death she felt afraid, so one day she ran to beg my mother to, please, save her husband from killing himself. My mother found him sitting beside the well, and told him he must live. What madness was this anyway, thinking he would be disgraced simply because he would earn a little less money and lose what had, after all, only been an interim position? No, he must be a man, a father, and follow the example of his wife and daughter . . . Pádua obeyed and said that he would somehow find the strength to carry out my mother's wishes.

"No, not my wishes, it's your duty."

"Duty, then. Yes, you're quite right."

In the days that followed, he continued to come in and out of the house, but always keeping close to the wall, his eyes fixed on the ground. He was not the same man as the one who had almost worn out his hat taking it off to the neighbors, smiling at all and sundry, even before he was given that interim post. As the weeks passed, the wound began to heal. Pádua started taking an interest in domestic matters again, looking after his birds, sleeping peacefully at night, and, in the afternoon, chatting and delivering the local gossip. Serenity returned, followed close behind by happiness in the form of two friends who invited him to play a game of solo whist one Sunday, for tokens only. He laughed and joked and was his old cheerful self; the wound had healed up completely.

Over time, an interesting phenomenon began to emerge. Pádua started to talk about that interim position, not only without a word of regret or shame, but with a certain degree of arrogance and pride. The time he had spent in the post became a kind of hegira, from which he counted forward and backward.

"During my time as administrator . . ."

Or:

"Ah, yes, I remember now, it was before my time as administrator, a couple of months before . . . No, wait, I started as administrator in . . . that's right, a month and half before, yes, a month and a half before."

Or even:

"Exactly. I had already been administrator for six months by then . . ."

Such is the posthumous savor of interim glories. José Dias declared roundly that it was more like proof of perennial vanity. Father Cabral, however, who always referred everything back to the Scriptures, said that their neighbor Pádua was a living example of Eliphaz's lesson to Job: "Happy is the man whom God correcteth; He woundeth, and His hands make whole."

≡ Chapter XVII / *The worms*

"HE WOUNDETH and His hands make whole!" When later on I learned that even Achilles's spear had healed a wound it made, I was almost tempted to write a dissertation on that topic. I even went so far as to pick up old books, dead books, buried books, to open and compare them, scrutinizing text and meaning, hoping to find the common origin of the pagan oracle and the Israelite thought. I went so far as to consult the bookworms themselves, to find out what they had to say about the texts they had gnawed at.

"Sir," said one long, fat worm, "we know absolutely nothing about the texts we gnaw, nor do we choose what we gnaw, nor do we love or loathe what we gnaw; we simply gnaw."

I could get nothing more out of him. The other worms, as if the message had been passed from worm to worm, all repeated the same refrain. Perhaps their discreet silence about the texts they gnawed was yet another way of gnawing the gnawed.

≡ Chapter XVIII / *A plan*

NEITHER HER MOTHER nor her father came to look in on us when Capitu and I met in the drawing room and talked about the seminary. With her eyes fixed on me, Capitu demanded to know the news that had so upset me. When I told her, she turned pale as wax.

"But I don't want to go," I said at once. "I don't want to go to any seminary, and I won't, they can insist all they like, but I won't go."

At first Capitu said nothing. She withdrew her eyes, turned them in on herself, and stood there, her pupils vague, dumb, her mouth half-open, totally stopped and silent. In order to give what I had said more force, I let out a whole stream of powerful oaths, swearing on my own life and death. I swore on the very hour of my own death. May the light be taken from me at the hour of my death, I said, if I go to the seminary. Capitu seemed neither to believe nor disbelieve, she didn't even appear to be listening; she was like a figure carved out of wood. I wanted to shout at her, to shake her, but I lacked the courage. That young creature who had played with me, had skipped and danced and even, I think, slept in the same bed as me, left me standing there, my arms bound and timorous. Finally, she came to, but her face was bright red and she burst out with these furious words aimed at my mother:

"Pew-warmer! Pope-lover! Wafer-eater!"

I was astonished. Capitu was so fond of my mother, and my mother so fond of her, that I couldn't comprehend such an explosion of rage. It's true that Capitu was also fond of me, indeed fonder, much fonder, or fond in a different way, fond enough, at least, to explain the fury aroused in her by the threat of separation; but how to explain those insults, how could she call my mother such vile names, and how could she denigrate religious customs which were, after all, her own? She, too, went to mass, and my mother had sometimes taken her there in our old carriage. She had also given her a rosary, a gold crucifix, and a book of hours . . . I tried to defend my mother, but Capitu wouldn't let me, and continued to call her "pope-lover" and "wafer-eater" so loudly that I was afraid her parents might hear. I had never seen her so angry; she seemed in a mood to say absolutely anything to anyone. She clenched her teeth and shook her head . . . I was so alarmed that I didn't know what to do; I kept repeating my oaths, and promised I would go home that very night and tell my mother that nothing on earth could make me go to the seminary.

"You? Oh, you'll go."

"No, I won't."

"Just you wait."

Capitu fell silent then, and when she spoke again, she had changed; she still wasn't the Capitu I knew of old, but almost. She was serious, but not agitated, and she spoke very softly. She asked me to tell her about that overheard conversation, and I told her everything, except the part about her.

"And why do you think José Dias brought the matter up? What's in it for him?" she asked me at last.

"Nothing, as far as I can see. He was just stirring up trouble. He's a nasty piece of work, and he'll pay for it, don't you worry. When I'm the master of the house, the first thing I'll do is kick him out in the street, you'll see. Mama is far too kind and takes his advice far too seriously. Tears were shed, apparently."

"Who by? José Dias?"

"No, by Mama."

"But what made her cry?"

"I don't know. I just heard Uncle Cosme telling her not to cry, that there was nothing to cry about. Anyway, José Dias did eventually apologize, and then he left. And that was when I left my hiding place and ran out onto the veranda, because I was afraid of being found snooping. But don't you worry, I'll get my revenge!"

I clenched my fist when I said this, and uttered other threats. When I think of this now, I don't find myself ridiculous; adolescence and childhood are not, in that regard, ridiculous; that's one of their privileges. Feeling ridiculous is an ill or a danger that begins in youth, increases in middle age, and reaches its apogee in old age.

When you're fifteen, there's a certain pleasure in issuing lots of threats and never carrying them out.

Capitu was thinking hard. This was not unusual for her, and you could always tell when she was thinking because she squeezed her eyes shut tight. She asked me for a few more details, the exact words used by this or that person, and the tone of voice used. Since I did not want to reveal that she had been the starting point of the conversation, I couldn't give her a full account of what had been said. Capitu was particularly intrigued by my mother's tears, which she simply could not understand. In the middle of all this, she declared that my mother's wish to make me a priest was certainly not born of spite; it was that old promise she had made and which she, being a God-fearing woman, could not break. I was so relieved to see her spontaneously withdraw those earlier heart-felt insults that I grabbed her hand and squeezed it hard. Capitu laughed and let me hold her hand; and the conversation gradually dozed off of its own accord and fell asleep. By then, we were standing by the window; a black man who had been hawking coconut candy outside for a while now stopped by and asked:

"Missy like some candy today?"

"No," said Capitu.

"Ve' good candy."

"Go away," she said softly.

"Give me two pieces," I said, holding out my hand.

I bought one for each of us, but had to eat both; Capitu refused to be tempted. I realized that, even in the midst of the crisis, I still had room for some coconut candy, which could just as easily be seen as a flaw or a virtue, but this is not the time for such definitions. Let's just say that my friend, although she was once more perfectly calm and lucid, wasn't interested in candy, and yet she loved the stuff. On the contrary, the seller's cry, so familiar locally and so reminiscent of far-off childhood afternoons:

Hey, girl, why you cryin'?
Just 'cause you ain't got a dime?

seemed, rather, to annoy her. It wasn't the tune, though, which she knew by heart and had sung for years; she used to sing it when we played together as children, laughing and skipping, swapping roles, one moment playing the seller, the next the buyer of that nonexistent candy. I think it was the words, intended to provoke childish pride, that irritated her now, because she said:

"If I was rich, you could just run away, get on a steamship, and sail to Europe."

She looked me in the eye then, but I don't think my eyes told her anything, or perhaps they merely expressed their gratitude for her kind intentions. Indeed, it was such a friendly thought that I could forgive the extravagant nature of that proposed adventure.

As you see, the fourteen-year-old Capitu already had some very bold ideas, although nowhere near as bold as the ideas she had later on; however, they were only bold in their conception, in practice they became sly, insinuating, secretive, and achieved their aim not with one bound, but with a series of smaller bounds. Do you see what I mean? Imagine a great plan carried out little by little. Let's stay with that vague, hypothetical desire to sail off to Europe; in order to fulfill that desire, Capitu would not have me board that steamship and flee just like that; instead, she would arrange for there to be a whole line of canoes stretching from here to there, in which, while I appeared to be setting off for the fort on the nearby island of Laje on a kind of moving bridge, I would, in fact, be heading for Bordeaux, leaving my mother waiting for me on the beach. That was the way Capitu's mind worked, and so it was hardly surprising that, in rejecting my plan of open resistance, she opted instead for subtler means: perseverance, words, slow, persistent persuasion, and assessing which people we could count on for support. She rejected Uncle Cosme; he would do anything for a quiet life, and even if he didn't approve of my ordination, he was incapable of lifting a finger to stop it. Cousin Justina was better than him, and best of all was Father Cabral, because he had authority, but he was unlikely to work against the Church, or only if I confessed to him that I had no vocation . . .

"Could I do that?"

"Of course, but that would be too direct, there's a better way. José Dias . . ."

"What about José Dias?"

"He could use his influence . . ."

"But he was the one who mentioned me going to the seminary . . ."

"That doesn't matter," said Capitu. "Now he'll change his mind. He's really fond of you. Speak to him openly. You mustn't allow him to think that you're afraid, just let him know that one day you'll be master of the house, tell him what you want and what you intend to do. Make it clear you're not asking him for a favor. And flatter him; he loves to be flattered. Dona Glória will listen to him, but the main thing is that, once he's on your side, he'll speak more persuasively than anyone else."

"I don't agree, Capitu."

"Then go to the seminary."

"Oh, anything but that."

"But what do you lose by trying? Come on, let's try: Do as I say. Dona Glória might change her mind, and if she doesn't, then we'll try something else, there's always Father Cabral. Don't you remember how it was that you were allowed to go to the theater for the first time two months ago? Dona Glória didn't want you to go at all, and that should have been enough for José Dias not to insist. But because *he* wanted to go, he made a great speech, don't you remember?"

"I do. He said that the theater was a school of manners."

"Exactly. He talked so much that your mother finally gave in and even paid for both your tickets . . . Go on, ask, insist. Look, tell him you want to go and study law in São Paulo."

A shiver of pleasure ran through me. São Paulo was merely a fragile screen, destined to be removed one day, not like the thick, eternal spiritual wall of priesthood. I promised to speak to José Dias in the terms she suggested. Capitu repeated these, emphasizing the most important ones, and then questioned me about them to make sure I had understood properly and wasn't getting one mixed up with another. And she said I should ask politely, but as if I were asking for a glass of water from someone who was under no obligation to bring me one. I give all these details, so that you will have a clear idea what my friend was like in the morning of her life, which will soon be followed by an afternoon, and together morning and afternoon will make the first day, just as in Genesis, where seven days were made, one after the other.

Chapter XIX / *"Without fail"*

IT WAS DARK BY THE TIME I went home. I was walking fast, but not fast enough to keep me from thinking about the terms in which I would speak to José Dias. I formulated my request in my head, choosing the words I would say and the tone in which I would say them, somewhere between brusque and benevolent. In the backyard, before going into the house, I repeated them to myself, then out loud, to see if they sounded right and were in keeping with Capitu's recommendations: "I need to speak to you tomorrow—

without fail. Just tell me a time and a place." I said these words slowly, especially the words "without fail," as if to underline them. I repeated them again, and this time found them too brusque, almost rude, and, frankly, they were not the kind of words a boy would say to a grown man. I stopped walking for a moment and tried to find others.

In the end, I told myself that the words were fine, I just had to say them in a way that would not offend. And the proof is that, when I repeated them over again, they sounded almost supplicating. I must be neither too pushy nor too saccharine, but somewhere in between. "And Capitu is right," I thought, "the house is mine and he is a mere retainer . . . He's clever, though, and could very well work on my behalf to undo Mama's plan."

Chapter XX / *A thousand Paternosters and a thousand Ave Marias*

I RAISED MY EYES to the heavens, which were beginning to cloud over, but I did not do so in order to see if it was overcast or not. It was to that other heaven that I lifted up my soul; to my refuge, to my friend. And then I said to myself:

"I promise to say a thousand Paternosters and a thousand Ave Marias if José Dias manages to ensure that I don't have to go to the seminary."

This was a huge number. And to make matters worse, I was already laden down with unfulfilled promises. I had recently promised to say two hundred Paternosters and two hundred Ave Marias if it didn't rain on a certain afternoon outing to Santa Teresa. It didn't rain, and I had still not said my prayers. I had been in the habit, ever since I was little, of asking heaven for favors and promising to say prayers if those favors were granted. I would say the first few and postpone the others, and the more they mounted up, the more I forgot them. And thus I reached twenty, thirty, fifty. Then I got into the hundreds, and now it was the thousands. It was a way of bribing the divine will with sheer quantity; and each new promise was made with the earnest intention of paying off the old debt. But what can you do with a soul that has been idle since the cradle and whose idleness has remained undiminished by life! Heaven granted me the favor, and I postponed payment. In the end, I simply lost count.

"A thousand," I repeated to myself. "A thousand."

The importance of what I was asking for this time was enormous, though: neither more nor less than the salvage or shipwreck of my entire existence. A thousand, a thousand, a thousand. It needed to be a number that would pay off all the arrears. Annoyed at so many forgotten prayers, God might very well refuse to hear me without a big bribe . . . Serious-minded reader, you may find these childish anxieties irritating, not to say ridiculous. Sublime they were not. I thought long and hard about how to pay off that spiritual debt. I could find no other currency in which—as was my intention—all would be repaid, and the accounts of my moral conscience signed off without a deficit. Paying for a hundred masses, crawling up the hill to the Igreja da Glória on my knees to hear mass, visiting the Holy Land, and all those other famous promises the old slavewomen used to tell me about, all these things came into my mind, but none stayed. It was hard work crawling up a hill on your knees; you were bound to end up injuring them. And the Holy Land was a very long way away. And a hundred masses were an awful lot of masses, and I could easily find my soul in hock yet again . . .

≋ Chapter XXI / *Cousin Justina*

I FOUND COUSIN JUSTINA pacing up and down the veranda. She came over to the steps to ask where I had been.

"I was just next door chatting to Dona Fortunata, and I forgot the time. Is it very late? Was Mama asking for me?"

"Yes, she was, but I said you had already come in."

This lie shocked me as much as the frankness with which she owned up to it. Cousin Justina was never one to mince words; she would happily tell Pedro precisely what she thought of Paulo, and Paulo what she thought of Pedro, but saying openly that she had lied, that was new. She was a pale, scrawny woman in her forties, with thin lips and inquisitive eyes. My mother had invited her to live with us out of a combination of kindness and self-interest; she wanted to have a lady companion, and preferred that person to be a relative rather than a stranger.

For a few minutes, we walked up and down the lamplit veranda together. She asked if I had forgotten about my mother's ecclesiastical ambitions for me, and when I said I had not, she asked how I felt about becoming a priest. I gave a suitably evasive response:

"Well, a priest's life is a very nice one."

"Yes, but my question is, do you want to be a priest?" she said, laughing.

"I want whatever Mama wants."

"Cousin Glória really does want you to be ordained, but even if she didn't, there is someone in this house who keeps putting the idea in her head."

"Who's that?"

"Oh, really! Who do you think? It's not Cousin Cosme, who doesn't care one way or the other, and it's not me."

"You mean José Dias?" I asked.

"Of course."

I frowned and looked suitably perplexed, as if I knew nothing about this. Cousin Justina completed her report by saying that José Dias had reminded my mother of her old promise that very afternoon.

"Cousin Glória might, in time, forget her promise, but how can she if there's always someone at her elbow going on and on about the seminary? And the speeches he makes in praise of the Church, about how the life of the priest is this and that, using all those long words he alone knows and in that affected voice of his . . . And he does it purely in order to cause mischief, because he's about as religious as that lamp over there. Yes, even today. And don't pretend you know nothing about it . . . The things he said today, well, you can't imagine . . ."

"Was he just talking nonsense?" I asked, wanting to know if she would reveal what he had said about me falling in love with our young neighbor.

She did not answer, but the look on her face made it clear that there was another matter she could say nothing about. She again urged me not to play the innocent, and listed all the reasons why she thought José Dias was such a bad person, and it was quite a long list: he was an intriguer, a flatterer, a busybody, and beneath that veneer of politeness, he was vulgarity itself. After a few moments, I said:

"Cousin Justina, could you do something for me?"

"What's that?"

"Could you . . . suppose I didn't want to be a priest, could you ask Mama—"

"Oh, no," she said before I could even finish. "Cousin Glória has the idea fixed firmly in her head, and the only thing that could make her change her mind is time. You were still a baby when she told everyone about her promise, close friends and mere acquaintances. I'm not going to bring the subject up myself, although I would never do anything to bring misfortune on others, but to suggest to her that she should break her promise, no, I couldn't do it. If she were to ask me, fine; if she were to say: 'Cousin Justina, what do you think?' my response would be: 'Cousin Glória, I think that if he wants to be a priest, he should go to the seminary, but if he doesn't, then he should stay.' That's what I would say if she were ever to ask me. But what I won't do is mention the matter without being asked."

≡ Chapter XXII / *Other people's feelings*

I COULD GET NOTHING MORE out of her, and, in the end, I regretted having asked: I should have followed Capitu's advice. Then, when I made as if to go inside, Cousin Justina detained me for a few more minutes, talking about the heat and about the forthcoming Feast of the Immaculate Conception, about the shrines I used to make as a child, and, finally, about Capitu. She said nothing critical; on the contrary, she suggested that she could turn out to be a very pretty young woman. Since I already thought her utterly gorgeous, I would have roundly declared her the most beautiful creature in the world had caution not counseled discretion. However, when Cousin Justina began praising Capitu's manners, her seriousness, her sensible habits, what a help she was in the house, her fondness for my mother, all this prompted me to praise her too. If not in actual words, then with the approving nods with which I greeted all her comments, and, even more, with the happy glow on my face. I did not realize that I was thus confirming José Dias's "revelation," which she had heard that afternoon in the drawing room, assuming she did not already have her suspicions. No, this only occurred to me once I was in bed. Only then did I recall how, whenever I spoke, Cousin Justina's eyes had seemed to touch me, hear me, smell me, taste me, her eyes doing the work of all the senses. It couldn't have been jealousy; there was no place for jealousy between a young whippersnapper like me and a forty-year-old widow. It's true that, after a while, she did modify her praise of Capitu, and even made a few critical comments, saying that she could be sly and wouldn't always look you in the eye; I still don't believe it could have been jealousy, though. No, I think Cousin Justina saw in the spectacle of other people's feelings a vague resurrection of her own, for one can also take pleasure from lips talking about their own pleasure.

Chapter XXIII / *The deadline*

"I NEED TO SPEAK TO YOU TOMORROW, without fail. Just tell me a time and a place."

I think José Dias was rather taken aback by my way of speaking. My voice did not sound as imperative as I had feared, but the words did, and the fact that I wasn't inquiring or hesitating, as one would expect from a child and as had been my habit until then, must certainly have made him think he was dealing with a new person and a new situation. I spoke to him in the hallway, as we were going in for tea; José Dias was still full of the Walter Scott novel he was reading to my mother and to Cousin Justina. He read in a rhythmic, melodic fashion. The castles and the gardens all emerged from his lips somehow larger, the lakes contained more water, and the "celestial vault" was filled with thousands more twinkling stars. In the dialogues, he alternated the sounds of the voices, either soft or slightly gruff, depending on the sex of the speakers, subtly conveying tenderness and anger.

When he took his leave from me on the veranda, he said: "Let's meet tomorrow away from the house. I have a few purchases to make, and you could come with me. I'll ask your mother. You don't have a class, do you?"

"No, that was today."

"Good. I won't ask you what this is all about, but I can see it's some grave, very real matter."

"It is, sir."

"I'll see you tomorrow, then."

Everything worked out perfectly. There was just one setback; my mother thought it too hot for me to walk, so we caught the omnibus outside the house.

"No matter," said José Dias. "We can get off when we reach the gates to the Passeio Público."

<hr />

Chapter XXIV / *Mother and servant*

JOSÉ DIAS always treated me with a mixture of motherly solicitude and attentive servility. The first thing he did, as soon as I started going into town on my own, was to get rid of my lackey, and he then took the lackey's place and accompanied me whenever I went out. He took care of all my things at home: my books, my shoes, my general hygiene, and my grammar. When I was eight, my plurals sometimes lacked the correct endings, and he would put me right, half-seriously to give himself the necessary authority, half-jokingly as a way of apologizing for correcting me. In this way, he proved helpful to the tutor charged with teaching me to read and write. Later, when Father Cabral was teaching me Latin, doctrine, and sacred history, José Dias would attend those lessons, too, making suitably ecclesiastical comments and, at the end, he would say to Father Cabral: "Don't you think our young friend is making rapid progress?" He called me "a prodigy"; he told my mother that he had known other very intelligent boys, but that I was streets ahead of them, and that, for a boy my age, I already possessed a number of solid moral qualities. While I did not really grasp the importance of these latter qualities, I enjoyed the praise. Well, praise is praise.

Chapter XXV / *In the Passeio Público*

WE ENTERED the Passeio Público. A few aged, ailing, or merely idle faces were scattered melancholically along the path that leads from the gate to the terrace. We headed straight for the terrace. As we walked, and in order to steady my nerves, I spoke about the gardens:

"I haven't been here for ages, possibly a year."

"Forgive me," he said, "but we were here not three months since with our neighbor Pádua. Don't you remember?"

"Yes, you're right, but it was such a brief visit . . ."

"He asked your mother to let him take you with him, and she, being as she is, as kind as the Blessed Virgin herself, gave her consent. But while we're on the subject, it really isn't right that you should be seen out in the street with Pádua."

"But I've been out and about with him several times . . ."

"Yes, when you were younger, when you were a child, that was fine, because he could pass for your servant. But you're very nearly a young man now, and, frankly, he's becoming rather overfamiliar. And Dona Glória can't possibly want that. Not that the Páduas are bad people. Capitu, despite those devilish eyes of hers . . . Have you noticed her eyes? They're like a gypsy's eyes, oblique and sly. Anyway, despite that, she would be just about acceptable, if she didn't put on such airs and wasn't such a flatterer! Goodness me, how she flatters! Now, Dona Fortunata is an estimable woman, and I won't deny that Pádua himself is an honest fellow, has a good job, owns his own house, but honesty and respectability are not enough, and such qualities lose most of their value when one sees the bad company he keeps. Pádua has a real penchant for vulgar types. He only has to get a whiff of some ill-bred fellow to immediately become bosom pals with him. I'm not saying this out of personal animus, mind, nor because he's been known to make rude comments about me and to titter, as he did the other day, at my down-at-the-heels shoes—"

"I'm sorry," I said, interrupting him and coming to a halt, "but I've never once heard him speak ill of you; on the contrary, one day, not long ago, he said to someone, in my presence, that you were 'a very capable man' and that you talked 'like a member of the Chamber of Deputies.' "

José Dias beamed with delight, then, with a great effort, managed to recompose his features and say gravely: "Well, that's hardly a compliment, coming from him! Other men, of far superior breeding, have been kind enough to speak highly of me. But none of this means that he is other than I say he is."

We had continued walking, and were now on the terrace, looking out to sea.

"I can see that you only have my best interests at heart," I said after a few moments.

"How could it be otherwise, Bentinho?"

"In that case, may I ask you a favor?"

"A favor? Of course, anything, I am yours to command. What is it?"

"Mama . . ."

For a while I was unable to complete my sentence, however brief, and which I knew by heart. José Dias asked again what this favor was, and even shook me gently, lifted my chin, and, just as Cousin Justina had done the day before, keenly fixed his eyes upon me.

"What about Mama?"

"Mama wants me to become a priest, but I just can't do it," I said at last.

José Dias drew back in alarm.

"I can't," I said, no less alarmed than he was. "I have no vocation; the life of a priest is simply not the life for me. I'll do anything she wants, and Mama knows that, she knows I'll be whatever she wants me to be, even the driver of an omnibus. But not a priest, I can't be a priest. It's a very fine vocation, but not for me."

This whole speech did not emerge from my mouth as naturally and imperiously as it might seem when written down, but, rather, in mangled fragments, in a shy, somewhat muffled voice. Nevertheless, José Dias listened with a look of horror on his face. He obviously wasn't expecting such resistance, however timidly expressed, but what astonished him even more were my concluding words:

"I'm counting on you to save me."

His eyes opened wide, his eyebrows rose, and there was not a sign in either of those muscles of the pleasure I was expecting him to feel at being chosen as my protector. His whole face was barely large enough to contain his stupefaction. My speech had revealed in me a new soul; why, even I did not recognize myself. But it was those last two words, "save me," that brought a new vigor to the matter. José Dias was stunned. When his eyes returned to their normal size, he asked:

"But what can *I* do?"

"A great deal. You know how respected you are by everyone at home. After all, Mama often asks you for your advice, doesn't she? And Uncle Cosme says that you're a man of great gifts . . ."

"Oh, they're just being kind," he replied, flattered. "The generous words of worthy people, who deserve all one's . . . Ah, you see? No one will ever hear me say a word against them. And why? Because they are both excellent, virtuous people. Your mother is a saint, your uncle a perfect gentleman. I've known other distinguished families, but none with more nobility of feeling. The gifts your uncle sees in me come down to just one, a gift for recognizing what is good and worthy of admiration and esteem."

"Surely that gift should involve protecting your friends, like me."

"But, my angel, how can I help you? I cannot dissuade your mother from a project that is not just a promise, but an ambition and a dream nurtured over many years. Even had I been able to, it is now too late. Only yesterday, she did me the honor of saying: 'José Dias, I must send Bentinho to the seminary.' "

Timidity is not as bad as it might seem. Had I been bolder, the indignation I felt then would probably have made me explode with rage and call him a liar, but then I would have had to confess that I had been eavesdropping from behind the door, and which of those actions was worse? I contented myself with saying that, no, it was not too late.

"It isn't too late, there's still time, if you still want to help me."

"If I still want to help? What more could I possibly want, if not to serve you? What more could I wish for than that you should be as happy as you deserve to be?"

"Well, there is still time. And I'm not just being lazy. I'm ready to do anything. If Mama wants me to study law, then I will go to São Paulo . . ."

Chapter XXVI / *"The law is a beautiful thing"*

SOMETHING LIKE THE FLICKER of an idea crossed José Dias's face— an idea that cheered him enormously. He said nothing for a few moments; I kept my eyes fixed on him, while he stared out to sea. Then, when I repeated what I had said, he replied:

"It really is too late to do anything, but just to prove my willingness to help, I will go and talk to your mother. I can't promise I'll succeed, but I will do my best. I'll work heart and soul to convince her. You really don't want to be a priest? Well, the law is a beautiful thing. You could go to São Paulo or Pernambuco or even farther away. There are good universities all over the world. Yes, if the law is your true vocation, then study law. I'll talk to Dona Glória, but don't rely solely on me; talk to your uncle too."

"I will."

"And consult God as well, God and the Holy Virgin," he concluded, pointing skyward.

The sky was growing dark and overcast. Above the beach, large black birds were circling, either flapping their wings or gliding, then diving down to skim the water with their feet, before rising up, only to dive down again. But neither the darkness in the sky nor the fantastical dances of the birds could divert my mind from my interlocutor. Having said that I would do as he suggested, I added:

"God will do your will."

"Now, don't blaspheme. God is lord of all; he alone is the earth and the sky, the past, present, and future. Ask him for your happiness, for that is all I wish for too . . . If you cannot be a priest and prefer the law . . . yes, the law is a beautiful thing, which is not to undervalue theology, which, of course, is the best of all things, just as the ecclesiastical life is the holiest . . . Why shouldn't you go and study law elsewhere? Best to enroll in some university abroad and then travel as you study. We could go together; we'll see foreign lands, we'll hear English, French, Italian, Spanish, Russian, and even Swedish. Dona Glória probably won't be able to go with you; even if she could and did, she wouldn't want to have to deal with bureaucracy and paperwork, matriculations and accommodations, and to travel with you here, there and everywhere . . . Oh, yes, the law is a beautiful thing!"

"So it's agreed, then, you'll ask Mama not to send me to the seminary?"

"I'll certainly ask, but to ask is not necessarily to receive. Angel of my heart, if wishes were commands, then we would already be there, we'd already be on board! Oh, just wait until you see Europe. Ah, Europe!"

He raised one leg and performed a pirouette. One of his ambitions was to return to Europe, he had often spoken of it, but had never succeeded in tempting either my mother or Uncle Cosme, however warmly he spoke of the climate there and the many beautiful sights . . . The possibility of going to Europe with me and staying for however long my studies might last had never before occurred to him.

"We're already on board, Bentinho, we're on board!"

Chapter XXVII / *At the gates*

AT THE GATES of the Passeio Público, a beggar held out his hand to us. José Dias walked straight past, but, thinking about Capitu and the seminary, I took a two-*vintém* coin out of my pocket and gave it to the beggar. He kissed the coin, and I asked him to pray to God that all my wishes would be granted.

"Yes, my angel!"

"Oh, and my name's Bento," I added, just so that he would know.

Chapter XXVIII / *In the street*

JOSÉ DIAS was so happy that he slipped off his usual serious public persona and instead donned his more pliable, restless self. He was constantly pointing, talking, stopping outside every shop window or studying every theater poster. He told me the plots of various plays, recited monologues in verse. He did all his errands, paid bills, collected rent arrears, and bought a very cheap lottery ticket for himself. Finally, though, the stiff, stilted self won out over the pliable one, and he went back to speaking very slowly and using many superlatives. I didn't realize that this change was natural and feared that he might have gone back on our agreement, so I began treating him very affectionately, in words and gestures, until we got on the omnibus.

≡ Chapter XXIX / *The Emperor*

ON THE WAY, we met the Emperor, who was just leaving the School of Medicine. The omnibus we were traveling in stopped, as did every other vehicle; all the passengers got out and doffed their hats, until the imperial carriage had passed. When I returned to my seat, a fantastical idea entered my head: I would go and see the Emperor, explain the whole situation, and ask him to intervene. I wouldn't tell Capitu, though. "If His Majesty were to ask Mama, then she would be sure to give in," I thought.

I imagined the Emperor listening to me, reflecting on what I had told him, and finally agreeing to go and talk to my mother; I would tearfully kiss his hand. And I imagined myself back at home, waiting for the sound of the outriders and the cavalry escort: "It's the Emperor! It's the Emperor!" Everyone would rush to the windows to see him pass by, except that he wouldn't pass by. The carriage would stop outside our front door, the Emperor would get out and go inside. Great excitement among the neighbors: "The Emperor has gone into Dona Glória's house! What on earth is going on?"

Our family would come out to welcome him; my mother would be the first to kiss his hand. Then the Emperor, all smiles, either went into the drawing room or didn't—I can't quite remember, daydreams are often very confusing—and asked my mother not to force me to become a priest—and she, flattered and obedient, promised that she would not.

"How about medicine? Why don't you have him study medicine?"

"If that is what Your Majesty wants . . ."

"Yes, have him study medicine; it's a fine career, and we have excellent teachers here. Have you never visited our School of Medicine? A splendid place. We already have first-class doctors, who are a match for the best doctors anywhere in the world. Medicine is a mighty science, all that's needed to restore the health of others, to diagnose their illnesses, to combat and cure them . . . You yourself must have seen such miracles. True, your husband died, but then he had a fatal illness, and did not take proper care of himself . . . Yes, a fine career. Send him to our School of Medicine. Will you do that for me? Would you like that, Bentinho?"

"If that's what Mama wants."

"It is, my son. His Majesty commands it."

Then the Emperor again offered her his hand to kiss and left, and we all accompanied him out into the street to find it packed with people, every window crammed with onlookers, a stunned silence: the Emperor was getting into his carriage, nodding and waving and still saying: "Yes, Medicine, our School of Medicine." And the carriage left amid an atmosphere of envy and gratitude.

I saw and heard all this. No, Ariosto's imagination is no more fertile than that of children and lovers, and all an impossible vision requires is a corner of an omnibus. I took solace in this for a few moments, or perhaps minutes, until my plan crumbled and I turned to see the dreamless faces of my fellow travelers.

Chapter XXX / *The Blessed Sacrament*

YOU WILL HAVE REALIZED that the Emperor's imagined suggestion that I should study medicine was merely an indication of my own reluctance to leave Rio. Daydreams are just like any other kind of dream, they are woven out of our own inclinations and ideas. Going to São Paulo was one thing, but Europe . . . it was too far away, with all that sea and time in between. Hurrah for medicine! I would tell Capitu about my new hopes.

"It looks like they're about to bring out the Blessed Sacrament," said someone on the omnibus. "I can hear a bell, yes, I think it's coming from Santo Antônio dos Pobres. Stop the omnibus, Mr. Conductor!"

The conductor gave a tug on the cord connected to the driver's arm, the omnibus stopped, and the man got off. José Dias glanced first to the right, then to the left, before grabbing my arm and making me get off with him. We, too, would accompany the Blessed Sacrament. The bell was indeed calling the faithful to the sacrament of extreme unction. There were already a few people in the sacristy. This was the first time I had been present at such a solemn occasion; I obeyed, feeling slightly embarrassed at first, but then rather pleased, less because of the devout nature of my actions, and more because I was taking on a man's role. When the sacristan began handing out the surplices, another fellow rushed in, very out of breath; it was my neighbor Pádua, who had also come to accompany the Blessed Sacrament. He saw us there and came over to say hello. José Dias looked annoyed and gave only a brusque, monosyllabic response, keeping his eyes fixed on the priest washing his hands. Then, when he saw Pádua talking softly to the sacristan, he went to join them, and I followed suit. Pádua was asking the sacristan if he could carry one of the poles of the canopy. José Dias asked if he could do the same.

"There's only one available," said the sacristan.

"I'll take that one," said José Dias.

"But I asked first," said Pádua.

"You may have asked first, but you arrived late," retorted José Dias. "I was already here. You can carry a candle."

Despite Pádua's fear of José Dias, he nevertheless insisted in muffled tones on his right to carry one of the poles. The sacristan thought it best to placate the rivals, taking it upon himself to ask one of the other carriers to surrender his pole to Pádua, who was well known in the parish, as was José Dias. He did so, but José Dias immediately upset that apple cart too. No, since there was another pole available, surely I, a "young seminarian," was more deserving of such a distinction. Pádua turned as pale as the wax candles. This was a test of a father's heart. Out of curiosity, the sacristan, who had often seen me there with my mother on Sundays, asked if I really was a seminarian.

"Not yet, but he will be," said José Dias, winking at me discreetly. But it didn't help; I was still furious.

"Fine, then, let our Bentinho carry the pole," said Capitu's father with a sigh.

For my part, I would willingly have left it to Pádua; I knew that he usually only carried a candle when accompanying the Blessed Sacrament, but that on the last occasion he had been allowed to carry one of the poles. Anyone could carry a candle, but the special distinction of being allowed to carry a pole lay in having to cover and protect the priest and the Sacrament beneath the canopy. He had told me this himself, smiling and full of pious pride. This explains the haste with which he had entered the church; for this was the second time he would help carry the canopy, and he had gone straight up to the sacristan to ask that he be given this honor. In vain. He was relegated to being a mere candle-bearer again, another interim position snatched from him. He returned to his former post. I would happily have let him carry the pole, but José Dias foiled that act of generosity on my part and asked the sacristan to give us, José Dias and me, the two front poles, so that we would lead the procession.

Surplices on, lit candles distributed, priest and ciborium ready, the sacristan carrying the aspergillum and the bell, the procession went out into the street. I felt quite moved as we walked past the faithful, who knelt as we passed. Pádua, however, was gnawing bitterly on his candle.

That is a metaphor, by the way, but I can find no more vivid way of describing my neighbor's pain and humiliation. Not that I had much time to look at him or at José Dias, although the latter, walking alongside me, had his head held high as if he were the god of armies. I soon began to feel tired; my arms drooped; but, fortunately, the house was close by, in Rua do Senado.

The person to whom we were taking the Sacrament was a widow dying of consumption, and her fifteen- or sixteen-year-old daughter was standing at the bedroom door, weeping. The girl was neither beautiful nor even attractive; her disheveled hair fell loose about her shoulders, and her eyes were red and puffy from crying. And yet the whole scene spoke to and touched the heart. The woman made her confession to the priest, and he gave her Communion and administered the holy oils. The girl's sobbing redoubled then, and, feeling my own eyes growing moist, I hurried over to a window. Poor child! Grief was in itself infectious, and, complicated by the memory of my own mother, it felt even more painful to me, and when my thoughts turned to Capitu, I felt like sobbing, too, and escaped out into the hallway, where I heard someone say:

"Don't cry!"

I carried the image of Capitu with me, and my imagination, which, moments before, had attributed tears to her, now filled her mouth with laughter; I saw her writing our names on the wall, talking to me, walking around with her arms above her head; I distinctly heard my name spoken in a voice of intoxicating sweetness, and it was her voice. The lit candles on that grim occasion took on a nuptial glow, whatever that means. I had no idea, but it was something contrary to death, and I can think of nothing more contrary to death than a wedding. This new feeling so took hold of me that José Dias joined me in the hallway and whispered in my ear:

"Stop smiling like that!"

I immediately grew serious again. It was time to leave. I took up my pole; and since I already knew how far we had to go and we were heading straight back to the church—which shortened the distance—I found the pole now weighed almost nothing. Besides, everything was conspiring to fill my soul with a new lightness of spirit: the sun outside, the bustle in the street, the boys my own age eyeing me enviously, the faithful rushing to their windows or into their hallways and kneeling as we passed.

Pádua, on the other hand, looked still more humiliated. Even though he had given up his place to me, he could not reconcile himself to carrying a candle, a wretched candle. And yet other men were carrying candles, and did so with the seriousness befitting the occasion; they were not exactly thrilled, but nor were they sad. It was clear they considered it an honor.

Chapter XXXI / *Capitu's curiosity*

FOR CAPITU anything was better than the seminary. Instead of being plunged into despair by the threat of a long separation—assuming the idea of going to Europe became a reality—she seemed really pleased. And when I told her about my imperial dream, she responded:

"No, Bentinho, let's leave the Emperor in peace. Let's make do for now with José Dias's promise. When did he say he'd speak to your mother?"

"He didn't say when, but he promised he would go and see her, and would do so as soon as he could, and that meanwhile I should pray to God."

Capitu insisted that I repeat everything José Dias had said, as well as describing any changes in his facial expression, and, of course, that pirouette, which I had only mentioned in passing. She even wanted to know about the way in which he had pronounced certain words. She was very thorough and attentive to detail; everything, the story in itself and the conversation, was grist to her mill. It was as if she were filing away my account of events in her memory, to be compared, labeled, and pondered later. The second image is probably better than the first, but neither is perfect. Capitu was Capitu, that is, a most unusual creature, more of a woman than I was a man. If I haven't said that before, there it is. If I have said it before, there it is again. Some concepts should insinuate themselves into the reader's soul by dint of repetition.

She was also more curious than I was. Indeed, her many curiosities merit a whole chapter to themselves. They were explicable and inexplicable, useful and useless, some grave, others frivolous; she wanted to know everything. At school, where, from the age of seven, she had learned reading, writing, and arithmetic, as well as French, religious doctrine, and needlework, she had not, for example, learned how to make lace, and so she asked Cousin Justina to teach her. The only reason she didn't learn Latin with Father Cabral was because he, who had playfully suggested the possibility, then concluded by saying that Latin was not a language for girls. Capitu admitted to me one day that this only increased her desire to learn Latin. To compensate, she tried learning English with an old friend of her father's—a teacher and his partner at whist—but she did not get very far. Uncle Cosme, however, taught her to play backgammon.

"Come on, Capitu, let's see if you can beat me," he would say.

She would do as he asked, and she played easily, attentively, almost, one might say, lovingly. One day, I found her drawing a portrait in pencil; she was just adding the final touches and asked me to wait until she had finished, then see whether I thought it a good likeness. It was a portrait of my father, copied from the painting my mother had in the drawing room, and which I still have with me now. It was far from perfect; on the contrary, she had given him somewhat bulging eyes, for example, and his hair consisted of little scribbled circles superimposed one on the other. However, given that she had no artistic training, and had done the drawing from memory in a matter of minutes, I thought it was really very good; you must allow, of course, for my age at the time and my fondness for the artist. Nevertheless, she would clearly have picked up painting in no time, just as she learned music later on. She already enjoyed tinkering on the piano in our house, a useless old thing kept purely for its sentimental value. She read all the novels we had, leafed through our books of engravings, eager to know about ruins, people, military campaigns, the name, history, and location of everything. José Dias proudly gave her this information as if he were genuinely erudite, although his erudition was about on a par with his rather primitive knowledge of homeopathy.

One day, Capitu asked about the men whose heads adorned the living room ceiling. He gave her a brief summary, lingering a little longer over Caesar, with many exclamations and a few Latin phrases:

"Caesar! Julius Caesar! A great man! *Et tu, Brute!*

Capitu did not find Caesar's face attractive, but the feats described by José Dias filled her with admiration. She stood studying him for a long time. A man who could do anything! And who had done everything! A man who had given a lady a pearl worth six million sesterces!

"What was a sesterce worth?"

Since José Dias did not know offhand the value of a sesterce, he replied enthusiastically:

"Yes, the greatest man in history!"

Capitu's eyes lit up when she heard the story of the pearl Caesar gave to his mistress. It was on that same occasion that Capitu asked my mother why she no longer wore the jewels she was wearing in the portrait; she meant the one hanging in the drawing room, alongside the painting of my father, and in which she was wearing a large necklace, a diadem and earrings.

"Ah, they, like me, are widows, Capitu."

"When did you wear them?"

"For the coronation celebrations."

"Oh, do tell me about that!"

She already knew what her parents had told her, but, naturally enough, she figured they knew little more than what went on in the streets. She wanted to hear about the special pews in the imperial chapel and about the balls. She had been born long after those famous celebrations. Having often heard tell of the crisis surrounding the Emperor's Majority, she insisted one day on being told about that, too, and, when it was explained to her, she declared that the Emperor had been quite right to accede to the throne when he was just fifteen. Everything was worthy of Capitu's curiosity: antique furniture, old ornaments, customs, stories about Itaguaí, my mother's childhood and adolescence, a saying, an idea, a proverb . . .

Chapter XXXII / *Eyes with an undertow*

YES, EVERYTHING was worthy of Capitu's curiosity. There was one case, though, when I can't be sure if she acted as student or teacher or both, like me, but I'll tell you about that in another chapter. In this one I will say only that, a few days after my talk with José Dias, I went to see Capitu; it was ten o'clock in the morning. Dona Fortunata, who was in the backyard, didn't even wait for me to ask where her daughter was.

"She's in the drawing room combing her hair," she said. "Creep in there and give her a fright."

I approached as slowly as I could, but either my foot or the mirror gave me away. It can't have been the latter, because it was just a small gimcrack mirror with a rough-and-ready frame (forgive the vulgarity) bought from an Italian street vendor, and which was suspended between the two windows from a small brass ring. If it wasn't the mirror, then it was my foot. One or the other, but the fact is that I had barely entered the room when comb, hair, and Capitu herself flew into the air, and all I heard was this question:

"Has something happened?"

"No, nothing," I said, "I just popped in to see you before Father Cabral arrives for my lesson. Did you sleep well?"

"Yes, fine. José Dias still hasn't spoken to your mother, then?"

"It seems not."

"When will he, then?"

"He said he intends to raise the subject today or tomorrow; he won't jump straight in, he'll take a more roundabout route, drop a hint or two. Then he'll get down to business. He first wants to find out if Mama is still firmly resolved to—"

"Oh, she is, she is," said Capitu, breaking in. "That's why we need someone to broach the subject and win her around, otherwise there'd be no point in talking to her. I'm not convinced now if José Dias will have that much influence. I'm sure he'll do his best if he really thinks you don't want to be a priest, but can he do it? She does listen to his advice, but . . . Oh, this is dreadful! Keep nagging him, Bentinho."

"I will. Today's the day."

"Do you swear?"

"I swear. Let me look at your eyes, Capitu."

I had suddenly remembered José Dias's description of her eyes "like a gypsy's eyes, oblique and sly." I didn't know what "oblique" meant, but I knew the word "sly," and I wanted to see if that was a fair description. Capitu allowed herself to be studied and scrutinized, asking only why I wanted to look at them, had I never seen them before? I found nothing remarkable, just the familiar color and sweetness. I think my prolonged contemplation of them made her think I had some other intention; she imagined that this was simply an excuse to look at them more closely, with my eyes fixed long and hard on hers, and which is, I think, why they became larger and larger and more somber, with an expression that . . .

Come, lovers' rhetoric, and bring me a precise, poetic comparison that could convey exactly what Capitu's eyes were like. No image comes to mind capable of describing those eyes and their effect on me, not without offending stylistic proprieties. Eyes with an undertow? Yes, that's it. It's precisely what comes to mind when I recall that new expression in her eyes. They contained some kind of mysterious, energetic fluid, a force that drew me in, like a wave withdrawing from the beach on stormy days. In order not to be dragged into her eyes, I clung to other neighboring parts, her ears, her arms, her hair hanging loose about her shoulders, but as soon as I returned to her eyes, the wave rising up out of them grew and grew, a dark cave threatening to overwhelm me, seize hold of me, and swallow me up. How many minutes did we spend playing that game? Only heaven's clocks could have measured a period of time that was at once infinite and brief. Eternity has its own time-pieces; just because it is itself never-ending doesn't mean that it takes no interest in the duration of our human joys and torments. The pleasure of the blessèd in heaven must be redoubled when they find out how many torments their enemies will have suffered in hell; and the sheer quantity of delights experienced by the latter's foes in heaven will only increase the agonies felt by those condemned to hell. This was one torment Dante failed to include, but I am not here to correct the poets. I am here to describe how, after an incalculable length of time, I finally fixed on Capitu's hair, this time not just with my eyes, but with my hands, and I said to her—just in order to say something—that I could comb her hair for her if she liked.

"You?"

"Yes, me."

"You'll get it all tangled."

"If I do, you can always untangle it afterward."

"Go on, then."

⟹ Chapter XXXIII / *The coiffure*

CAPITU TURNED TO FACE the mirror, and sat with her back to me. I took hold of her waist-length hair, gathered it up in my two hands, and began combing it from the roots to the tips. This didn't really work while she was standing up: don't forget, she was a tiny bit taller than me, but it would have been problematic even had she been the same height. I asked her to sit down.

She did. "All right, let's see the great coiffeur at work," she said, laughing. I continued to comb her hair very carefully, then divided it into two equal sections to make two braids. I didn't do this quickly, as a professional hairdresser would, but slowly, very slowly, savoring my contact with those thick tresses, with that part of her. I worked rather clumsily, sometimes out of sheer ineptitude, and sometimes on purpose so that I could undo what I had done and redo it. My fingers sometimes brushed the back of her neck or touched her shoulder blades beneath her cotton dress—a delightful feeling. Eventually, though, however much I would have liked that process to last forever, I ran out of hair. I didn't pray to heaven that her hair could be as long as Aurora's hair, because I didn't yet know that divinity, to whom I was only introduced later on by the old poets, but I wished I could comb her hair for all eternity and create two braids that could wind about the infinite a countless number of times. If this seems exaggerated, unfortunate reader, that is because you have never combed the hair of a young girl, never placed your adolescent hands on the young head of a nymph . . . A nymph! Ah, I've gone all mythological! A little earlier, I wrote the name "Thetis," then crossed it out, so let us also cross out "nymph"; let us say, rather, a beloved creature, a phrase equally potent in the Christian and the Pagan worlds. Anyway, I did finally finish those two braids. Where was the ribbon I needed to tie up the ends? On the table lay a grubby little scrap of ribbon. I put the ends of the two braids together and tied them up with a single bow, then put the finishing touches, primping and smoothing, before exclaiming:

"There you are!"

"Does it look good?"

"Look in the mirror."

Instead of going to the mirror, what do you think Capitu did?

Don't forget that she was sitting facing away from me. Capitu leaned her head back, so far that I had to reach out to stop her from falling; it was, after all, a low-backed chair. I then bent over her so that we were face-to-face, but upside down, each with our eyes on the level of the other's mouth. I begged her to raise her head, because she might get dizzy or hurt her neck. I even said she looked ugly like that, but this still did not move her.

"Sit up, Capitu!"

She refused to raise her head, and we remained like that, gazing at each other, until she pursed her lips, and I moved mine closer, and . . .

The kiss had a dramatic effect: Capitu sat bolt upright, and I retreated to the wall, feeling almost dizzy, unable to speak, my vision slightly blurred. When I could see clearly again, I saw that Capitu was staring down at the floor. I did not dare to say a word; even if I had wanted to, I was completely tongue-tied. Unable to move, too stunned to speak, I could not dredge up enough energy to unglue myself from the wall and heap Capitu with a thousand warm, loving words . . . Do not mock my fifteen-year-old self, precocious reader. At seventeen, Des Grieux—yes, Des Grieux, no less—was still not even aware that there were two sexes.*

---

* Des Grieux is one of the main protagonists in Antoine François Prévost's novel *Manon Lescaut*. He runs away to Paris with the eponymous heroine when he is only seventeen.

Chapter XXXIV / *I'm a man!*

WE HEARD FOOTSTEPS in the hallway; it was Dona Fortunata. Capitu quickly regained her composure, so quickly that she was already shaking her head and laughing when her mother appeared at the door. Her color had returned, and she showed not a hint of shame or embarrassment, her laughter bright and spontaneous as she explained gaily:

"Mama, look what this gentleman coiffeur has done! He asked if he could do my hair, and here you have the result. Have you ever seen such braids?"

"Why, what's wrong with them?" asked her mother, overflowing with kindness. "They're lovely. No one would think they were the work of an amateur."

"Oh, come, now, Mama! This?" retorted Capitu, unraveling the braids. "Really, Mama!"

And with the charming, willful pout she sometimes adopted, she took up the comb and returned her hair to its usual smooth self. Dona Fortunata said she was being silly and told me to take no notice, it was just her daughter's usual nonsense. She gazed fondly at me and at Capitu. Then it seemed to me that she sensed something was wrong. Seeing me so stiff and silent, my back to the wall, she perhaps felt there was between us something more than just a coiffure, and she smiled, pretending not to have noticed . . .

I also wanted to say something in order to disguise my unease, and I did manage to summon up a few words, which arrived promptly, but in such a rush that they crammed my mouth so full that none could emerge. Capitu's kiss had sealed my lips. However hard they tried, not a single exclamation, not even a mere article could burst out. And all the words withdrew into my heart, muttering: "Well, he's not going to get very far in the world if he lets his emotions get the better of him like that . . ."

Thus, caught by her mother, our one became two, and opposites at that, with Capitu covering up with words what I made public with my silence. Dona Fortunata rescued me from my hesitant state, saying that my mother had sent for me; it was time for my Latin lesson and Father Cabral was waiting. This offered me an escape route: I said goodbye and slipped off down the hallway. As I went, I heard mother scolding daughter for her bad manners, but the daughter said nothing.

I ran to my room and picked up my books, but I did not go straight to the classroom; I sat down on my bed, remembering how I had combed her hair and remembering everything else as well. Shivers ran through me, I drifted in and out of consciousness, losing all awareness of myself and the things around me, as if I existed who knows where or how. Then I returned to myself, and saw the bed, the walls, the books, the floor, heard vague sounds from outside, near or far, and then it all vanished again and all I could feel were Capitu's lips . . . I felt them pressed firmly to my equally firm lips, joined as one. Suddenly, unwittingly, unthinkingly, these proud words emerged from my mouth:

"I'm a man!"

Fearing that someone must have heard me, because I had spoken these words out loud, I ran to my bedroom door. There was no one there. I came back into my room and very softly repeated that I was a man. I can still hear the words echoing in my ears. Saying those words gave me enormous pleasure. Columbus could not have felt more pleasure on discovering America, and please forgive the banal comparison, which is nonetheless very apt: for in every adolescent there is an undiscovered world, an admiral, and an October sun. I made other discoveries later on, but none as dazzling as that. José Dias's revelation had certainly excited me, as had the lesson from the old coconut palm; the sight of our two names scratched by her on the backyard wall had truly shaken me too; but nothing could compare with that kiss. Those other things could all be lies or illusions. And if they were true, they were only the bare bones of the truth, not its flesh and blood. Even our hands touching, clasped as tightly as if fused together, could not say everything.

"I'm a man!"

When I repeated these words for the third time, I thought about the seminary, but only as one might think of a danger that had passed, an evil averted, a nightmare extinguished; all my senses were telling me that men do not become priests. My blood was of the same opinion. Again I felt Capitu's lips. Perhaps I'm making too much of these oscular reminiscences, but then that is the very nature of nostalgia: going over and over old memories. Of all my memories from that time, I believe the memory of that kiss is the sweetest, the most novel, the most comprehensive, the one that revealed me entirely to myself. I have other memories, vast and numerous and, yes, sweet, too, memories of various kinds, many of them intellectual and equally intense. Even had I gone on to become a great man, though, the memory of my greatness would pale into insignificance beside that kiss.

Chapter XXXV / *The Protonotary Apostolic*

I DID FINALLY PICK UP MY BOOKS and rush off to my lesson. Well, I didn't exactly rush; halfway there, I stopped, realizing that I must be very late, and that the look on my face might betray me. I considered lying and saying I'd had a dizzy spell while in my room, but I rejected this idea when I thought of how alarmed my mother would be. I considered making a promise to say dozens more Paternosters; however, I had only recently made such a promise and had another favor pending . . . So, let's see; I approached cautiously, heard cheerful voices talking loudly. And when I entered the room, no one scolded me.

The previous day, Father Cabral had received a message asking him to visit the internuncio; he duly went and learned that, by pontifical decree, he had just been named protonotary apostolic. This papal title was a cause of great contentment to him and to us all. Uncle Cosme and Cousin Justina kept repeating it in slightly awed tones; it was the first we had heard of such a title, being more familiar with canons and monsignors, bishops, nuncios, and internuncios; but what was a protonotary apostolic? Father Cabral explained that it wasn't so much the appointment to the Curia that mattered as the *honor*. Uncle Cosme clearly felt that he somehow shared in the glory of his partner at the card table.

"A protonotary apostolic!"

Then turning to me, he said:

"Prepare yourself, Bentinho. You, too, might be a protonotary apostolic one day."

Cabral enjoyed hearing his new title repeated over and over. He was standing up, and occasionally took a few steps back and forth, smiling or drumming his fingers on the lid of his snuffbox. The sheer length of the title somehow made it doubly magnificent, since it was far too long to be attached to his name; Uncle Cosme was the first to point this out. Father Cabral explained that it really wasn't necessary to say the whole thing, they could just call him Protonotary Cabral, with the "apostolic" understood.

"Protonotary Cabral."

"Yes, you're right, Protonotary Cabral."

"But, Protonotary Cabral," said Cousin Justina, so as to become accustomed to using the title, "does this mean you'll have to go to Rome?"

"No, Dona Justina."

"No, it's a purely honorific title," said my mother.

"Of course," said Father Cabral, who was still taking it all in, "this doesn't mean that the full title, protonotary apostolic, will not be used on ceremonial occasions, at public events, in formal letters, and so on. In everyday use, though, plain protonotary will be sufficient."

"Of course," we all said.

José Dias, who entered the room shortly after me, also applauded the distinction, and recalled, apropos, Pius IX's early liberalism and the hope this had given Italy, but no one pursued the topic; my old Latin teacher was the man of the hour and the place. Recovering from my fear, I suddenly realized that I, too, should congratulate him, and my applause was no less heartfelt. He patted my cheek in fatherly fashion and said I could have the day off. For that one hour, our happiness was entirely mutual. A kiss and a holiday! I think my face must have spoken for me, because Uncle Cosme, his large belly quivering with laughter, called me a lazybones; but José Dias put a stop to such jollity, saying:

"One should never celebrate idleness, besides, Latin will always be useful, *even if he doesn't become a priest.*"

There was my man. This was the first word, the first seed sown, as if in passing, with the intention of getting the ears of the family accustomed to the idea. My mother smiled at me, a smile full of love and sadness, then said:

"But he *will* be a priest, and very handsome one."

"Don't forget, sister," said Uncle Cosme, "he will be a protonotary as well. A protonotary apostolic."

"Protonotary Santiago," added Father Cabral.

I don't know if my Latin teacher was simply practicing using the title along with a name, but I do know that when I heard my own name linked to that title, I had to stop myself from blurting out some inappropriate comment. This impulse, though, was just an idea, a wordless idea, which remained still and silent, along with other ideas . . . But these demand a chapter of their own. Let us conclude by saying that my Latin teacher spoke briefly about my ecclesiastical ordination, albeit without any great enthusiasm. He was merely looking for some other topic of conversation to show that he had quite forgotten about his own moment of glory, which, however, was what continued to dazzle him. He was an even-tempered, skinny old fellow with many good qualities. He did have his faults, though, the worst being greed; not that he was a glutton, for he ate very little, but he did enjoy certain refined delicacies, and our cuisine, though simple, was more varied than his. And so when my mother invited him to stay to supper so that we could drink to his health, the smile with which he accepted this invitation may have been that of a protonotary, but it was far from apostolic. And in order to please my mother, he again turned to me, describing my ecclesiastical future, and asking if I would be going to the seminary now or the following year, and offering to speak to "His Excellency the Bishop," and punctuating everything with the words "Protono-tary Santiago."

Chapter XXXVI / *An idea with no legs and an idea with no arms*

I LEFT HIM, SAYING that I was going off to play, and went back to pondering that morning's adventure. This was the best thing to do, without Latin or even with Latin. After five minutes, it occurred to me to run next door, grab Capitu, undo her braids, redo them, then conclude in that very particular manner, lips pressed to lips. That's it, let's go, that's it . . . It was only an idea, though. An idea with no legs! My own legs wanted neither to run nor to walk. Only much later did they very slowly leave my house and go over to Capitu's. When I arrived, I found her in the same room, sitting on the settee, a cushion on her lap, peacefully sewing. She didn't look me squarely in the face, but only furtively and fearfully, or, if you prefer José Dias's terminology, obliquely and slyly. Her hands stopped moving each time they stuck the needle in the cloth. Standing where I was, on the other side of the table, I didn't know what to do; and again the words I had brought with me fled. A few long minutes passed, until she stopped sewing completely, stood up, and looked at me expectantly. I went over to her and asked if her mother had said anything; no, she hadn't. The mouth with which she answered was such that I fear I may have made as if to go closer. The fact is that Capitu recoiled slightly.

This was the moment to seize her, draw her to me, and kiss her . . . Again, this was only an idea! An idea with no arms! My arms hung limp and dead by my sides. I knew nothing of the Scriptures. If I had, it's likely that the spirit of Satan would have encouraged me to give the mystical language of the Song of Songs a more direct and natural meaning. Then I would have quoted the very first line: "O that you would kiss me with the kisses of your mouth!" And as for my inert arms, I would simply have had to follow verse 6 of chapter 2: "O that his left hand were under my head, and that his right hand embraced me!" There you have the sequence of gestures. It was simply a matter of putting them into practice; but even had I known the text, Capitu looked so withdrawn and aloof that I might well have just stayed there, rooted to the spot. In the end, it was she who rescued me from that situation.

Chapter XXXVII / *The soul is full of mysteries*

"DID YOU KEEP Father Cabral waiting very long?"

"I didn't have a lesson today. I've been given a holiday."

I explained the reason for that holiday. I also told her that Father Cabral had talked about my entering the seminary, in support of my mother's resolve to send me there, and I said a few harsh, cruel things about him. Capitu thought for a moment, then asked if she could go to my house that afternoon to congratulate him.

"Of course, but why?"

"Papa is bound to want to come, too, of course, but it would be better, more fitting, if he went instead to the priest's house. I couldn't do that, not now that I'm nearly a young woman," she concluded with a laugh.

That laugh gave me courage. Her words appeared to be a joke aimed at herself, given that, since that morning, she was a woman, just as I was a man. I found her remark very charming, and wanted to prove to her that she was indeed a young woman. I gently took hold of her right hand, then her left, and stood there, motionless and trembling. This was an idea with hands. I wanted to draw Capitu's hands toward me and thus force her to follow, but once more my actions did not match my intentions. Nevertheless, I felt strong and bold. I wasn't imitating anyone; I didn't live with other boys who could tell me stories about love. I knew nothing of the rape of Lucretia. All I knew about the Romans was that they spoke as they did in Father Pereira's Latin grammar, and were the fellow countrymen of Pontius Pilate. I'm not denying that the conclusion of that morning's coiffure was a major step along the road to amorous success, but what Capitu did then was precisely the opposite of what she was doing now. In the morning, she had leaned her head back, now she was avoiding me; and that was not the only way in which these two encounters differed; in another way, too, where there could have been repetition, there was only contrast.

I think I made as if to pull her toward me. I can't swear to that, because I was starting to feel so flustered that I wasn't fully aware of my actions, but I assume that I did, because she pulled away and tried to release her hands from mine; then, perhaps because she could not withdraw any farther, she put one foot in front of the other and leaned back with her whole upper body. This forced me to hold on still more tightly. She finally tired of that position and gave in, but her head did not, and with her head still thrown back, she rendered all my efforts futile, because, dear reader, I was making a real effort by then. Since I did not know the Song of Songs, it did not occur to me to place my left hand under her head; besides, such a gesture presupposes a meeting of minds, and Capitu, who was resisting me now, would have taken advantage of that gesture to free herself from my other hand and escape me entirely. We remained locked in that struggle, necessarily noiseless because, despite being engaged in a game of attack and defense, we were still taking care not to be heard; the soul is full of mysteries. Now

I know that I *was* pulling at her, and she continued to keep her head thrown back, until she grew tired; then it was the turn of her mouth. Capitu's mouth went in the opposite direction to mine, turning away from whichever side I was aiming at. And there we were in that impasse, with me not daring to go any further, and all it would have taken was a little more . . .

At that point, we heard someone knocking at the front door and then calling out. It was Capitu's father, who had come home from the office slightly early, as he did sometimes. "Open the door, Nanata! Capitu, open the door!" This was apparently a repetition of what had happened in the morning when Capitu's mother found us there, but only apparently; this was quite different. Remember that in the morning, the kiss was all over and done with, and the sound of Dona Fortunata's footsteps served as a warning so that we could compose ourselves. Now, though, we were engaged in hand-to-hand combat, and nothing had even begun.

We heard the bolt on the front door slide back, as Capitu's mother opened it. And since I'm confessing everything, I say here and now that I did not have time to release my friend's hands; I considered it, and even tried to do so, but before her father could enter the room, Capitu did something most unexpected: She pressed her lips to mine. And she willingly gave what she had been battling so hard to refuse. As I say, the soul is full of mysteries.

Chapter XXXVIII / *"Goodness, you startled me!"*

WHEN PÁDUA entered the drawing room, Capitu was standing with her back to me, bent over her sewing as if to pick it up, and was asking me:

"But Bentinho, what *is* a protonotary apostolic?"

"Hello, you two!" exclaimed her father.

"Goodness, you startled me!"

Now the scene is the same as the previous one; but the reason I'm describing in detail those two scenes that took place forty years ago is simply to show that Capitu could not only control her feelings in the presence of her mother; she was equally undaunted by her father. In a situation that left me tongue-tied, she spoke quite naturally and innocently. I'm sure her heart beat neither faster nor slower. She claimed to be startled, and did even look slightly frightened; but, knowing the situation as I did, I saw that it was all a lie, and was filled with envy. She immediately greeted her father, who came over to me and shook my hand, wanting to know why his daughter was talking about a protonotary apostolic. Capitu repeated what I had told her, and said that her father should go to Father Cabral's house to congratulate him, and she would go to mine. Then, gathering up her sewing materials, she set off down the hallway, calling out in a childish voice:

"Mama, supper, Papa's home!"

Chapter XXXIX / *The vocation*

FATHER CABRAL was at that very early stage after receiving an honor when even the smallest words of congratulation feel like odes. Later, recipients receive such praise blank-faced, and without a word of thanks. The excitement of that early stage is much to be preferred; a state of mind that can see a tree bowing in the wind as a congratulatory message from the flora of the world provokes deeper, more delicate sensations than any other. Father Cabral listened to Capitu's words with infinite pleasure.

"Thank you, Capitu, thank you very much. I'm touched that you should feel so pleased for me. And Papa is well? And your Mama? I hardly need ask how you are; your face alone tells me that you're brimming with good health. And are you saying your prayers regularly?"

Capitu answered all his questions promptly and correctly. She was wearing a neat little dress and her outdoor shoes. She didn't enter the room in her usual familiar fashion, but paused at the door before going over to kiss my mother's hand and that of Father Cabral. When she had addressed the latter as protonotary twice in a matter of five minutes, José Dias, not to be outdone, launched into a brief speech in honor of "Pope Pius IX's most august and fatherly heart."

"You're a great speechifier," said Uncle Cosme when he had finished.

José Dias did not take offense at this, but merely smiled. Father Cabral echoed José Dias's words of praise, minus the superlatives; and José Dias then added that Cardinal Mastai had clearly been intended for the papal tiara from the beginning of time.* Then, winking at me, he concluded:

"Vocation is all. The ecclesiastical state is a most perfect thing as long as the priest is destined to embrace that state from the cradle. Where there's no vocation, and I mean real, genuine vocation, a young man could just as easily study the humanities, which are also useful and honorable."

Father Cabral responded, saying:

"Vocation is very important, but God's will is supreme. A man can dislike the Church and even persecute it, until, one day, God speaks to him and he becomes an apostle. Think only of Saint Paul."

"Oh, I agree, but that isn't what I mean. What I mean is that one can also serve God without becoming a priest, out in the world. Is that not so?"

"It is."

"Aha!" José Dias exclaimed in a triumphant voice, looking around him. "Without vocation there can be no good priest, but one can serve God, as we all should do, in any liberal profession."

"Absolutely, but vocation does not only start in the cradle."

"But surely it's better if it does."

"A young man with no taste for the ecclesiastical life can still become a very good priest; it is all as God determines. I hesitate to give myself as an example, but I was born with a vocation for medicine. However, my godfather, who was coadjutor at the church of Santa Rita, kept nagging my father to send me to the seminary, and,

---

* Pope Pius IX (formerly Cardinal Mastai) was head of the Catholic Church from 1846 to 1878. At the time of his election, he was seen as a champion of liberalism and reform, but the Revolutions of 1848 decisively reversed his policies, and he became increasingly conservative. His 1864 *Syllabus of Errors* condemned many Enlightenment ideas such as secularization and separation of Church and state.

in the end, my father agreed. Well, I so enjoyed my studies and the company of the priests that I ended up taking orders myself. What if things hadn't turned out like that and I hadn't changed vocations? What would have happened? I would have studied certain subjects well worth knowing, and which are always taught better at the seminary than anywhere else."

Here Cousin Justina butted in:

"You mean you can enter the seminary and not come out a priest?"

Of course, Father Cabral said, and then, turning to me, he spoke of my vocation, which was evident to everyone; my childhood games had always been centered around the church and I loved divine service. Not that this proved anything, for in my day all children were devout. Father Cabral added, though, that the rector of São José, whom he had recently told of my mother's promise, held my birth to be a miracle; and he was of the same opinion. Capitu, keeping close to my mother, ignored my anxious glances, indeed, she appeared not to be listening to this conversation about the seminary and its consequences, and yet, as I found out later, she had absorbed all the principal arguments. Twice I went over to the window, hoping she would follow, so that we could be alone and at ease until the end of the world, if the world ever did end, but still Capitu did not move. She only left my mother's side in order to go home. It was time to say her rosary, she said.

"You go with her, Bentinho," said my mother.

"There's no need, Dona Glória," Capitu said, laughing. "I know the way. Goodbye, Senhor Protonotary . . ."

"Goodbye, Capitu."

Having taken one step as if to cross the room, it was clear that my duty, my desire, every impulse of age and the occasion, were urging me to cross the whole room, to follow Capitu into the hallway and out into the backyard, where I could give her a third kiss and say goodbye. I didn't mind that she had rejected my company—which I took anyway to be a mere ruse—and went into the hallway; Capitu, who was walking very briskly, stopped in her tracks and gestured to me to go back. I refused and went over to her.

"No, don't come. We'll talk tomorrow."

"But I just wanted to say—"

"Tomorrow."

"Listen!"

"Stay there!"

She was speaking softly; she took my hand, then placed her finger on her lips. A slave woman, who had come inside to light the lamp in the hallway, caught us in that pose and laughed sympathetically, murmuring something we could not quite catch. Capitu whispered to me that the slave woman suspected something and might tell the other women. Again she told me to stay where I was and then left; and I just stayed there, fixed, nailed, riveted to the spot.

Chapter XL / *A mare*

LEFT ALONE, I spent some time pondering, and a fantasy came into my head. You will, by now, be familiar with my fantasies. I told you about the Emperor's visit; I told you about this house in Engenho Novo being a replica of the house in Rua de Matacavalos . . . My imagination has kept me company throughout my life, lively, quick, restless, sometimes timid and with a tendency to stall, but more often capable of galloping furiously across country, eating up the miles. I seem to recall reading in Tacitus that Iberian mares were made pregnant by the wind; or if it wasn't Tacitus, it was some other classical author, who saw fit to include this superstition in one of his books. In this respect, my imagination was a great Iberian mare; the slightest breeze produced a foal, which immediately turned into Alexander's stallion, but enough of such bold metaphors, which are so unlikely in a fifteen-year-old. Let us put the case simply. My fantasy at that moment was to reveal all to my mother: my love for Capitu and the fact that I had no ecclesiastical vocation. The discussion about vocation came back to me now in all its detail, and although it frightened me, it also opened a door, a way out. "Yes," I thought, "I'll go and tell Mama that I have no vocation, and that Capitu and I are in love; if she's not convinced, then I'll tell her about the other day, about me braiding Capitu's hair and what happened next . . ."

Chapter XLI / *The secret audience*

THAT "WHAT HAPPENED NEXT" kept me standing in the hallway as I considered the matter further. I saw Dr. João da Costa arrive, and preparations for the customary game of ombre being made. My mother emerged from the drawing room and, finding me there, asked if I had taken Capitu home.

"No, Mama, she went on her own."

Then, almost launching myself at her, I said:

"Mama, there's something I want to tell you."

"What?"

All alarmed, she asked where it hurt, was it my head, my chest, my stomach, she put her hand on my forehead to see if I was feverish.

"No, I'm not ill, Mama."

"What is it, then?"

"It's something that . . . But listen, it would be better to talk after we've had tea . . . yes, after tea . . . It's nothing bad. You get so worried about the slightest thing, and it's nothing to be frightened about."

"You're not ill?"

"No, I'm not."

"That cold of yours has come back, hasn't it? You're hiding it because you don't want to take your medicine, but you've definitely got a cold. I can hear it in your voice."

I tried to laugh, as proof that I was fine. However, she still wouldn't allow me to postpone my confession, and, taking my arm, she led me into her bedroom, where she lit a candle and ordered me to tell her everything. Then, as a starting point, I asked her when I would be going to the seminary.

"Next year, after the holidays."

"Will I have to stay there?"

"What do you mean?"

"Won't I be allowed to come home?"

"You'll come home on Saturdays and during the holidays, it's better like that. And when you're ordained, you can come and live with me."

I wiped my eyes and blew my nose. She stroked my head, then tried to scold me, but I think her voice quavered, and it seemed to me that her eyes were moist with tears. I said that the idea of being separated from her made me sad, too. She said that we wouldn't be separated, or only briefly because of my studies, and that after the first few days I would soon get used to my fellow students and to the teachers, and would even come to enjoy living with them.

"You're the only person I really love, Mama."

There was no calculation behind these words, but I was nonetheless pleased to have said them, so as to have her believe that she was my one true love and thus divert suspicion away from Capitu. How many immoral intentions hitch a ride, halfway through the journey, on a pure, innocent sentence like that! It's enough to make one think that lying is often as involuntary as sweating. On the other hand, dear reader, have you noticed that there I was trying to divert suspicions away from Capitu when I had summoned my mother precisely in order to confirm those suspicions; but then the world is full of such contradictions. The truth is that my mother was as innocent as the first dawn before original sin raised its ugly head; she lacked the necessary sixth sense to even make such a deduction, that is, she would never conclude from my sudden opposition to entering the seminary that I had been whispering in corners with Capitu, as José Dias put it. She remained silent for a few moments; then she responded, but not in an imposing or authoritative manner, and this encouraged me to resist further. I spoke about the sense of vocation that had been discussed that very afternoon, and confessed that I felt no such vocation.

"But you always loved the idea of becoming a priest," she said. "Don't you remember asking to go and see the seminarians leaving church in their cassocks? And, at home, when José Dias used to call you Most Reverend Sir, you would laugh and laugh! So why is it that now . . . No, I can't believe it, Bentinho. And besides . . . vocation comes with habit," she went on, repeating what she had heard Father Cabral say.

When I sought to disagree, she scolded me, not harshly, but quite forcefully, and I reverted to being the obedient son that I was.

Then she spoke at some length and with great solemnity about the promise she had made; she did not mention the circumstances or the occasion or her motives, about which I learned only later on. She repeated her main argument, namely that she had to keep her promise to God.

"Our Lord came to my aid when he saved your life, and I can neither lie to him nor fail him, Bentinho; such things cannot be done without committing a sin, and God, who is great and powerful, would not let me off lightly, Bentinho; I know that I would be punished, severely punished. Becoming a priest is a good and saintly thing; you know lots of priests, for example Father Cabral, who lives contentedly with his sister; one of my uncles was a priest, too, and, so they say, was very nearly made a bishop. Oh, do stop blubbering, Bentinho."

I think the look I gave her was so sorrowful that she quickly withdrew that word; no, I wasn't blubbering, I couldn't be, she knew how much I loved her, and that I would be incapable of pretending to feel something I didn't. She meant soppy, that I should stop being so soppy, that I should be a man and do as she asked, for her sake and for the good of my own soul. All this and other things were said rather hurriedly, and her voice sounded muffled, veiled, as if she were choking back tears. However, I saw that although her emotions were again threatening to overwhelm her, she was not to be moved; even so, I ventured to ask:

"And what if you were to ask God to release you from your promise?"

"No, I can't do that. Don't be so silly, Bentinho. Besides, how would I know that God had released me?"

"In a dream, perhaps. I sometimes dream of angels and saints."

"So do I, my dear, but it's no use. Look, it's getting late, let's go down to the drawing room. Anyway, just to be clear: in the first or second month of next year you will go to the seminary. What

I want now is for you to concentrate on getting to grips with the books you're studying. It's such a lovely thing, not just for you, but for Father Cabral too. The people at the seminary are very keen to meet you, because Father Cabral has been singing your praises."

She went over to the door, and we left the room together. Before we did, though, she turned to me, and I could see that she was almost about to throw her arms around me and say that I didn't have to become a priest after all. For, as the time for me to leave grew nearer, this was what she really wanted. She needed to find a way of repaying the debt she had incurred, but with another form of coinage that would be worth as much or more; alas, though, she could find none.

≡ Chapter XLII / *Capitu thinking*

THE FOLLOWING DAY, I went next door as soon as I could. Capitu was just saying goodbye to two friends who had come to visit her, Paula and Sancha, her classmates, the former fifteen and the latter seventeen. Paula was the daughter of a doctor, and Sancha the daughter of a dealer in merchandise from the Americas. Capitu was feeling rather tired and had a scarf wrapped tightly about her head; her mother told me that she had been reading too much the previous evening, before and after tea, in the drawing room, and then in bed, until long past midnight, and by lamplight too . . .

"Well, if I'd lit a candle, Mama, you would have told me off. Anyway, I'm fine now."

And as she began to untie the scarf, her mother suggested timidly that it might be best to keep it on, but Capitu declared that she didn't need it now because she was feeling fine.

We were left alone in the drawing room; Capitu confirmed her mother's version of events and added that she had felt unwell because of what she had heard at my house.

I then told her what had happened to me, the conversation with my mother, my pleas, her tears, and her final decisive words: in two or three months' time, I would be going to the seminary. Now what were we going to do? Capitu listened with rapt attention, which shifted from earnest to somber. By the time I had finished, she was struggling to control her breathing, as if she were about to explode with rage.

This happened so long ago now that I cannot say for certain if she really did cry or merely dabbed at her eyes; no, I think the latter. When I saw her do this, I took her hand to comfort her, but really I needed comforting too. We fell back on the sofa, and sat staring into space. No, that's not true; she was staring down at the floor. As soon as I noticed this, I did the same. But while I think Capitu was actually looking deep inside herself, I really was staring at the floor, at the worm-eaten cracks, two flies strolling about, and a chipped chair leg. It wasn't much, but it took my mind off my troubles. When I looked at Capitu again, I saw that she wasn't moving, and I was so afraid that I shook her very gently. Capitu came to and asked me to tell her again what had happened with my mother. I did so, toning down my account a little, so as not to upset her. Don't call me a liar, call me empathetic; and while it's true that I did fear losing Capitu if all her hopes were dashed, it really did hurt me to see her suffer. The ultimate truth, the truth of truths, is that I was already regretting having spoken to my mother before José Dias had had a chance to try his luck; when I think about it now, I wish I hadn't heard that disappointing but probably inevitable verdict, even if that had only meant putting it off. Capitu meanwhile was thinking, thinking, thinking . . .

Chapter XLIII / *"Are you afraid?"*

SUDDENLY SHE STOPPED THINKING and fixed me with those undertow eyes of hers and asked if I was afraid.

"Afraid?"

"Yes, I'm asking if you're afraid."

"Afraid of what?"

"Afraid of getting beaten, imprisoned, afraid of struggling, moving on, working . . ."

I didn't understand. If she had just said straight out, "Let's run away!" I may or may not have agreed, but at least I would have understood. But I couldn't grasp what that vague, random question meant.

"Sorry, I don't understand. Get beaten?"

"Yes."

"But beaten by whom? Who would give me a beating?"

Capitu looked slightly annoyed. Those undertow eyes did not move, but appeared to grow larger. Not knowing quite what to think, and not wanting to ask her again what she meant, I started wondering where that beating would come from, and why, and also why I would be taken prisoner, and by whom. Oh, dear God! I imagined myself in jail, a dark, insalubrious place. I also saw myself aboard a prison ship, in the Barbonos barracks, and the House of Correction. All these charming social institutions wrapped me in their mystery, and yet Capitu's undertow eyes continued to grow larger and larger until they drove everything else from my mind. Capitu's mistake was in not letting them keep on growing ad infinitum, but, instead, allowing them to resume their usual size, and their usual way of moving. Capitu returned to her normal self and said that she was just joking and didn't mean to alarm me; then, with a charming look on her face, she tapped my cheek and, smiling, said:

"Scaredy-cat!"

"Me? But . . ."

"Don't be silly, Bentinho. Who's going to beat you or imprison you? I'm just a bit crazy today, I was trying to make a joke, and—"

"No, Capitu, you're not joking. Neither of us is in the mood for jokes."

"Yes, you're right, it was just me being crazy. Anyway, see you later."

"What do you mean, 'see you later'?"

"My headache's coming back. I'm going to apply a couple of slices of lemon to my temples."

She did just that, and again wound the scarf tightly around her head. She then accompanied me out into the backyard to say good-bye; once there, though, we sat for a few minutes on the edge of the well. It was windy and the sky was overcast. Capitu again spoke of our separation as a certain, definitive fact, however hard I, fearing precisely that, tried to find reasons to reassure her. When she wasn't talking, Capitu kept sketching noses and faces on the ground with a twig. Ever since she had started drawing, this was one of her ways of passing the time; anything and everything served as pencil and paper. Remembering how she had written our names on the wall, I wanted to repeat this experience on the ground, and asked her to give me the twig. She either didn't hear me or else ignored me.

≈ Chapter XLIV / *The first child*

"GIVE IT HERE, let me write something too."

Capitu looked at me, but in a way that reminded me of José Dias's words, oblique and sly; she somehow looked up at me without actually looking up. In a slightly faint voice she asked:

"Tell me something, and I want you to tell me the truth, no beating about the bush; you must answer with your hand on your heart."

"What is it? Tell me."

"If you had to choose between me and your mother, who would you choose?"

"Who would I choose?"

She nodded.

"I would choose . . . but why should I have to choose? Mama would never ask me such a thing."

"Yes, but I'm asking you now. Imagine you're in the seminary and you get news that I'm dying . . ."

"Don't say that!"

". . . or that I'll pine away if you don't come at once, and your mother wouldn't let you come, tell me, would you come anyway?"

"I would."

"And disobey your mother?"

"Yes, and disobey my mother."

"You would leave the seminary, leave your mother, leave everything in order to see me on my deathbed?"

"Don't talk about dying, Capitu!"

Capitu gave a wan, incredulous little laugh, and wrote something on the ground with the twig. I leaned over and read the word: "liar."

This was all so strange that I could think of no response. I couldn't fathom what she meant by what she had written or what she had said. If I could have thought of some insult, large or small, I might have scratched it in the earth there and then, with that same twig, but absolutely nothing occurred to me. My head was empty. At the same time, I was gripped by a fear that someone might hear us or read that word. But who, when we were utterly alone? Dona Fortunata occasionally came to the door, but immediately went back inside. Our solitude was complete. I remember that a few swallows flew over the backyard, heading off toward the Santa Teresa district; that was it. In the distance, a vague hubbub of voices; in the street, the clatter of hooves; from the courtyard, the twittering of Pádua's caged birds. Nothing else, or only this curious phenomenon, that the word she had written was not only winking scornfully up at me from the ground, but even seemed to echo in the air. Then I had a very mean idea: I told her that, all things considered, the life of a priest wasn't such a bad one, and that I wouldn't find it so very hard to accept. This was a very childish act of revenge, but I harbored the secret hope that she would fling her arms around me, her face bathed in tears. Instead, Capitu merely opened her eyes very wide and said:

"Oh, yes, being a priest is definitely a good thing, no doubt about it; even better than being a priest, though, is being a canon, because they get to wear purple stockings. And purple's such a lovely color. Yes, when I think about it, being a canon is better."

"But you can't be a canon without first being a priest," I said, biting my lips.

"Fine, begin with the black stockings, and the purple ones will follow. What I really don't want to miss is your first mass; do give me plenty of notice so that I can make a fashionable dress for the occasion, with a hoop skirt and lots of frills . . . Although by then, of course, the fashion might have changed. And it will have to be in a big church, Carmo or São Francisco."

"Or Candelária."

"Yes, Candelária would be good, too, just as long as I get to hear your first mass. I'll make a real impression. Lots of people will ask: 'Who is that elegant young woman wearing that beautiful dress?'—'Oh, that's Dona Capitolina, a girl who used to live in Rua de Matacavalos . . .' "

"Used to live? Are you thinking of moving?"

"Who knows where one might live tomorrow?" she said in a slightly melancholy tone, which immediately turned sarcastic: "And you at the altar in your alb and your gold cape, singing . . . *Pater noster* . . ."

Ah, how I wish I were a romantic poet and could say this was a duel of ironies! I would describe my barbed comments and her ripostes, the sheer wit of one and the quickness of the other, my blood racing, passion in my soul, until my final rejoinder, which was this:

"Of course you will hear my first mass, Capitu, but on one condition."

To which she responded:

"Speak, Most Reverend Father."

"Promise me one thing."

"Which is?"

"No, first, you must promise."

"Since I don't know what it is, I can't promise."

"Actually, there are two things," I went on, for another thing had just occurred to me.

"Two things? What are they?"

"The first is that you will only confess to me so that I may administer a penance and grant absolution. The second is . . ."

"I can promise you the first thing," she said when she saw me hesitate, adding that she was eager to know the second thing.

I found it really hard to say, and I wish the words had never left my mouth; I would not then have heard what I did hear, and I would not have to write here something that might seem to the reader quite simply unbelievable.

"The second . . . yes . . . Promise me that I will be the priest at your wedding?"

"At my wedding?" she said, slightly taken aback.

Then she turned down the corners of her mouth and shook her head.

"No, Bentinho," she said, "that would mean a long wait, and besides, you're not going to become a priest overnight, that takes many years . . . Look, I'll promise you something else: I promise that you will baptize my first child."

Chapter XLV / *Shake your head, dear reader*

SHAKE YOUR HEAD, dear reader; look as incredulous as you like. Even put the book down, if you haven't already done so out of sheer tedium; after all, anything is possible. However, if you haven't put the book down until now, I trust you will pick it up again and open it at the same page, even though you don't believe a word of what the author wrote. And yet, that is exactly what happened. That is precisely what Capitu said, using those words and in that tone of voice. She spoke of her first child as if it were her first doll.

I was, as you can imagine, very shocked, but that shock was mingled with another strange sensation. A kind of fluid ran through

me. The threat of that first child, Capitu's first child, of her marrying someone else, which would mean our permanent separation,
loss, annihilation, all this affected me so deeply that I could find neither word nor gesture; I stood there stunned. Capitu was smiling,
and I could see her first child playing on the ground . . .

Chapter XLVI / *Making peace*

WE MADE PEACE as quickly as we had made war. Were I hoping to
glorify myself to you in this book, I would say that I was the one to
open negotiations, but, no, she did that. Moments later, seeing me
with my head bowed, she, too, bowed her head, but raised her eyes
so as to be able to see mine. I played hard to get, then made as if
to stand up and leave; but I didn't stand up, nor did I leave. Capitu
was looking at me so tenderly—and the way she was looking at me
made that gaze seem all the more tender and supplicating—that
I stayed, put my arm around her waist, and then she touched my
fingertips, and . . .

Dona Fortunata once more appeared at the door, I don't know
why; I didn't even have time to remove my arm from around Capitu's waist before she vanished again. She might just have been
doing what she felt was her duty, a ceremonial gesture, like the
obligatory prayers one gabbles through without any real religious
feeling; unless she merely wanted to confirm with her own eyes
what her heart knew was reality . . .

Whatever the truth of the matter, my arm continued to squeeze
her daughter's waist, and that is how we made our peace. What
was so touching was that we each wanted to take the blame and

reciprocally begged forgiveness. Capitu blamed her insomnia, her headache, her low spirits, and, finally, "one of my sulking fits." I— for I was easily moved to tears at the time—felt my eyes growing moist . . . It was pure love, sympathy for my little friend's pain, the tenderness of reconciliation.

Chapter XLVII / *"The mistress isn't at home"*

"RIGHT, THAT'S IT," I said at last, "but just tell me one thing, why did you ask me if I was afraid of being beaten?"

"Oh, no reason," Capitu replied. "Why bring that up again now?"

"No, tell me. Was it because of the seminary?"

"Yes, I've heard that they beat the boys there. No? I don't believe it either."

This explanation pleased me; there could be no other. If, as I now believe, Capitu was not telling the truth, I have to admit that she had no choice, and it was a lie like how maids tell visitors that "the mistress isn't at home" when, in fact, the mistress just doesn't want to speak to anyone. There is a peculiar pleasure in that complicity; that shared sin makes mistress and servant equal for a moment, not to mention the pleasure of seeing the look of disappointment on the faces of those deceived visitors, and their departing backs as they retreat down the steps . . . The truth did not come out, it remained at home, in Capitu's heart, drowsily pondering its repentance. And I left feeling neither sad nor angry; I thought the maid delightful, positively alluring, far more so than her mistress.

The swallows were flying in the opposite direction now, or perhaps they weren't the same ones. We were definitely the same Bentinho and Capitu; there we sat, counting up our hopes, our fears, and beginning to count up our regrets too.

Chapter XLVIII / *The oath by the well*

"NO!" I said suddenly.

"No, what?"

A few minutes of silence had elapsed, during which I had thought deeply and come up with an idea; my "No," however, was so loud that I startled Capitu.

"No, that's not what's going to happen," I went on. "They say we're too young to marry, that we're just children, mere babes in arms according to them. Well, two or three years will pass quickly enough. Will you swear an oath? Will you swear that you will marry me and no one else?"

Capitu did not hesitate, and I even saw her cheeks flush with pleasure. She swore twice, then a third time:

"Even if you marry someone else, I will keep my oath and never marry."

"If I marry someone else?"

"Anything's possible, Bentinho. You might meet another girl who loves you, fall in love with her, and marry. Why should I expect you to remember me then?"

"But I've sworn the same oath, and I swear by Our Lord God that I will only marry you, Capitu. Is that enough?"

"It should be," she said, "and I daren't ask for more. Yes, you have sworn an oath, but let's swear a different oath: let's swear that we will marry each other, come what may."

Do you see the difference? This was more than just choosing a partner, it was an affirmation that we would be joined in matrimony. My friend had a very clear, quick-thinking mind. And the previous formula was too limited, merely exclusive. We could both end up unmarried, like the sun and the moon, without breaking that oath by the well. This was a far better formula and had the advantage of fortifying my heart against ever becoming a priest. We swore that second oath, and felt so happy that all our anxieties about future perils disappeared. We were devout believers, we had the heavens as our witness. I no longer feared the seminary.

"If they insist, then I'll go, but I'll just pretend it's the same as any other school. And I won't take holy orders."

Capitu feared our separation, but accepted this proposal as the best one available. This way, we would not have to make my mother suffer, and time would pass quickly enough until the day came when we could marry. Indeed, any resistance to going to the seminary would only confirm José Dias's revelation. This last idea was not mine, but hers.

Chapter XLIX / *A candle every Saturday*

AND SO, AFTER MANY A STORM, we finally reached the harbor where we should have taken shelter straightaway. Don't be too hard on us, you evil old pilot, one cannot navigate a heart as one can the other seas of this world. We were contented, we began talking about the future. I promised my wife a lovely, tranquil life in the countryside or on the outskirts of the city. We would come into town just once a year. If we chose a suburb, it would be far from the center, where no one could bother us. The house, in my view, should be neither large nor small, but a compromise, something in between; I would plant flowers, choose furniture, a carriage, and a shrine. Yes, we would have a beautiful shrine, tall and made of jacaranda wood, containing the image of Our Lady of the Conception. I spent more time on that than on anything else, partly because we were both religious, partly to make up for the cassock I was intending to discard among the nettles; but there was also a part that I attribute to a secret, unconscious desire to ensure heaven's protection. We would light a candle every Saturday . . .

⸻ Chapter L / *A compromise*

MONTHS LATER, I set off for the seminary of São José. If I could count the tears I shed on the eve of the morning of my departure, they would come to more than all the tears shed since Adam and Eve. This is a slight exaggeration, but a little exaggeration now and then is a good thing, for it makes up for my unfortunate obsession with exactitude. And yet, if I summon up the memory of what I felt then, I would not be so very far from the truth; when one is fifteen, everything is infinite. However mentally prepared I was to leave, I really did suffer. So did my mother, but she suffered inwardly, wholeheartedly; what's more, Father Cabral had come up with a compromise to test my vocation; if, after two years, I still showed no vocation for the priesthood, then I would follow some other career path.

"Promises should only be kept according to God's wishes. Suppose that Our Lord does not give your son a vocation, and life at the seminary does not please him as it did me; this would mean that the divine will has chosen otherwise. You could not place in your son, before he was even born, a vocation that Our Lord denies him . . ."

This was a concession of Father Cabral's. He was giving my mother a pardon in advance, passing on the Divine creditor's forgiveness of the debt. Her eyes shone brightly, but her mouth continued to say no.

José Dias, having missed his chance to go to Europe with me, seized the next best option, and gave his support to "the protonotary's proposal," although he felt that one year at the seminary would be enough.

"I am sure," he said with a wink at me, "that within a year our Bentinho's ecclesiastical vocation will reveal itself clearly and decisively. He will make an excellent priest. Then again, if that doesn't happen after a year at the seminary . . ."

And later, in private, he said to me:

"Go for a year. A year passes quickly enough. If you really don't like it, then, as Father Cabral says, that means it is not God's will, in which case, my young friend, the best remedy will be to go to Europe."

Capitu gave me the same advice when my mother announced to her my definite departure for the seminary:

"Daughter of mine, you are about to lose your childhood playmate . . ."

Capitu was so thrilled to be called "daughter" (the first time my mother had done so) that she didn't even have time to feel sad; she kissed my mother's hand and told her that I had already forewarned her. Capitu particularly urged me to put up with everything with great patience; by the end of that first year, everything would be different, and a year was no time at all. This was not yet our farewell; that happened on the eve of my departure in a way that demands a chapter of its own. All that I will say here is that, just as Capitu and I were drawing closer to each other, so she became more and more attached to my mother. She became more attentive and more affectionate, was always at her side, had eyes for no one else. My mother was kind by nature, and sensitive too; the smallest thing could cause her joy or pain. She began to find new qualities in Capitu, fine, rare gifts; she gave her a ring and a few other trinkets. When Capitu asked her to be photographed so that she could have a portrait of her, my mother refused, but she did have a miniature of herself, painted when she was just twenty-five, and, after some hesitation, she decided to give this to Capitu. When Capitu received this treasure, her eyes were quite simply indescribable, they were not oblique, they had no undertow, they were direct, clear, lucid. She bestowed a passionate kiss on the portrait, and my mother bestowed just such a kiss on her. All these things remind me of our farewell.

Chapter LI / *Between dusk and darkness*

BETWEEN DUSK AND DARKNESS, everything must be as brief as that moment in time. Our farewell did not take long, although we made it last as long as we could, in her house, in the drawing room before the candles were lit; that is where we said our final farewell. We again swore that we would marry each other, and this contract was sealed not just with a handclasp, as in the backyard, but by the meeting of our loving lips . . . I might strike that out in the printed version, unless I change my mind in the meantime; if I don't, it can stay. Yes, it will stay, because it is, after all, our defense. The divine commandment requires that we do not take God's name in vain. I would not be lying to the seminary, given that I had a contract signed and sealed before heaven itself. As for the seal, God, who gave us clean hands, also gave us clean lips—and any evil thoughts are in *your* perverted mind, not in the minds of that pair of adolescents . . . Oh, my sweet childhood companion, I was pure, and remained pure. I entered the São José seminary pure, apparently seeking my investiture as a priest, and before that, my vocation. But you, Capitu, were my vocation, you were my investiture.

⟨ Chapter LII / *Old Pádua*

I WILL NOW ALSO DESCRIBE my farewell to Capitu's father, old Pádua. He came to our house very early in the morning. My mother told him to come and speak to me in my room.

"May I?" he asked, poking his head around the door.

I shook his hand, and he embraced me fondly.

"Be happy!" he told me. "You will be much missed by myself and by all my family. We are very fond of you, as is only right and proper. Should anyone ever say otherwise, don't believe them. They are mere malicious gossips. When I married, I, too, was the victim of such gossip, but it all came to nothing. God is great and will reveal the truth. If you should one day lose your mother and your uncle, something which, by heaven's light, I hope will never happen, because they are good people, excellent people, and I am deeply grateful for all their kindnesses . . . No, I am not like certain other men, certain parasites, outsiders determined to sow discord in families, vile sycophants, no, I am of quite a different stripe; I do not eat at another man's table or live in his house for free . . . Still, such men are the fortunate ones!"

"Why is he telling me this?" I wondered. "He must know that José Dias often speaks ill of him."

"As I was saying, if you should one day lose your family, you can always count on us for our company. I know it would be small recompense, but we are so very fond of you. Whether you become a priest or not, our door is always open. I just hope you will not forget old Pádua . . ."

He sighed and went on:

"No, don't forget your old friend Pádua, and if you have some small thing that you could leave me as a souvenir, a Latin textbook, anything, a button from a vest, something no longer of any use to you. The value lies in the memories it will bring me."

I was quite taken aback. I had just wrapped up in a piece of paper a long, beautiful lock of my own hair, which I had cut off the night before, intending to take it to Capitu before I left. However, it occurred to me that if I gave it to her father, Capitu would be sure to put it in a safe place. I picked up the small package and gave it to him.

"Here. Please keep it."

"Oh, a lock of your hair!" cried Pádua, opening then closing the package. "Oh, thank you! Thank you on behalf of myself and my family! I'll give it to my wife so that she can put it away somewhere safe, or to my daughter, who takes more care over such things. How lovely! How could you bear to cut off such a beautiful lock of hair? Let me embrace you! Again! And again! Farewell!"

His eyes really were filled with tears; his expression, though, was that of a disappointed man, like someone who has saved up and placed all his saved-up hopes on one lottery ticket only to have the wretched number come up blank—and it was such a nice number too!

Chapter LIII / *En route!*

OFF I WENT TO THE SEMINARY. I won't bother describing the other farewells. My mother clasped me to her bosom. Cousin Justina sighed. She may have shed a few tears or none. There are some people to whom tears do not come easily, if at all; it's said that they suffer more than others. Cousin Justina was doubtless suppressing any inner sorrow she felt, dealing instead with whatever my mother had forgotten, giving me advice, and issuing orders. When I kissed Uncle Cosme's hand, he said, smiling:

"Away you go, my boy, and be sure to come back a pope!"

José Dias, composed and grave-faced, said nothing at first; we had spoken the previous evening in his room, where I went to ask him if it was still possible for me to avoid going to the seminary. It no longer was, but he gave me some hope and, more importantly, cheered me up enormously. In less than a year, we would be on board ship. When I said that this seemed rather soon, he said:

"Well, they do say it's not a good time to cross the Atlantic. I'll make inquiries. Otherwise, we'll set off in March or April."

"I could always study medicine here."

José Dias pursed his lips and impatiently ran his fingers up and down his suspenders, before formally dismissing this proposal.

"I would happily approve such an idea," he said, "were it not for the fact that, at the School of Medicine, all they teach is that vile nonsense allopathy. Allopathy is the great error of the age, and will inevitably die; it is murder, a lie, an illusion.* If people tell you that

* Allopathy was a derogatory term, coined by the inventor of homeopathy, for conventional science-based medicine.

at the School of Medicine you can learn the part of science common to all systems, they are quite right; allopathy, however, is a therapeutic error. Physiology, anatomy, pathology are neither allopathic nor homeopathic, but it's best to learn everything all at once, from books and from the lips of men who cultivate the truth . . ."

This is what he had said in his room on the eve of my departure. Now he said nothing, or merely proffered some aphorism on religion and the family; I remember this one: "To share something with God is to have it still." When my mother gave me one final kiss, he said with a sigh: "Ah, the most affecting of scenes!"

It was a beautiful morning. The slave boys were whispering to each other; the slave women were offering me their blessings: "Blessings on you, Master Bentinho! Don't forget your old friend Joana! Miquelina will be praying for you!" Out in the street, José Dias repeated his hopes for the future:

"Put up with it for a year, and by then, everything will be settled."

= Chapter LIV / *Panegyric for Santa Mônica*

AT THE SEMINARY . . . Ah, no, I'm not going to describe life at the seminary, that would take more than one chapter. No, my friend; one day, I might write a brief account of what I saw and experienced there, the people I met, the customs, and so on. This itch to write, when it takes hold of you in your fifties, simply won't let go. In youth, a man can cure himself of it; indeed, to look no further, right there in the seminary one of my fellow students wrote poetry in the style of Junqueira Freire, the poet-monk whose book of poetry had recently been published. He went on to be ordained a priest; years later, I met him in the choir at the church of São Pedro, and I asked to read his latest verses.

"What verses?" he said, somewhat alarmed.

"Yours. Don't you remember how in the seminary—"

"Ah!" And he smiled.

Yes, he smiled, meanwhile searching in a book to find out what time he was due to sing the following day, and he confessed that, since being ordained, he hadn't written a single line of poetry. It had been a youthful itch; he scratched it and it went away, and he was well again. And he spoke in prose about an infinite number of banal everyday things, the high cost of living, a sermon given by Father X . . . a vicarship in Minas . . .

On the other hand, there was one seminarian who did not take up a career in the church. His name was . . . No, there's no need to give his name, just the facts. He had composed a *Panegyric for Santa Mônica*, which was praised by some and even read by his fellow seminarians. He received permission to have it printed and dedicated it to Saint Augustine. This is all ancient history now, but it took on a more youthful aspect one day, in 1882, when I had to go to the Admiralty to deal with some business or other and I met that same student, now head of an administrative department there. He had left the seminary, abandoned literature, married, and he'd forgotten everything, apart from his *Panegyric for Santa Mônica*, all twenty-nine pages of it, which he had continued to press on other people throughout his life. Since I needed some information, I decided to consult him, and I could not have found anyone more willing to help; he told me everything I needed to know, clearly, accurately, and copiously. Naturally, we talked about the past. Personal memories, interesting incidents, mere trifles, a book, a word, a nickname, yes, all the old stuff emerged, and we laughed together and sighed companionably. For a while we relived our old seminary days. And, either because those memories were very much of that time and place or because we were young then, they brought back such potent happiness that, had there ever been some shadow over them in the past, it did not reappear. He confessed that he had lost touch with all his fellow students.

"Me, too, or almost all. Those who were ordained, of course, returned to their provinces, and those who were from Rio found vicarships elsewhere."

"Ah, yes, they were good times!" he said with a sigh.

Then, after a moment's thought, he fixed me with a sad, searching look and asked:

"Do you still have a copy of my *Panegyric*?"

I didn't know what to say; I tried to speak, but no words came out. Finally, I asked:

"Panegyric? What panegyric?"

"My *Panegyric for Santa Mônica*."

I did not immediately remember, but that explanation must have been enough to jog my memory. After a few moments of mental rummaging, I replied that I had kept my copy for many years, but what with moving house various times and traveling . . .

"I'll have to bring you a copy."

Less than twenty-four hours later, he came to my house bearing the pamphlet, a grubby twenty-six-year-old pamphlet, stained by time, but with every page intact, and with a respectful, handwritten dedication.

"It's my penultimate copy," he said. "Now I only have one copy left, which I can't give to anyone."

And, seeing me leafing through, he said:

"See if there are any lines you particularly remember."

A twenty-six-year gap can be the death of far closer and more assiduous friendships, but it was courteous, almost charitable, to remember the occasional page; I read one, emphasizing certain lines to give him the impression that they really did find some echo in my memory. He agreed that they were very beautiful, although there were others he preferred, and he went on to point these out to me.

"So you do remember them?"

"Oh, yes, perfectly. Your *Panegyric for Santa Mônica*! That really takes me back to my youth! I've never forgotten the seminary, you know. The years pass, events crowd in on us, as do feelings. I made new friendships, which also subsequently vanished, but that's life . . . No, my friend, nothing has erased those times we spent together, the priests, the lessons, our games . . . oh, do you remember our games? And Father Lopes, oh, Father Lopes . . ."

He was gazing into space, and he must have been listening and must have heard what I said, but his only response, after a longish silence, was to close his eyes and say with a sigh:

"Yes, my *Panegyric* has brought pleasure to so many!"

 Chapter LV / *A sonnet*

HAVING SAID THIS, he clasped my two hands with all the force of his immense gratitude, then said goodbye and was gone. I was left alone with the *Panegyric*, and the memories evoked by its pages deserve a chapter or more. First, though, and because I, too, had my own panegyric, I will tell you the story of a sonnet I never wrote; it was when I was in the seminary, and the first line was this:

O Flower of heaven! Flower so innocent and pure!

How and why this line came into my head, I do not know; it just surfaced while I was lying in bed, like a random exclamation, and when I realized that it had the necessary feet to be a line of poetry, I thought I should make something of it, a sonnet. Insomnia, that muse with the wide staring eyes, kept me awake for a long hour or two; the itch needed to be scratched and I scratched long and hard. I didn't immediately choose to write a sonnet; at first I tried a different form, toying with rhymes and then with free verse; finally, though, I plumped for a sonnet. It was a short, practical form. As for the idea, the first line was not yet an idea, it was an exclamation; the idea would come later. And so, snuggled up in bed, I tried my hand at versifying. I felt as excited as a mother when she feels her child moving inside her, her first child. I was going to be a poet, I was going to compete with that monk from Bahia, who had only recently appeared and was currently all the rage; I, a seminarian, would speak in verse of my sadnesses, just as he had spoken of his in the cloister. I learned that first line by heart, and repeated it softly to the sheets; I thought it was very fine, and even now I rather like it:

O Flower of heaven! Flower so innocent and pure!

Who was this flower? Capitu, of course; but it could equally be virtue, poetry, religion, or any other concept to which the metaphor of a flower, a flower of heaven, could be applied. Still repeating that first line, and lying now on my right side, now on my left, I waited for the rest of the poem to come; finally, I lay on my back, eyes fixed on the ceiling, but still nothing came. Then I noticed that the most highly praised sonnets were those that concluded with a "golden key," that is, with one of those lines that encapsulates everything in meaning and form. I decided that I needed to come up with just such a key, thinking that if I wrote the last line in chronological order, following the first thirteen, it would be hard to achieve the necessary perfection; I imagined that such keys were probably cut before the lock. And so I decided to compose the last line of the sonnet and, after much effort, this is what came out:

A life may be lost, but the battle will be won!

I don't mean to boast, but looking at that line with an entirely impartial eye, I thought it quite magnificent. It had a real ring to it. And it contained an idea, victory gained at the cost of one's own life, a lofty, noble idea. It may not have been entirely new, but nor was it banal; and I still cannot explain by what mysterious route it entered my young head. At the time, I thought it sublime. I recited that golden key over and over; then repeated the two lines one after the other, and prepared to connect them with the twelve intervening ones. Given that last line, it seemed to me that it would be better not to have Capitu as the central idea; instead the idea would be justice. It was more appropriate to say that, in the fight for justice, one might lose one's life but win the battle. It also occurred to me to use "battle" in its literal sense and make it, for example, the struggle for one's country; in that case, the flower of heaven would be freedom. This meaning, though, given that the poet was a seminarian, might be less fitting than the first, and I spent some minutes deciding between the two. I thought justice was the better idea, but, in the end, I opted definitively for another idea entirely, that of charity, and I recited those two lines, each in its own fashion, one languidly:

O Flower of heaven! Flower so innocent and pure!

and the other with great brio:

A life may be lost, but the battle will be won!

I had the feeling that a perfect sonnet was about to emerge. It was no small thing to find a good beginning and a good ending. In search of inspiration, I recalled a few famous sonnets, and noted that most were apparently extremely simple; the lines containing the idea flowed from one to the other so naturally that it was impossible to tell if the idea had produced those lines or if the lines had engendered the idea. I then returned to my sonnet, and once again repeated that first line and waited for the second to come; the second did not come, nor did the third or the fourth; not a single line came. I found this so infuriating that more than once I considered getting out of bed and fetching some paper and ink, for it could be that the verses would come more willingly with pen in hand, but . . .

Weary of waiting, it occurred to me to change the meaning of the final line, by simply swapping two words around:

The battle may be lost, but a life will be won!

The meaning was then exactly the opposite, but perhaps that in itself would bring inspiration. It could be taken as ironic: by not behaving charitably, you could save your life, but lose heaven's battle. I summoned up new resolve and waited. There was no window in my room; if there had been, I could have appealed to the night to send me an idea. And who knows, the fireflies flickering about down below might have proved to be rhymes sent to me by the stars, and that vivid metaphor might then bring me those elusive lines, complete with consonants and meanings.

I labored in vain, I searched, I sought, I waited, but still the lines did not come. Later in life, I wrote a few pages in prose, and now here I am writing this story, finding that there is nothing more difficult than writing, be it well or badly. But, dear readers, nothing can console me for that sonnet I did not write. However, since I believe that, for some metaphysical reason, sonnets emerge already written, like odes and plays, and other works of art, I donate these two lines to the first idle poet who wants them. On a Sunday, or if it's raining, or while marooned in the countryside, in a moment of leisure, he could have a go and see if the sonnet does emerge. It's merely a matter of coming up with an idea, then filling in the missing middle.

≡ Chapter LVI / *A seminarian*

THAT LITTLE DEVIL of a pamphlet, with its antiquated font and Latin quotations, kept reminding me of all those things. I saw rising up from its pages many of my fellow seminarians' faces, the Alburquerque brothers, for example, one of whom is now a canon in Bahia, while the other went on to study medicine and has, so they say, discovered a remedy for yellow fever. I saw Bastos, a skinny boy, who is now a vicar in Meia-Ponte, if he hasn't died in the meantime; Luís Borges, despite being a priest, went into politics and ended up becoming a senator of the Empire . . . And how many other faces stared out at me from the *Panegyric*'s cold pages! No, they weren't cold; they brought with them the warmth of nascent youth, the warmth of the past, my own warmth. I wanted to reread them, and did manage to understand some parts, which seemed as fresh as they had the first time, albeit shorter. It was a delight to leaf through it; sometimes, unwittingly, I would turn the page as if I really were reading; I think this happened when my eyes fell on the final word on that page, and then my hand, accustomed to helping my eyes, performed its usual job . . .

Here's another seminarian. His name was Ezequiel de Sousa Escobar. He was a slender lad, and his pale eyes were rather mercurial, as were his hands, his feet, his words, everything. If you didn't know him, he could make you feel almost uncomfortable, unsure quite what to make of him. He never looked you in the eye, never spoke clearly or coherently; his hand never clasped someone else's hand, nor did it allow itself to be clasped, because his fingers were so slim and short that, just when you thought you had them in your grasp, there was nothing there. The same could be said of his feet, which could just as quickly be here as there. This difficulty in staying put was the major obstacle to him embracing seminary life. His smile was equally of the moment, but he could also laugh long and loud. In one aspect, though, he was less mercurial, and that was when he was thinking; we would often find him sitting alone, absorbed in thought. He always told us that he was meditating on some spiritual matter, or going over yesterday's lesson. When we became friends, he would often ask me to repeat things in detail, and he had the kind of retentive memory that stored away everything, even the actual words used. That ability may have proved detrimental to his other skills.

He was three years older than me, the son of a lawyer in Curitiba who was related to a merchant in Rio de Janeiro, who acted as his father's agent. The father was a devout Catholic. Escobar had a sister, who, he said, was an angel.

"She's not just angelic in her physical beauty, she's also kindness itself. You couldn't meet a kinder person. She often writes to me. I'll have to show you some of her letters."

Her letters were indeed simple and affectionate, full of fond words and advice. Escobar told me interesting stories about her, all of which focused on her kindness and intelligence: so much so that, were it not for Capitu, I might have ended up marrying her. She died not long afterward. Seduced by Escobar's words, I was almost tempted to blurt out my own story straightaway. I felt shy at first, but he soon won my trust. His mercurial manner stopped when he wanted it to, and time and the environment we found ourselves in helped to slow him down. Escobar flung wide his soul to me, from the front door to the far end of the backyard. For, as you know, the soul is laid out like a house, often with windows on all sides, with lots of light and pure air. Some souls are dark and enclosed, with no windows or only a few and those few have bars on them, like the windows of convents and prisons. Others can be chapels or bazaars, simple lean-tos or sumptuous palaces.

I don't know what kind of house my soul was. I had not yet become a grumpy Dom Casmurro. It was fear that inhibited frankness on my part, but, since the doors to my soul had neither keys nor locks, all Escobar had to do was give them a push, and in he came. And there he was and there he stayed, until . . .

Chapter LVII / *By way of preparation*

AH, BUT IT WASN'T ONLY the seminarians who rose up out of the *Panegyric*'s fading pages. They also brought me lost sensations, so intense, so numerous, that I could not possibly list them all, because there would be no space for anything else. I will describe one such sensation, one of the first, and I only wish I could do so in Latin. Not because there are no honest words in our own language to describe the matter, for our language is as chaste for the chaste as it can be sordid for the sordid. Yes, you, gentlest and most chaste of lady readers—as my long-departed José Dias would have said— can read to the end of the chapter without fear of being alarmed or embarrassed.

No, I'll put the story in another chapter. However modest and composed my retelling of it might be, there is, as with everything, a less sober side, which calls for a few lines of repose and preparation. Let this chapter serve that purpose. And that is no small thing, dear reader; when the heart ponders what the future might hold, the sheer number and magnitude of those possible events, it grows robust and stalwart, and then any evil that might befall us seems less evil. If the heart doesn't grow strong then, it never will. Do you see how clever I have been? For, when you read what you are about to read, you will probably find it far less shocking than you expected.

Chapter LVIII / *The pact*

IT HAPPENED THAT, one Monday, when I was returning to the seminary, I saw a lady fall over in the street. My first response, in such a case, should have been either pity or laughter; it was neither because (and this is the part I wish I could write in Latin) the lady was wearing a pair of spotlessly clean stockings, which she did not dirty when she fell, and silk garters, which remained in place. Several people rushed to her aid, but they did not arrive in time to help her to her feet; for she got up looking highly embarrassed, brushed herself down, thanked her would-be helpers, and headed off down the next street.

"This desire to imitate the French ladies on Rua do Ouvidor," José Dias said, as he walked along beside me, commenting on the incident, "is quite clearly mistaken. Our young women should walk as they always did, slowly and patiently, not tick-tacking along in the French style . . ."

I barely heard what he said. The lady's stockings and garters were spiraling palely before me, walking and falling, getting up and striding off. When we reached the corner, I looked down the side street, and, in the distance, saw the unfortunate lady, who was still proceeding at the same pace, tick-tack, tick-tack . . .

"She doesn't seem to have hurt herself," I said.

"Lucky for her, but she must have grazed her knees. Rushing along like that is nothing but a bad habit . . ."

I think that's what he said, but I was still ruminating on those grazed knees. From then on, all the way to the seminary, I longed for every woman I saw to fall over too; some of them, I felt sure, would be wearing very close-fitting stockings and very tight garters . . . There might have been some who weren't even wearing stockings . . . surely not . . . Or perhaps . . . That, too, was possible . . .

All these ellipses are just to give you an idea of how diffuse and confused my thoughts were, although I'm probably not "giving" you anything. My head felt hot and my legs unsteady. At the seminary, the first hour of class was simply unbearable. The priests' cassocks rustled like skirts, and reminded me of that lady falling over. I didn't just imagine one lady falling over now; all the women I had seen in the street that morning were offering me a glimpse of their blue garters, yes, blue. That night, I dreamed about them. A multitude of abominable creatures came and danced around me, tick-tack, tick-tack . . . They were beautiful, some slender, some fat, all of them as nimble as the very devil. I woke up and tried to drive them away with words of exorcism and other such ploys, but as soon as I fell asleep again, they returned, joined hands, and danced around me, forming a vast circle of skirts, or clambered up into the air and then rained down feet and legs upon my head. And so it went, on into the early hours. I couldn't get back to sleep; I repeated a whole string of Paternosters, Ave Marias, and credos, but, since this book is the pure truth, I must confess that I had to interrupt my prayers more than once in order to accompany a distant figure moving off into the darkness, tick-tack, tick-tack . . . I would then quickly resume my prayers, always in the middle so that it dovetailed perfectly as if there had been no interruption, but I'm sure I never managed to quite connect new words with old.

When this malaise continued into the morning, I tried to overcome it, but in such a way that it would not be lost entirely. Scriptural scholars, can you guess how I did that? Like this. Unable to keep those pictures at bay, I drew up a pact between my conscience and my imagination. From then on, I would consider those female visions as mere embodiments of the vices, and studying them would, therefore, be the best possible way of fortifying my character and toughening it up for life's most taxing battles. I didn't put it in those precise words, nor did I need to; this pact was made tacitly, with a certain degree of repugnance, but there it was. And for a few days, I called up those visions in order to make myself stronger, and I did not reject them, or at least only when they themselves grew weary and left of their own accord.

Chapter LIX / *Guests with good memories*

THERE ARE SOME reminiscences that will not rest until either the pen or the tongue have made them public. Some ancient author warned us to avoid guests with good memories. Life is full of such guests, and I am possibly one of them, although as proof of how poor my memory is, I cannot now recall the name of that ancient author, except that he was definitely ancient, so let that suffice.

No, I don't have a good memory. On the contrary, it is rather like someone who has lived in various types of lodgings and can put neither names nor faces to them, and only very rarely the reasons for his stay. Whereas if you have spent your whole life in the same family house, with its eternal furniture and customs, people and affections, you will have all of that engraved on your memory out of sheer continuity and repetition. How I envy those who have never forgotten the color of the first pair of trousers they wore! I can't even remember the color of the trousers I put on yesterday. I know only that they were not yellow, a color I loathe; but again that could just be forgetfulness and confusion.

And I would prefer forgetfulness to confusion. Let me explain. You cannot easily correct a confusing book, but you can add almost anything to a book full of omissions. Whenever I read one of the latter sort, I don't mind in the least. What I do when I reach the end is close my eyes and imagine all the things I didn't find in it. What a host of fine ideas come to me then! What profound thoughts! The rivers, mountains, churches I did not find in its pages all appear to me with their flowing waters, their trees, their altars, along with the generals who now wield swords that had hitherto stayed in their scabbards, while the trumpets sound notes that had been sleeping until then in their metal skins, and everything proceeds with unexpected vim and vigor.

Because, dear reader, everything can be found outside an inadequate book. And just as I fill in someone else's lacunae, you can do the same with mine.

Chapter LX / *Dear pamphlet*

THIS IS WHAT I DID with that *Panegyric for Santa Mônica*, and I went even further; I added not only missing information about the saint, but other things that had nothing to do with her. You have seen the sonnet, the stockings, the garters, the seminarian Escobar, and possibly several other seminarians too. You are now about to see what else emerged from the yellowing pages of that opuscule.

Dear pamphlet, you were not worth much in yourself, but then the same could be said of an old pair of slippers. And yet, that same pair of slippers often harbor something like the faint aroma and warmth of two feet. Though worn and shabby, they are still a reminder that someone used to put them on in the morning when he got out of bed, or take them off at night when he got into bed. And if that really doesn't work as a comparison, because the slippers are still a part of the person and were in contact with his feet, here are other memories, like the stone in the road, the front door of the house, a particular whistle, the cry of a street vendor, like that man hawking coconut candy whom I told you about in Chapter XVIII. Indeed, when I wrote about that particular vendor, I was so filled with nostalgia that I even mentioned it in a letter to a friend, a music teacher, and glued it to the legs of the chapter. If I later amputated it, this was because another musician, to whom I showed the passage, admitted frankly that he didn't find it in the least nostalgic. So to prevent this from happening to any other professionals who might read me, it would be best to save the editor both the trouble and the ink. As you see, I added nothing, nor will I. I no longer believe that it's enough for the cries of street vendors, or, in this case, a seminarian's pamphlet, to be a receptacle of people and sensations; you need to have known all those things yourself and to have experienced them in time, otherwise all is silent and drab.

But let us move on to the other things that emerged from those yellowing pages.

.

≡ Chapter LXI / *Homer's cow*

THERE WERE QUITE A LOT of "other things." From those yellow pages emerged memories of my first days away from home, dark, difficult days, despite the words of comfort offered me by the priests and the other seminarians, and the words from my mother and Uncle Cosme that José Dias brought to the seminary.

"Everyone misses you," he said, "but the one who misses you most, of course, is the one with the biggest heart, and who would that be?" he asked, the answer written in his eyes.

"Mama," I said.

José Dias squeezed my hands hard, then painted a picture of my mother's sadness, how she talked about me every day, at almost every hour. Since he would always agree with her and add some comment about the gifts God had given her, my mother's pride on those occasions was almost indescribable; and he told me all this full of tearful admiration. Uncle Cosme was also often moved to tears.

"Actually an interesting thing happened yesterday. I had just said to your mother that God had given her not a son, but an angel, and your uncle was so moved that the only way he could hold back his tears was by paying me one of those mocking, jocular compliments of his. Needless to say, Dona Glória furtively wiped away a tear, too, well, any mother would. She really has the most loving of hearts!"

"But Senhor José Dias, when will I be able to leave here?"

"I'm working on that. The trip to Europe is our first priority, and that can't happen until 1859 or 1860, so not at least for a year or two . . ."

"That long?"

"Obviously, it would be best if it was this year, but let's give it time. Be patient, keep studying; after all, there's no harm in picking up the odd bit of knowledge while you're here; and even if you don't become a priest, life in the seminary is still very useful, and it's no bad thing to enter the world anointed with the holy oils of theology . . ."

At this point—I remember it as if it were yesterday—José Dias's eyes gleamed so brightly that I felt quite alarmed. His eyelids closed immediately afterward, and remained so for a few moments, until they opened again, and then fixed upon the courtyard wall as if he were totally absorbed in pondering something, possibly himself; then his eyes detached themselves from the wall and began wandering about the courtyard. One might well compare him here to Homer's cow, walking around and around the calf to which she has just given birth, lowing all the time. I didn't ask him what was wrong, perhaps out of shyness or perhaps because two teachers, one of them the theology teacher, were heading in our direction. As they came past, José Dias, who knew them, greeted them in suitably deferential tones and asked how I was getting on.

"We can't make any promises just yet," said one of them, "but it looks like he'll turn out all right."

"That's what I was telling him just now," said José Dias. "I'm counting on hearing him say his first mass, but even if he doesn't take orders, this is still the best possible place to study. He will set out on the journey of life," he concluded, lingering over his words, "anointed with the holy oils of theology . . ."

This time, his eyes did not gleam quite so brightly, nor did his eyelids droop or his pupils shift about in the strange way they had before. On the contrary, he was all attention and interrogation: at most, a bright, friendly smile flickered across his lips. The theology teacher approved of the metaphor and said so; José Dias thanked him, saying that these ideas often came to him in the course of conversation, not that he was either a writer or an orator. I, on the other hand, did not like the metaphor at all; and as soon as the teachers had gone, I shook my head, saying:

"I don't care about the holy oils of theology, I just want to get out of here as soon as possible, preferably now . . ."

"No, my angel, now is quite impossible, but it could happen much earlier than we imagine. Perhaps this very year. I have a plan, and I'm already thinking how to put it to Dona Glória. I'm sure she'll agree and come with us."

"I really can't see Mama wanting to go abroad."

"Maybe, maybe not. Mothers are capable of anything. With her or without her, though, I'm sure we will go, and, don't worry, I will strain very sinew. Patience must be our motto, though. And don't do anything here that might give rise to criticism or complaint; be all docility and contentment. Didn't you hear what the teacher said? That's because you've behaved yourself so far. Keep it up."

"But 1859 or 1860 are such a long way off."

"It will be this year," said José Dias.

"In three months' time?"

"Or six."

"No, three."

"All right. I have a plan now, which seems to me the very best of plans. And that is to combine the lack of any ecclesiastical vocation with the need for a change of air. Why don't you cough?"

"Why don't I cough?"

"No, no, not now. I'll tell you when to start coughing, when it's necessary, building up gradually, starting with a dry little cough and a slight loss of appetite, then I'll report back to your excellent mother . . . After all, we're doing this for her sake. If her son cannot serve the Church as it should be served, then the best way to do God's will is to have him dedicate himself to something else. The world is also a church for the righteous . . ."

Again I couldn't help thinking of Homer's cow, as if "the world is also a church for the righteous" were another calf, the brother of those "holy oils of theology." However, I didn't give him time to wallow in his motherly feelings, and said:

"Ah, I see! You mean pretend that I'm ill so that I can go abroad!"

José Dias hesitated slightly, then said:

"No, I simply intend to show her the truth, because, frankly, Bentinho, I've been worried about your chest for months now. You have a real problem. As a child, you often had fevers and a slight wheeze . . . You recovered, of course, but in the last few days, you've been looking rather pale. I'm not saying you're ill now, but illness can come on very fast. A house can fall in an instant. That's why, if the dear lady doesn't want to go with us, or simply as a way of encouraging her to set off sooner, I think that a good cough . . . And if you're going to have a cough, then it would be best to hurry it along . . . But leave it for now. I'll tell you when . . ."

"All right, but when I do leave here, I'm not going to get straight on the boat. First I leave here, then we'll plan our departure. That can wait for a year. Don't they say that the best time to set off is April or May? Let's say May, then. First, though, I want to be out of the seminary two months from now . . ."

And then, because the words were sticking in my throat, I suddenly spun around and asked him point-blank:

"How's Capitu?"

=== Chapter LXII / *A touch of Iago*

THIS WAS AN UNWISE question to ask, especially after I had just spoken of postponing our trip to Europe. It was tantamount to admitting that Capitu was my main or only reason for disliking the seminary so intensely, and would make him think that our journey was unlikely to happen. I realized this as soon as I had spoken; I desperately wanted to correct this impression, but didn't know how, nor did he give me time.

"Oh, she's her usual cheery, giddy young self. Just waiting for some local dandy to fall for her and marry her . . ."

I think I must have turned pale; I certainly felt a cold shudder run through my whole body. This was the effect of learning that, while I was crying myself to sleep every night, she was perfectly happy, and my heart beat so violently that I swear I can still hear it now. This is a slight exaggeration, but that is what human discourse is like, a combination of wild excess and modest restraint, two opposites that offset and eventually accommodate each other. On the other hand, if we bear in mind that the audience here is not our ears but our memory, we will arrive at the real truth. My memory can still hear the way my heart was beating at that moment. Don't forget, this was first love. I was almost at the point of asking José Dias to explain why Capitu was so happy, what she was up to, if she was always laughing, singing, or skipping, but I stopped myself in time; and then came another idea.

No, not an idea, but a cruel, previously unknown feeling, pure jealousy, O reader of my innermost self. That is what gnawed at me as I repeated to myself José Dias's words: "some local dandy." I had never contemplated such a calamitous event. I lived so much in her, of her, and for her that the arrival of a local dandy was like a notion lacking all reality; it had never occurred to me that there were such things as local dandies, of varying ages and appearances, often to be seen out on afternoon strolls. Now I recalled seeing some of those dandies casting admiring glances at Capitu—but at the time, I had felt so utterly confident that she was mine alone, it had felt as if they were actually looking at me with due admiration and envy. Now that we were separated from each other by space and time, that evil seemed to me not only possible but certain. And Capitu's happiness merely confirmed my suspicions; if she was happy, that was because she was already flirting with another young man, watching him as he walked past in the street, talking to him at her window in the evenings, exchanging flowers and . . .

And . . . what? You know perfectly well what else they might be exchanging; and if you don't, then there's little point in you reading the rest of this chapter or this book, you won't understand even if I spell it out for you, etymologies and all. If, however, you did grasp my meaning, you will understand why, after that cold shudder, my first impulse was to rush out of the seminary doors and race down the hill to the Pádua family home, where I would seize hold of Capitu and demand to know how many, how many, how many that local dandy had given her. I did nothing, though. During those few minutes, the same dreams I'm telling you about now lacked any such logic of thought or movement. They were disjointed, patched and clumsily re-patched, half-finished, lopsided, all confusion and turmoil, blinding and deafening me. When I returned to my senses, José Dias was just completing a sentence, the beginning of which I hadn't heard, and the ending of which was vague: "the account she'll give of herself." What account and who? I assumed, needless to say, that he was still talking about Capitu, and was tempted to ask him, but that urge died as soon as it was born, like so many other generations before it. I merely asked José Dias when I could go home to see my mother.

"I really miss Mama. Can I go this week?"

"Go on Saturday."

"Saturday? Ah, yes, yes! Ask Mama to send for me on Saturday! Saturday! This Saturday, right? Yes, ask her to send for me, without fail."

Chapter LXIII / *Two halves of a dream*

I COULD HARDLY WAIT for Saturday to arrive. Until then, I was pursued by dreams, even while I was awake, and I won't describe them here so as not to make this part of the book even longer. I will tell you just one, and in as few words as possible, or perhaps two dreams, because one was born of the other, unless both were two halves of the same dream. I know this is all very obscure, lady reader, but it's entirely the fault of you, the fairer sex, for troubling the adolescence of a poor seminarian. If it weren't for you, this book would perhaps be a simple parish sermon were I a priest, or a pastoral letter were I a bishop, or an encyclical were I a pope, as Uncle Cosme had urged me to become: "Away you go, my boy, and be sure to come back a pope!" Ah, why did I not grant his wish? Ever since Napoleon, who was both lieutenant and emperor, anyone can become anything in this century of ours.

As for the dream, here it is. I was spying on some local dandies, when I saw one of them standing outside Capitu's window, chatting. I ran toward him, but he fled; I went over to Capitu, but she wasn't alone, her father was by her side, wiping away tears and gazing down at a sad lottery ticket. Having no idea what was going on, I was about to ask for an explanation, when he himself gave it to me; the dandy had just brought him the list of lottery winners, and his ticket was not among them. His number was 4004. He told me that the symmetry of that number was mysterious and beautiful, and that something had obviously gone wrong with the lottery wheel; it was simply impossible that he could have failed to win the big prize. While he was speaking, Capitu was giving me all sorts of prizes, large and small, with her eyes. The biggest prize of all should have been given with her lips. And this is where the second part of the dream comes in. Pádua disappeared, along with his hopes for his lottery ticket. Capitu leaned out of the window, and I looked up and down the street, which was deserted. I clasped her hands then, mumbled some unintelligible words, and woke up alone in my bedroom.

The interesting thing about what you have just read lies not in the substance of the dream, but in the huge effort I made to try and go back to sleep and re-enter that dream. You will never ever know the energy and persistence I devoted to closing my eyes tight shut and driving every thought from my mind in order to sleep, but to no avail. These labors kept me awake into the small hours. Only as day was breaking did I finally manage to fall asleep again, but no dandies appeared, no lottery tickets, no prizes large or small— absolutely zero of zero came into my head. I did not dream again, and performed badly in class.

━━ Chapter LXIV / *An idea and a scruple*

REREADING THAT LAST CHAPTER, an idea and a scruple came to
mind. The scruple was whether or not to write down the idea, since
there was nothing on earth more banal—not even the banal rising
and setting of the sun and moon that the heavens present us with
each day and each month. I abandoned my manuscript and stared
at the walls instead. As you know, this house in Engenho Novo
replicates my old house in Rua de Matacavalos, in its dimensions,
its paintings and the distribution of its rooms. Also, as I told you in
Chapter II, my aim in imitating that other house was to connect the
two ends of my life, something I have completely failed to do. Well,
the same thing happened to that dream at the seminary, however
hard I tried to sleep and did sleep. From which I conclude that one
of man's tasks is to close his eyes and keep them tightly closed in
order to see if, in his old man's night, he can recommence the trun-
cated dream of his youth. That is the idea, at once banal and new,
that I did not want to set down here, and which I must do now, but
only provisionally.

Before concluding this chapter, I went over to the window to
ask the night why dreams have to be so very fragile that the slightest opening of the eyes or turning of the body causes them to fray
and vanish into nothing. The night did not answer me at once. It
was deliciously beautiful, the hills were turning pale in the moon-
light, and the air was utterly still and silent. When I asked again,
the night informed me that dreams do not fall under her jurisdic-
tion. When they lived on the island that Lucian gave them, where
the night had her palace, and whence she sent them forth with their
many and varied faces, then she could have given me a possible

explanation. But time had changed everything. The old dreams were sent into retirement, and the modern ones are now unique to each individual's brain. These modern dreams would be incapable of imitating the old ones even if they wanted to; the island of dreams, like the island of love, and like all the islands in all the seas, is now the object of the ambitions and rivalry between Europe and the United States.*

This was an allusion to the Philippines. Anyway, since I am no lover of politics, still less international politics, I closed the window and came back to my desk to finish this chapter before going to bed. I don't want Lucian's dreams now, nor any others, the offspring of memory or our digestive system; all I want is a peaceful night's sleep. Tomorrow, in the cool of morning, I will tell you the rest of my story and its characters.

⟹ Chapter LXV / *The deception*

SATURDAY CAME, then more Saturdays, and eventually I adjusted to my new life, alternating between home and seminary. The priests liked me, the other boys liked me, and Escobar liked me the most of all. After five weeks I was on the verge of telling him all my hopes and fears; Capitu dissuaded me.

"Escobar's a very good friend of mine, Capitu!"

"But he isn't my friend."

* The island of dreams is one of several fantastical lands described by Lucian of Samosata (ca.125–ca.180) in his parody *A True Story*. The island of love, just as fantastical, forms the climax of Luís de Camões's sixteenth century epic poem *The Lusiads*.

"He could become one; he's already said he wants to meet Mama."

"It doesn't matter; you have no right to tell him a secret that isn't yours alone, and I don't give you permission to tell anything to anyone."

She was right. I held my tongue and obeyed. Another example of my obeying her demands occurred on my very first Saturday home from the seminary when I went over to her house and, after only a few minutes' conversation, she advised me to leave.

"Don't stay too long today; go back to your own house and I'll pop around there shortly. Dona Glória will naturally want to have you to herself for as long as she can."

Capitu showed such clarity of mind in all of this that I could easily dispense with citing a third example, but examples are made to be cited, and this one is so good that it would be a crime to leave it out. It was on my third or fourth visit home. Once I had answered my mother's battery of questions about my studies, my friends, discipline, how they were treating me, any aches or pains, was I sleeping well, and all the other questions a mother's affection invents to weary a son's patience, she turned to José Dias and said:

"Senhor José Dias, do you still doubt that he'll make a good priest?"

"Senhora, I *most* humbly—"

"As for you, Capitu," my mother said, interrupting him and turning to Capitu, who had joined them in the drawing room, "don't you think our Bentinho will make a good priest?"

"I think he will, Senhora," Capitu replied with great conviction.

I did not like that conviction. I told her so the following morning in her backyard, recalling her words of the previous evening, and, for the first time, throwing in her face her apparent happiness since I had entered the seminary, while I was consumed with longing for her. Capitu grew very serious, and asked me how I expected her to behave, given that we were already under suspicion; she, too, endured nights of despair, and her days, spent sitting at home, were as forlorn as mine: I just had to ask her mother or father. Her mother had even suggested, in veiled terms, that she should stop thinking about me.

"When I'm with Dona Glória and Dona Justina I naturally put on a brave face, so as to cast doubt on José Dias's accusations. If they believed him, they would try to drive us even further apart, and might even ban me from the house . . . For me, it's enough that we have sworn an oath to marry each other."

There it was: we must deceive in order to deflect any suspicion, and at the same time enjoy all our previous liberties, while calmly planning for our future. However, the example would be incomplete without something I heard over lunch the following day; when Uncle Cosme said he was looking forward to seeing how convincing I would be at blessing the congregation during mass, my mother remarked that a couple of days earlier, while talking about girls who marry young, Capitu had told her: "Well, as for me, it will be Father Bentinho who'll marry me; I'm waiting for him to be ordained!" Uncle Cosme laughed at the joke, while José Dias managed not to *not*-smile, and Cousin Justina frowned and shot me a quizzical glance. I looked around at all of them, and, unable to hold Cousin Justina's gaze, tried to busy myself with my food. I could hardly eat, though; I was so pleased with Capitu's great deception that I couldn't focus on anything else, and, as soon as lunch was over, I rushed to tell her about the conversation and congratulate her on her sharpness of mind. Capitu smiled gratefully.

"You're right, Capitu," I concluded. "We'll pull the wool over all their eyes."

"We will indeed," she said simply.

Chapter LXVI / *Intimacy*

CAPITU WAS BY NOW GAINING my mother's affections. They spent most of their time together, talking about me, or about the weather, or about nothing at all; Capitu went there in the mornings to sew; sometimes she stayed for lunch.

Cousin Justina did not join my mother in extending such courtesies, but nor did she treat my friend entirely badly. She was honest enough never to hold back anything bad she had to say about someone, but then again she had nothing good to say about anyone. With the possible exception of her husband, but her husband was dead; in any event, no man could compete with him in affection, hard work and honesty, good manners and keenness of mind. This opinion, according to Uncle Cosme, had been formed posthumously, because in life they were always quarreling, and had lived apart during his final six months. All the better for her sense of righteousness: praising the dead is a form of praying for them. She must also have liked my mother, or if she did think ill of her, she kept such thoughts to herself and her pillow. One can understand why, outwardly, she paid her due respect. I do not think she aspired to any legacy; people who do that usually go beyond their natural obligations, and make a special effort to be more cheerful, more assiduous, showering other people with care and attention, even outdoing the servants. All of which went contrary to Cousin Justina's sour, nitpicking nature. Since she lived with us for free, it is understandable that she did not scorn the lady of the house and kept any resentments to herself, or spoke ill of her only to God and the Devil.

Even if Cousin Justina did resent my mother, this was not a

reason to detest Capitu, nor indeed did she require any additional reason. Nevertheless, Capitu's intimacy with my mother made Cousin Justina loathe her all the more. She did not initially treat my friend badly, but, over time, her manner changed and eventually she avoided her completely. Capitu, perspicacious as ever, would inquire after her and seek her out. Cousin Justina tolerated these attentions. Life is full of obligations that we accept even though we would, out of petulance, prefer to ignore them. Moreover, Capitu had at her disposal a certain seductive charm; Cousin Justina would end up smiling, however sourly, but when alone with my mother she would always take the opportunity to make some unkind comment about the girl.

When my mother fell ill with a fever that left her at death's door, she wanted Capitu to nurse her. Even though this relieved Cousin Justina of that tedious responsibility, she could not forgive my friend's intervention. One day, she asked Capitu if she had nothing to do in her own house; another day, with a smile, she fired this epigram in her direction: "No need to chase so hard; whatever's to be yours will come to you."

Chapter LXVII / *A sin*

BEFORE I HAUL the poor patient out of her bed, let me first tell you what happened to me. After five days, my mother woke up feeling so unwell that she gave orders for me to be fetched home from the seminary. Uncle Cosme tried in vain to dissuade her:

"My dear sister, you're worrying yourself needlessly. The fever is subsiding . . ."

"No! No! Send for him! I could die at any moment, and my soul will not be saved if Bentinho is not at my side."

"We'll only frighten him."

"Then don't tell him anything. But fetch him, right now, without delay."

They thought this was her delirium speaking; but since it was easy enough to bring me home, José Dias was entrusted with the task. He arrived at the seminary looking so upset that he really did alarm me. He explained the situation privately to the rector, and I was given permission to go home. We walked quietly through the streets, he maintaining his usual plodding pace—premise before consequence, consequence before conclusion—but head down and sighing, so that I was afraid that I could read in his face some harsh and incontrovertible news. He had told me about the illness as a simple and straightforward matter; but my being summoned home, his silence, and his sighs must mean something more. My heart was thumping and my legs were shaking; indeed, more than once I thought I might fall over . . .

My impatience to hear the truth was all tangled up inside me with my fear of knowing it. This was the first time that death had appeared so close, all around me, staring at me with its dark piercing eyes. The farther we walked along Rua dos Barbonos, the more terrified I became at the idea of arriving home, going inside, hearing wailing voices, seeing a dead body . . . Oh! I could never describe here everything I felt during those terrifying moments. Even though José Dias walked superlatively slowly, the street seemed to slip away beneath my feet, the houses flying by on both sides, and the sound of a bugle emanating from the barracks of the Municipal Guard rang in my ears like the trumpet at the Last Judgment.

I carried on, reached the Arcos da Lapa, and turned into Rua de Matacavalos. The house was much farther along, well beyond the corner of Rua dos Inválidos, almost as far as Rua do Senado. Three or four times I wanted to question my companion, but didn't dare open my mouth; by then, all desire to do so had left me. I carried on walking, resigned to the worst, as an act of fate, a necessity of the human condition, and it was then that Hope, in mortal combat with Fear, whispered to my heart, not in these precise words, for it articulated nothing resembling words, but rather an idea that could be translated as follows: "If Mama dies, that'll put an end to the seminary."

Reader, it was like a flash of lightning. No sooner had it lit up the night sky than it vanished, and the darkness grew still darker due to the feelings of remorse enveloping me. It was a thought born of licentiousness and egotism. My filial piety faded just for a moment at the prospect of certain freedom, through the passing away of both debt and debtor; it was a moment, less than a moment, one hundredth of a moment, and yet it was enough to add remorse to my affliction.

José Dias kept sighing. At one point, he looked at me so dolefully that it seemed to me he must have guessed my thoughts, and I felt like asking him not to say anything to anyone, that I would do penance myself, and so on. But there was so much affection in his sadness that it could not be sorrow at my sin; it must therefore be my mother's death . . . I felt an overwhelming sense of loss, a lump in my throat, and, unable to stop myself, I burst out crying.

"What's the matter, Bentinho?"

"Is Mama . . . ?"

"Of course she isn't! What an idea! Her condition is *most* serious, but not life-threatening, and God can do all. Dry your eyes; it isn't becoming for a boy your age to be seen crying in the street. It's nothing at all, only a fever . . . Fevers vanish as suddenly as they appear . . . Now, don't use your fingers, boy; where's your handkerchief?"

I dried my eyes, although of all José Dias's words only two stuck in my mind: "most serious." I realized later that he had only meant to say "serious," but prolonged use of the superlative slackens the mouth, and for the love of a fine phrase, José Dias had added to my woes. If, reader, you find in this book any other instances of a similar sort, please let me know so that I may correct it in the second edition; there is nothing worse than giving the *longest* of legs to the *briefest* of ideas. As I said, I dried my eyes and carried on walking, eager now to reach home, and beg my mother's forgiveness for the terrible thought I had entertained. At last, we arrived; trembling, I climbed the six steps, and soon afterward, leaning over her bed, I heard my mother, as she clasped my hands, tenderly addressing me as her dear son. She was burning hot, her eyes seared into mine, her whole body seemed consumed by an inner volcano. I knelt beside the bed, but as the bed was rather high, I was still too far from her caresses:

"No, son, stand up! Stand up!"

Capitu was also in the bedroom, and, as she told me later, she enjoyed watching me enter the room, enjoyed my gestures, words, and tears; but, naturally, she did not suspect the cause of my distress. Later, alone in my own room, I contemplated telling my mother everything, once she was better, but the idea did not appeal to me; it was a fleeting thought, something I would never carry out, however heavily the sin weighed upon me. So, carried away with remorse, I once again resorted to my old method of making spiritual promises, and begged God to forgive me and spare my mother's life, and that I would say two thousand Paternosters in return. To any priest reading this, forgive my chosen method; this was the very last time I employed it. And it was all because of the crisis in which I found myself, as well as habit and faith. That was two thousand more Paternosters, and where were all the earlier ones? I had paid neither the old ones nor the new, but when issued by pure and honest souls such promises are like fiat currency—for as long as the debtor does not pay them, they're worth whatever the debtor says they are worth.

≡ Chapter LXVIII / *Postponing virtue*

FEW WOULD BE BRAVE ENOUGH to confess to the thought I had entertained as I walked along Rua de Matacavalos. I will confess to everything that is relevant to my story. Montaigne wrote of himself: *Ce ne sont pas mes gestes que j'escris; c'est moi, c'est mon essence.** Well, there's only one way of writing one's own essence, which is to tell all, both the good and the bad. This is what I am doing, by summoning up memories that help to construct or reconstruct myself. For example, now that I've told you of a sin, I would very much like to recount a good deed from around the same time, if I could remember one. But I can't, so it will have to wait for another opportunity.

You will lose nothing by waiting, my friend; on the contrary, I have just remembered that . . . Not only are good deeds good on any occasion, they are also both possible and probable, according to my theory of sins and virtues, a theory that is as simple as it is clear. It comes down to this: Each person is born with a certain number of sins and virtues, each one paired in matrimony so as to balance each other out in life. When one of these spouses is stronger than the other, then it alone guides the individual, and that individual,

---

* From Montaigne's *Essais:* "It is not my deeds that I write down, it is myself, my essence."

having neither practiced such a virtue nor committed such a sin, cannot claim to be free of either one or the other. However, the general rule is that both are practiced simultaneously, to the overall benefit of their host, and occasionally to the greater glory of heaven and earth. It's a pity that I cannot substantiate this evidence involving other people, but I don't have time.

As regards myself, it is certainly the case that I was born with one of those pairs within me, and, naturally, they're still there. Even here in Engenho Novo, there was one time when, suffering from a terrible headache at night, I wished that the train whistling its way along the railway line would blow up far out of earshot and block the line for many hours, even if that meant someone dying. Then, the following day, I missed my train on the very same line because I went over to give my walking stick to a blind man who didn't have a white cane. *Voilà mes gestes, voilà mon essence.**

<hr/>

Chapter LXIX / *The mass*

ONE OF THE DEEDS that best expresses my essence was the devotion with which I rushed the following Sunday to hear mass at São Antônio dos Pobres. José Dias wanted to go with me, and started getting dressed, but he was so slow with his straps and suspenders that I could not wait for him. Also, I wanted to be alone. I felt the need to avoid any conversation that might divert my thoughts from the goal I had set: to reconcile myself with God

* These are my deeds, this is my essence.

after the events of chapter LXVII. It was not merely to ask him to forgive my sin, but also to give thanks for my mother's recovery, and, since I am revealing everything, to ask him to let me off the payment of my promise. Jehovah, despite his divinity, or perhaps because of it, is a much more human Rothschild; he doesn't just offer a moratorium, he forgives debts entirely, provided that the debtor genuinely desires to change his ways and reduce his expenses. I wanted nothing more; from then on, I would make no more promises I could not repay, and I would repay promptly those I did make.

I heard mass; at the moment of elevation of the Host, I gave thanks for the life and health of my mother; I then begged forgiveness for my sin and remission of my debt, and I received the priest's final blessing as a solemn act of reconciliation. At the end, I remembered that the Church instituted the confession box as the safest of depositories, and the act of confession as the truest of instruments for the settling of moral accounts between man and God. However, my irredeemable shyness closed that door to me; I feared not finding the right words to tell the confessor my secret. How a man can change! Today, here I am publishing it!

Chapter LXX / *After mass*

I PRAYED FOR A FEW MORE MINUTES, crossed myself, closed my missal, and walked toward the door. The congregation was small, but then the church wasn't very big, either, so I could only make my exit very, very slowly. There were men and women, old and young, silks and chintzes, and probably eyes both ugly and beautiful, but I saw neither one nor the other. I made my way toward the door along with the wave of people, listening to their greetings and whisperings. At the entrance, in the bright light of day, I stopped and gazed at all of them. I saw a girl and a man who left the church and then paused; and the girl looked at me while speaking to the man, and the man looked at me as he was listening to the girl. And I heard these words:

"But what is it you want?"

"I want to know how she is. Ask him, Papa."

It was Sancha, Capitu's school friend, wanting news of my mother. Her father came over to me; I told him that she was fully recovered. We turned to leave, he pointed toward his house, and, since I was going in the same direction, we left together. Gurgel, the father, was a man in his early forties, with a tendency to put on fat around his belly; he was very affable, and on reaching the door of his house, he was adamant that I join them for breakfast.

"Thank you, but Mama is waiting for me."

"I'll send one of our blacks over to tell her you're staying for breakfast, and that you'll be home later."

"No, I'll come another day."

Miss Sancha, intently watching her father, listened and waited. She was not bad-looking; the only family resemblance was in her nose, which was also somewhat large, but certain features take beauty from some and give it to others. She was very simply dressed. Gurgel was a widower and devoted to his daughter. Since I had declined breakfast, he insisted I come in and rest a few minutes. I couldn't refuse and went inside. He wanted to know how old I was, about my studies, my faith, and he gave me advice in the event that I became a priest; he told me the address of his emporium, on Rua da Quitanda. Finally, I said my goodbyes, and he accompanied me to the top of the steps; his daughter sent her fond regards to Capitu and my mother. From the street I looked up at the house; the father was at the window and remained there waving me a fond goodbye.

=== Chapter LXXI / *Escobar's visit*

AT HOME, THE FAMILY had already lied to my mother, telling her I had returned and was getting changed.

"The eight o'clock mass must have finished by now . . . Bentinho should be back . . . Do you think something has happened, Cosme? We must send someone . . ." She repeated this every other minute, until I entered the room and peace was restored.

It was a day of pleasant surprises. Escobar came to see me and inquire after my mother's health. He had not visited me before, as we were not yet as intimately connected as we would later become; but on finding out the reason for my departure three days earlier, he had used his Sunday to come and see me, and ask if my mother was still in peril. When I told him she wasn't, he gave a sigh of relief.

"I feared the worst," he said.

"Do the others know?"

"I think so. Some of them."

Uncle Cosme and José Dias liked the young man. José Dias told him he had met his father once, here in Rio. Escobar was very polite; and while he talked more then than he would in later life, he still wasn't as talkative as most boys our age; that day I found him a little more expansive than usual. Uncle Cosme asked him to stay for lunch. Escobar thought for a moment, then replied that his father's agent was waiting for him. Remembering Gurgel's words earlier, I repeated them:

"We'll send one of our blacks over to tell him you're having lunch here, and that you'll see him later."

"I don't want to be a bother!"

"No bother at all," interrupted Uncle Cosme.

Escobar accepted and stayed for lunch. I noticed that the twitching he successfully mastered in class he also mastered here, both in the drawing room and at the table. The hour he spent with me was one of honest friendship. I showed him the few books I possessed. He greatly admired the portrait of my father; after several moments' contemplation, he turned and said:

"One can see he had a pure heart!"

Escobar's eyes (pale, as I have already said), were *most* charming; this is how José Dias described them after Escobar left, and I will keep his choice of words, despite the forty years that have since passed. In this instance our family retainer was not exaggerating. Escobar's clean-shaven face revealed a smooth, fair complexion. His forehead, it must be said, was a little low, the parting in his hair coming down almost to his left eyebrow; but it was sufficiently high not to spoil his other features, nor diminish their charm. In fact, he had an interesting face, with thin, sardonic lips and a slender, curved nose. He had a habit of twitching his right shoulder every now and then, but promptly lost it when one of us remarked upon it one day at the seminary; it was the first example I've seen of a man being perfectly capable of curing himself of minor defects.

I never failed to feel a certain pride whenever my friends pleased everyone. At home they adored Escobar; even Cousin Justina thought him a very nice young man, despite . . . "Despite what?" José Dias asked her, when she didn't finish her sentence. No reply was forthcoming, nor could it be; Cousin Justina probably did not see any obvious or significant defect in our guest: the "despite" was a sort of caveat for something she might one day discover; or perhaps it was just an old habit that led her to find fault where none was to be found.

Escobar said his farewells soon after lunch; I took him to the door, where we waited for an omnibus. He said that his father's agent had his offices on Rua dos Pescadores, and would be open until nine o'clock; he, however, did not like to be out late. We parted fondly: he was still waving goodbye from inside the omnibus. I remained standing at the door, to see whether he would look back again, but he didn't.

"Who's your great friend?" a voice asked from a nearby window.

I scarcely need say that this was Capitu. These are things that can be guessed in life, just as in books, whether in novels or true stories. It was Capitu, who had been spying on us for some time from behind the venetian blinds, and had now opened the window fully and stood there before me. She had seen our fond, effusive farewells, and wanted to know who it was who deserved such attentions.

"That was Escobar," I said, walking over to stand beneath her window, and gazing up at her.

Chapter LXXII / *A dramatic reform*

NEITHER I, NOR YOU, NOR SHE, nor anyone else in this story could have said any more in reply, given that destiny, like all good playwrights, does not give advance notice of either plot twists or the final denouement. These arrive at their own pace, until the curtain falls, the lights are turned off, and the spectators go home to sleep.

It is a genre perhaps in need of reform, and I would like to propose, as an experiment, that plays should begin at the end. Othello would kill himself and Desdemona in the first act, the following three would be given over to his slow, ever-decreasing jealousy, and the final act would consist of the threat of an attack by the Turks, Othello's and Desdemona's dialogues, and the sage advice of cunning Iago: "Put money in thy purse." In this manner, the theatergoer would, on the one hand, experience the same charade he finds in newspapers, with subsequent acts explaining the outcome set out in the first (the "clue" to the drama, as it were), and, on the other hand, he would then go to bed with a heartening impression of tenderness and love:

> *She loved me for the dangers I had passed,*
> *And I loved her that she did pity them.*

Chapter LXXIII / *The stage manager*

DESTINY IS NOT ONLY A PLAYWRIGHT, it is its own stage manager, meaning that it determines when the characters should enter and leave the stage, hands them letters and other props, and provides the backstage sounds that complement the dialogue: a thunderclap, a passing carriage, a gunshot. When I was a young man, someone put on a play, at a theater I've now forgotten, that ended with the Last Judgment. The main character was Ahasuerus, who in the final scene concludes a monologue with this exclamation: "I hear the archangel's trumpet!" No trumpet was to be heard. An embarrassed Ahasuerus repeated the crucial word, this time more loudly, so as to catch the stage manager's attention, but still nothing. He then strode to the back of the stage, in vaguely tragic mode, but in fact for the sole purpose of speaking to the stagehand, and telling him in a stage whisper: "The cornet! The cornet! The cornet!" The audience heard and burst out laughing, until, when the cornet did finally sound, and Ahasuerus wailed for the third time that it was the archangel's trumpet, a joker in the orchestra stalls called out: "No, sir, it's the archangel's *cornet!*"

This explains how I came to be standing beneath Capitu's window when a young man on horseback, a "beau," as we used to say back then, passed by. He was riding a fine chestnut horse, his slim, erect figure sitting firmly in the saddle, reins in his left hand, right hand on his waist, and wearing patent-leather boots; the face was not unknown to me. Others had passed by before him, and others would come after him, all were going to visit their sweethearts. At the time, it was customary to go courting on horseback. Reread Alencar: "Because a student [says one of his characters in a play from 1858] cannot be without these two things: a horse and a sweetheart."* Reread Álvares de Azevedo. He uses one of his poems, from 1851, to explain that he lived in Catumbi, and in order to see his sweetheart in Catete, he had rented a horse for three *mil-réis* . . . Three *mil-réis!* Everything disappears in the mists of time!†

---

* José de Alencar (1829–1877), Brazil's greatest novelist of the Romantic period and a close friend of Machado de Assis. The quote is from *O Crédito*, a comedy centering on themes of marriage and money. It was a notable flop, and led to Alencar abandoning his work for the theater.

† Álvares de Azevedo (1831–1852), a leading Brazilian romantic poet who died tragically young following a fall from a horse. The quote is from his poem *Namoro a cavalo* (*Courting on Horseback*). Inflation had rendered three *mil-réis* almost worthless by the time Bento was reflecting on these events.

Well, the *beau* on the bay horse did not pass by like the others; he was the trumpet of doom, sounding right on time; Destiny, as you see, is its own stage manager and never misses a cue. The rider was not content merely to pass by, but turned his head toward us, toward Capitu, and he gazed at Capitu, and she at him; the horse moved on, but the man's head continued to turn as he passed by. This was the second tooth of envy to bite me. Strictly speaking, it's only natural to admire a fine silhouette, but that fellow was in the habit of passing by there every afternoon; he lived on what used to be Campo da Aclamação, and later . . . and later . . . You try thinking straight when your heart is on fire! I didn't say a word to Capitu; I rushed from the street into my own house, and, when I came to my senses, found myself in the drawing room.

<hr>

Chapter LXXIV / *The trouser strap*

IN THE DRAWING ROOM, Uncle Cosme and José Dias were deep in conversation, one seated, the other pacing up and down. The sight of José Dias reminded me of what he'd said to me at the seminary about Capitu: "Just waiting for some local dandy to fall for her and marry her . . ." He was doubtless alluding to the young man on horseback. Remembering his words added to the impression I had formed in the street; but then perhaps it was those very words, lurking in the back of my mind, that had inclined me to believe in the rider's mischievous gaze? I wanted to grab José Dias by the collar, drag him out into the hallway, and ask him whether he had been talking factually or hypothetically; but José Dias, who had briefly paused on seeing me enter the room, resumed his pacing and talking. I was impatient to return next door, imagining that Capitu would now have stepped away from her window in alarm, and would soon appear with questions and explanations . . . And the two of them carried on talking, until Uncle Cosme got up to go and see how the patient upstairs was doing, and José Dias came over to join me by the other window.

A moment earlier, I had wanted to ask him what was going on between Capitu and the local dandies; now, imagining that this was precisely what he had come to tell me, I was afraid to hear it. I wanted to stop his mouth. José Dias saw in my face something different from its usual expression, and asked me earnestly:

"What is it, Bentinho?"

I looked down to avoid his gaze, but as my eyes did so, they noticed that one of his trouser straps was undone, and, as he insisted on knowing what was wrong, I replied pointing with my finger:

"Look at your trouser strap. It needs buttoning up."

José Dias bent down, and I fled the room.

Chapter LXXV / *Despair*

I ESCAPED JOSÉ DIAS, and escaped my mother by not going to her room, but I did not escape myself. I rushed to my room, and followed myself in. I talked to myself, I tormented myself, I threw myself onto the bed and wrestled with myself, and cried, and stifled my sobs with one corner of the sheet. I swore not to go and see Capitu that afternoon, or ever again, and to make a priest of myself once and for all. I imagined myself already ordained, standing before her while she wept remorseful tears and begged my forgiveness, while I, cold and serene, would have nothing for her but scorn, deep scorn; I turned my back on her. I called her wicked. Twice I found myself gnashing my teeth, as if I held her between them.

From my bed I could hear her voice: she had come over to spend the rest of the afternoon with my mother, and, of course, with me, as on previous occasions; but, however shaken I had been by her attitude at the window, nothing would induce me to leave my room. Capitu was laughing loudly and speaking loudly, as if announcing her presence; I shut my ears, alone with myself and my scorn. It made me want to sink my fingernails into her neck, bury them deep, and watch her life's blood drain out of her . . .

≡ Chapter LXXVI / *Explanation*

AFTER SOME TIME HAD PASSED, I felt calm again, but totally drained. As I lay on the bed, my eyes fixed on the ceiling, I recalled my mother's advice not to lie down after lunch so as not to bring on some form of congestion. I sat bolt upright, but did not leave my room. By now Capitu was laughing less and talking more quietly; she was probably troubled by my absence, but not even this could sway me.

I had no supper and I slept badly. The following morning I felt no better, but I did feel different. My sorrow was now mingled with the fear of having gone too far, and of failing to examine the matter thoroughly. Since my head ached somewhat, I feigned a more serious malaise, with the intention of not returning to the seminary, and of speaking to Capitu. She might be angry with me; perhaps she no longer loved me and preferred the young man on horseback. I wanted to settle the whole thing, to hear what she had to say, and to judge her; she might have a defense or an explanation.

She had both. When she found out why I had shut myself away the previous evening, she told me I was doing her a great injustice; she could not believe that after our exchange of vows I had deemed her so frivolous as to believe . . . And here she burst into tears, and waved me away; but I rushed to her side, grasped her hands, and kissed them with such warmth and feeling that I felt them tremble. She wiped away her tears with her hands, and I kissed those fingers again, both for their own sake and for the tears they had wiped away; then she sighed, then shook her head. She confessed that she did not know the young man, any more than she knew the others who passed by every afternoon, on horseback or on foot. If she had looked at him, it was proof positive that there was nothing between them; if there had been, it would have been natural to pretend otherwise.

"Anyway, what could be going on, if he's getting married?" she concluded.

"Getting married?"

Yes, he was, and she told me to whom, a young lady from Rua dos Barbonos. This piece of information satisfied me more than anything else, and she saw this in my face; she nevertheless went on to say that, from now on, to avoid any further misunderstandings, she would not spend time at the window anymore.

"No! no! no! I won't ask you to do that!"

She agreed to withdraw her promise, but made another, which was the following: that at the first sign of suspicion on my part, everything would be over between us. I accepted her threat, and swore that she would never have to carry it out: this was my first suspicion and my last.

Chapter LXXVII / *Taking pleasure in old sorrows*

WHEN I DESCRIBE THIS CRISIS in my adolescent love, I feel something that I am perhaps not explaining very well, which is that my sorrows from that period became so distilled by time that they have mellowed into pleasures. I'm not being very clear, but then not everything is clear in life or in books. The truth is I feel a peculiar pleasure in mentioning my vexation at the time, even though it reminds me of others that I most definitely do not wish to remember.

Chapter LXXVIII / *Secret for secret*

BESIDES, AT THE TIME, I felt an overwhelming need to tell someone about what was happening between Capitu and me. Escobar was my chosen confidant, but I did not tell him everything, only a part. When I returned to the seminary that Thursday, I found him in a rather anxious state; he said that, if I had stayed at home for one more day, he was planning to come and see me. He asked me solicitously how I had been, and whether I was completely recovered.

"I am."

He listened, his eyes probing me. Three days later, he told me that people were commenting on how distracted I seemed; it would be a good idea to conceal this as much as possible. He had his own reasons for being rather distracted, but he was trying to remain focused.

"So you think it shows?"

"Oh, yes, sometimes you're completely off in your own world somewhere, staring into space. Learn to disguise your feelings, Santiago."

"I have my reasons . . ."

"I'm sure you do; no one becomes distracted without a reason."

"Escobar . . ."

I hesitated; he waited.

"What is it?"

"Escobar, you are my friend, and I'm your friend too; here in the seminary you are the person I feel closest to, and outside of here, other than family, I don't really have a friend."

"If I were to say the same thing to you," he replied, smiling, "it would lose its charm; I would seem merely to be repeating what you had said. But the truth is I have no real friend here either; you are the first, and I think the others have already noticed, not that this bothers me."

I was touched, and could feel the words rushing into my mouth.

"Escobar, can you keep a secret?"

"By asking me that, you are clearly doubting me, in which case . . ."

"I'm sorry, it was just a way of speaking. I know you are a serious fellow, and that talking to you is the same as confessing to a priest."

"If you need absolution, consider yourself absolved."

"Escobar, I cannot be a priest. I am here in the seminary, and my family believe and expect me to become one; but I cannot be a priest."

"Me neither, Santiago."

"Really?"

"Secret for secret: I don't intend to finish the course either. I want to go into commerce, but don't say a thing, not a word; this is strictly between us. It isn't that I'm not religious; I am, but commerce is my passion."

"Only commerce?"

"What more is there?"

I paced twice around the room and whispered the first word of my secret, so faintly and indistinctly that I didn't hear it myself; I know, however, that I said, "A person . . ." and paused. A person? . . . Nothing more was needed for him to understand. A "person" must be a girl. And don't go thinking he was shocked to find out I was in love; he thought it completely natural and shot me another piercing gaze. I then told him in outline what I could, although slowly enough to savor the pleasure of revisiting the subject. Escobar listened attentively; at the end of our conversation, he declared that my secret would go with him to the grave. He advised me not to become a priest. I could not bring to the Church a heart that belonged to earth and not to heaven; I would be a bad priest, indeed I wouldn't be a priest at all. On the contrary, God protected the sincere of heart; since I could only serve Him in the world, then that was where I should stay.

You cannot imagine the joy I felt once I had told him my secret. It was like piling happiness upon happiness. Having another youth-

ful heart hear me and agree with me lent the world an extraordinary new aspect. The world was large and beautiful, life was a
marvelous adventure, and I was nothing less than heaven's dar-
ling—this was how I felt. Note, however, that I didn't tell him
everything, not even the best bits; I didn't mention the chapter
about combing her hair, for example, nor other such matters; but I
did tell him a great deal.

Needless to say, we returned to the subject later. Indeed we
returned to it time and again; I praised Capitu's moral qualities,
a suitable attribute for a seminarian to admire, her simplicity,
her modesty, her love of needlework, and her religious devotions. I did not touch upon her physical charms, nor did he ask
me about them; I merely hinted at the advantage of him meeting
her in person.

"It isn't possible right now," I told him that first week back at the
seminary; "Capitu is going to spend a couple of days with a friend
in Rua dos Inválidos. When she returns, we'll go together; but you
can visit my home before then, anytime you like. Why didn't you
come to dinner yesterday?"

"You didn't invite me."

"Do I need to invite you? Everyone at home has taken a great
liking to you."

"And I have taken a great liking to all of them, but if it's possible to make a distinction, I have to say that your mother is an
adorable lady."

"Isn't she just?" I replied eagerly.

Chapter LXXIX / *Let's go straight to the chapter*

I CERTAINLY ENJOYED HEARING him talk like that. You know how I felt about my mother. Even now, putting down my pen to look at her portrait hanging on the wall, I think she had that very quality imprinted on her face. There's no other way of explaining Escobar's view of her, since they had only exchanged a few words. Just one word was enough to grasp her innermost essence: yes, my mother was indeed adorable. Even though she was at the time forcing me into a career I did not want, I still couldn't help but feel that she was as adorable as a saint.

And in any case, was it even true that she was forcing me into an ecclesiastical career? Here I come to a point I thought I would reach later on, so much so that I was already thinking about where I would put that chapter. I shouldn't really tell you something now that, in fact, I only discovered later, but since I've touched on the matter, better to get it over and done with. It is both grave and complex, delicate and subtle, one of those points on which the author must listen to the child, and the child must listen to the author, in order that both of them shall tell the truth, the whole truth, and nothing but the truth. It should also be noted that it is precisely this point that makes the saint all the more adorable, without prejudice (quite the contrary!) to her more human and earthly qualities. But enough of this preface; let's go straight to the chapter itself.

⟨ Chapter LXXX / *Here we are*

SO HERE WE ARE AT THE CHAPTER. My mother was a God-fearing woman; you know this already, and about her religious devotions, and the pure faith that inspired them. You are also aware that my ecclesiastical career was the subject of a promise made when I was conceived. All this was explained at the appropriate juncture. Likewise, you know that, in order to tighten the moral strictures of her solemn undertaking, she confided her motives and intentions to members of the family and the household. That promise, made fervently, accepted mercifully, was kept joyfully in the innermost reaches of her heart. I think I tasted the sweetness of that happiness in the milk I drank when she gave me suck. Had my father lived, he may well have altered those plans, and, since his own vocation was political, it is likely he would have guided me toward that alone, even though the two professions neither were nor are incompatible, and more than one priest has entered into the cut and thrust of partisan strife and the government of men. But my father had died knowing nothing of her promise, and my mother found herself the sole party to the contract, the sole debtor.

One of Benjamin Franklin's aphorisms is that for those who owe money to be paid at Easter, Lent is very short. Our Lent was longer than most, and although my mother had ensured I was taught Latin and the catechism, she began to put off my entry into the seminary. It's what they call, in commercial parlance, rescheduling a debt. But in this case the divine creditor was a multimillionaire and so not reliant on that particular payment for his daily bread, and he agreed to the deferral of the payment, without even increasing the rate of interest. One day, however, one of those household members who had endorsed the original promissory note mentioned the importance of paying the agreed amount: you'll find this in one of the early chapters. My mother agreed, and off I went to São José.

Now, in that same chapter she did shed some tears, which she wiped away without further explanation, and which none of those present, neither Uncle Cosme, nor Cousin Justina, nor José Dias, fully understood. From my hiding place behind the door, I understood no more than they did. On careful examination, despite the distance in time, it is now apparent that her tears came from an anticipatory sense of loss, the pain of separation—and perhaps also (and this is where the point begins), perhaps also a feeling of remorse for having made that promise. As a devout Catholic, she knew very well that promises are meant to be kept; the question was whether it was right and proper to keep every single one of them, and she, naturally enough, inclined toward the negative. Why would God punish her by denying her a second child? Perhaps my life was God's will anyway, with no need to dedicate it to Him *ab ovo*. But this was rather a belated argument; she should have thought of it on the day I was conceived. In any case, this was her initial conclusion; but since it was not sufficient to overturn her promise, everything remained as it was, and away I went to the seminary.

A momentary dozing of her faith would have resolved the question in my favor, but faith was wide awake with its large, ingenuous eyes. If she could, my mother would have swapped one promise for another, giving up some of her own years in order to keep me by her side, outside the clergy, married and with children; that's what I assume, just as I assume she rejected such an idea as a betrayal. This was how she always behaved in daily life.

My absence, however, was soon tempered by Capitu's assiduous attentions. She began to make herself indispensable to my mother. Gradually, my mother became persuaded that this girl would make me happy. Therefore (and here I conclude my point), the hope that our love, by making me absolutely incompatible with the seminary, would cause me to leave irrespective of either God or the Devil, this private, secret hope began to take hold of my mother's heart. In such an event, I would be breaking the contract, and she would not be to blame. She would have me by her side, but not by her own actions. It was as if, having entrusted the full amount of a debt to someone else to deliver it to the lender, that person then kept the money for himself and delivered nothing. In ordinary life, the actions of a third party do not release the contracting party; but the advantage of entering into a contract with heaven is that intention is just as good as money.

You must have known similar conflicts, and, if you are religious, you must have sought at some point to reconcile heaven and earth in an identical or at least analogous way. Heaven and earth always end up being reconciled; they are almost twins, heaven having been made on the second day and earth on the third. Like Abraham, my mother took her son to the mount of the Holy Vision, along with fire, the knife, and firewood for the burnt offering. And she placed the bound Isaac on top of the bundle of firewood, took the knife, and raised it aloft. Just as she was about to plunge the knife downward, she heard the angel's voice ordering her on behalf of the Lord: "Lay not thine hand upon the lad, neither do thou anything unto him: for now I know that thou fearest God." It was the very thing my mother had secretly hoped for.

Capitu was, of course, that angel of the Scriptures. By now my mother could not bear for her to be far from her side. Her growing affection showed itself in extraordinary ways. Capitu became the very flower of the household, the morning sun, the evening breeze, the moonlit night; she was there hour after hour, listening, talking, and singing. My mother probed Capitu's heart, searched deep in her eyes, and my name passed between them as the code word for their future lives.

Chapter LXXXI / *A few words*

NOW THAT I HAVE DESCRIBED what I would later discover, I can bring in here a few words spoken by my mother. You will now understand those words uttered on the first Saturday when I arrived home and was informed that Capitu was over at Rua dos Inválidos, with Miss Gurgel:

"Why don't you pay her a visit? Didn't you tell me Sancha's father said you were always welcome?"

"Yes, I did."

"Well, then? But only if you want to, mind. Capitu was due to come here today to finish off some needlework with me; no doubt her friend asked her to stay the night there."

"Perhaps they've been entertaining young gentlemen?" suggested Cousin Justina.

I refrained from killing her there and then because I had neither steel nor rope, pistol nor dagger at hand; but if looks could kill, the look I gave her would have made up for all those implements. One of Providence's errors was to endow mankind only with arms and teeth as a means of attack, and legs as a means of escape or defense. Eyes alone would suffice in the first category. A glance from them would halt or fell an enemy or rival, they would extract swift vengeance, with the added advantage of throwing justice off the scent, for the same murderous eyes would fill with pity, and promptly weep for their victim. Cousin Justina escaped my murderous glance, while I failed to escape the effects of her insinuation, and on that Sunday, at eleven o'clock, I rushed over to Rua dos Inválidos.

Sancha's father greeted me, looking downcast and disheveled. His daughter was ill; she had succumbed the previous day to a fever, which was gradually worsening. Since he loved his daughter above all else, he was already convinced she would die, and told me that if she did, he would kill himself too. This is turning into a chapter as mournful as a cemetery, complete with deaths, suicides, and murders. I was yearning for a ray of bright sunshine and a clear blue sky. It was Capitu who brought them to the doorway of the drawing room, coming down to tell Sancha's father that his daughter had sent her to fetch him.

"Is she getting worse?" asked Gurgel in alarm.

"No, senhor, but she wants to speak to you."

"Stay here a little longer," he said to Capitu, and, turning to me: "She's been nursing Sancha, since she won't have anyone else. I'll be back in a moment."

Capitu showed signs of exhaustion and anxiety, but as soon as she saw me she became quite her old self, the same young girl, fresh and sprightly and surprised in equal measure. She could hardly believe it was me. She talked to me, wanted me to talk to her, and indeed we spoke for several minutes, but in whispers so soft that even the walls couldn't hear, for walls have ears. Or at least if they did hear something, they understood none of it, neither the walls nor the furniture, which were as downcast as their owner.

Chapter LXXXII / *The settee*

OF ALL THE FURNITURE, only the settee seemed to have best understood our emotional condition, since it offered us the services of its wickerwork, and so insistently that we accepted and sat down. The high opinion in which I hold settees dates from that moment. They combine intimacy and decorum, and reveal the nature of the entire house without leaving the drawing room. Two men seated upon one can debate the destiny of an empire, and two women the elegance of a gown; but a man and a woman together would only by an aberration of the laws of nature discuss anything other than themselves. Which is precisely what Capitu and I did. I vaguely remember asking if her stay there would be a long one . . .

"I don't know; her fever seems to be subsiding . . . but . . ."

I also remember, vaguely, that I explained how my visit to Rua dos Inválidos had come about, namely that it was on my mother's advice.

"Your mother's advice?" Capitu murmured.

And with her eyes looking suddenly extraordinarily bright, she added:

"We're going to be happy!"

I repeated these words with just my fingers squeezing hers. The settee, whether it saw or not, continued to provide its services to our clasped hands and to our heads that were so close as to be almost touching each other.

Chapter LXXXIII / *The portrait*

GURGEL RETURNED to the drawing room and said to Capitu that his daughter was asking for her. I leaped to my feet and looked extremely embarrassed, my eyes fixed on the chairs. In contrast, Capitu stood up perfectly naturally and asked if the fever had worsened.

"No," he said.

Not the slightest sign of alarm or mystery from Capitu; she turned to me and told me to send greetings to my mother and Cousin Justina, and that she would see me soon. Then she shook my hand and slipped out into the hallway. I watched in envy. Why was it that Capitu could control herself so easily and I couldn't?

"She's quite the young lady now," observed Gurgel, also gazing after her.

"Yes, she is," I murmured. Capitu was indeed growing up by leaps and bounds, her figure filling out and firming up with remarkable speed; emotionally it was the same. She was a woman both inside and out; a woman from every possible angle, and from head to toe. Now that I was seeing her only every few days, she seemed to be growing and blossoming ever more quickly; whenever I went to her house, she was taller and more shapely; her eyes seemed to have a new gleam to them, and her mouth a new authority. Turning toward the portrait of a young lady hanging on the drawing room wall, Gurgel asked if I thought Capitu resembled the portrait.

It has been the habit of a lifetime always to agree with whatever was the likely opinion of my interlocutor, as long as the subject matter did not offend, irritate, or otherwise intrude upon me. So before examining whether or not the portrait did indeed resemble

Capitu, I replied that it did. He then informed me that the portrait was of his wife, and everyone who had known her said the same thing. He, too, thought many of her features were similar, especially the forehead and the eyes. As for her temperament, it was exactly the same; you would think they were sisters.

"And then there's her friendship with my dear Sanchinha; her own mother was no greater friend . . . Life is full of such strange resemblances."

Chapter LXXXIV / *Summoned*

IN THE HALLWAY and in the street, I was still debating with myself whether or not he suspected something, but I decided he didn't and set off walking. I felt satisfied with my visit, with Capitu's cheerfulness, and with Gurgel's praise, so much so that I did not at first hear a voice summoning me:

"Senhor Bentinho! Senhor Bentinho!"

Only after the voice grew louder and its owner appeared at a door did I stop to see who it was and where he was calling from. I was already in Rua de Matacavalos. I was outside a crockery shop, a bare, impoverished sort of place; the door stood ajar and the person calling out was a poor man with gray hair and shabby clothes.

"Senhor Bentinho," he said, weeping, "did you know that my son Manduca has just died?"

"Died?"

"Yes, he died half an hour ago; he'll be buried tomorrow. I've just sent a message to your mother, and she did me the kindness of sending some flowers to place on his coffin. My poor son! He had to die, and it was best that he did, poor lad, but even so it hurts terribly. What a dreadful life he had! He mentioned you just recently, and asked if you were at the seminary . . . Do you want to see him? Come in and see him . . ."

It pains me to say this, but better to say too much than too little. I wanted to tell him no, that I didn't want to see Manduca, and I even made as if to walk away. It wasn't fear—on any other occasion I might have gone inside out of mere curiosity—but just then I was feeling so very contented! Visiting a corpse after visiting one's sweetheart . . . some things just don't fit well together. Simply hearing the news was already a major upset. My golden thoughts had lost all their hue and shine, turning to drab, dark ashes, and everything became a blur. I think I managed to say that I was in a hurry, but I probably didn't say this clearly or even using human words, because the shopkeeper, leaning against the doorframe, beckoned me in, and I, lacking the courage either to go in or to run away, let my body decide, and my body decided to go in.

I don't blame the man; the most important thing for him at that moment was his son. But nor should you blame me; for me the most important thing was Capitu. The trouble was that the two things came together on the same afternoon, and the death of one had poked its nose into the life of the other. That was the real problem. If I'd passed by a little earlier or later, or if Manduca had waited a few more hours to die, then no discordant note would have interrupted the sweet melodies of my soul. Why had he died exactly half an hour ago? Any time of day suits death; you can as easily die at six in the evening as at seven.

Chapter LXXXV / *The dead body*

IT WAS WITH THESE AMBIVALENT FEELINGS that I entered the shop. It was dark inside, and the living quarters beyond even darker, since the shutters in that part were closed. I saw the boy's mother hunched in the corner of the dining room weeping; at the bedroom door two children stood staring fearfully in, fingers on lips. The corpse lay on the bed; the bed . . .

Let me put down my pen for a moment and go to the window to clear my thoughts. The scene was truly grim, both in terms of death itself and in terms of the dead body, which was horrible . . . Here, now, in Engenho Novo, things are very different. Everything I can see outside breathes life: the goat ruminating beside a cart, the hen pecking about in the dirt, the train whistling and billowing smoke as it puffs along the railway line, the palm tree reaching sky-ward, and even that church belfry over there, even though it lacks either muscles or foliage. A young lad playing with his paper kite in that alleyway over there isn't dead and isn't dying, although he, too, is named Manduca.

It's true that the other Manduca was older, a little older, than this one. He must have been eighteen or nineteen, but you might just as well say fifteen or twenty-two, for his face did not reveal his age, but rather concealed it in the folds of . . . Come, let's tell the whole story: he's dead, his relatives are dead, and if any are still alive they are not prominent enough to be embarrassed or upset. So here's the whole story: Manduca suffered from a cruel illness: leprosy, no less. Alive he was ugly; dead he seemed to me quite simply hideous. When I saw my neighbor's wretched body lying there on the bed, I was terrified and looked away. I don't know what hidden hand compelled me to look back, albeit briefly; I gave in and looked again, then shrank back and left the room.

"He suffered terribly," his father said with a sigh.

"Poor Manduca!" sobbed his mother.

I planned my escape, told them I was expected home, and said goodbye. The father asked if I would be so kind as to go to the funeral; I replied truthfully that I didn't know, and that I would do as my mother wished. I then rushed from the room, through the shop, and bounded out into the street.

≡ Chapter LXXXVI / *Young men, you must love!*

THE SHOP WAS SO CLOSE that within three minutes I was home. I paused in the hallway to catch my breath; I tried to forget the dead body, pale and misshapen, and a lot of other things I haven't mentioned so as not to give these pages an equally repugnant appearance, but which you can well imagine. In a matter of seconds I had removed everything from my sight; I needed only to think of that other house, to think about life and Capitu's fresh, lively face . . . Young men, you must love! And most of all, you must love pretty, vivacious young women: they are the one remedy for all ills, they bring fragrance to the fetid, they turn death into life . . . Young men, you must love!

Chapter LXXXVII / *The chaise*

I HAD REACHED THE TOP STEP, and a thought came into my head, as if it were waiting for me between the bars of the wrought-iron gate. I heard every word that Manduca's father had said when he asked me to go to the funeral the following day. I paused on the step. I thought for a moment; yes, I *could* go to the funeral; I would ask my mother to hire me a carriage . . .

Do not think that this was a desire to ride in a carriage, however much I enjoyed such things. When I was little, I remember that I would often go in the chaise with my mother on her social visits, and to mass if it was raining. It was an old chaise belonging to my father, which she held on to for as long as she could. When the coachman, who was our slave and as old as the chaise itself, saw me standing at the door, all dressed up and waiting for my mother, he would chuckle and say to me:

"Old João's goin' drive young massa!"

And I nearly always told him:

"Keep a firm grip on the mules, João. Take it slowly."

"S'nhora Glória don't like that."

"Even so, take it slowly!"

It goes without saying that this was in order to savor every moment of the ride and not out of vanity, because those traveling inside could not be seen from outside. It was the old-fashioned type, a two-wheeler, short and narrow, with two leather curtains at the front that you had to pull around to the sides to get in and out. Each curtain had a glass peephole, through which I liked to peer.

"Sit down, Bentinho!"

"Let me look, Mama!"

And when I was little, I would stand up, put my face to the glass, and I could see the coachman with his big boots, sitting astride the mule on the left and holding the other mule's reins; in his other hand he held the long, thick whip. It was all very cumbersome—the boots, the whip, and the mule—but he liked it and so did I. I watched the houses pass by on either side, some with shops, open or closed, with or without customers, and people coming and going in the street, or crossing in front of the chaise, with great strides or dainty steps. When there was a logjam of people or animals, the chaise would stop and the spectacle would become particularly interesting; people paused on the sidewalk or in the doorways of houses, looking at the chaise and whispering to each other, no doubt wondering who might be inside. As I grew older I imagined them guessing and saying: "It's that lady from Rua de Matacavalos, who has a son Bentinho . . ."

The chaise so suited my mother's reclusive lifestyle that we continued to use ours even after everyone else had gotten rid of theirs, and it became known in our street and neighborhood as the "old chaise." Eventually my mother agreed to stop using it, but still did not immediately sell it; she only finally got rid of it when the stabling expenses forced her to do so. Her reason for keeping it without using it was purely sentimental: it was a reminder of her husband. Everything that came from my father was kept as a piece of him, a vestige of his person, his very soul pure and whole. But using it was also a product of her conservative outlook, as she freely confessed to her friends. My mother was a fine example of loyalty to old habits, old manners, old ideas and old fashions. She had her museum of relics, outmoded combs, a lace mantilla, some copper coins from 1824 and 1825, and, so that everything could be antiquated together, she tried to make herself old as well; but as I have already mentioned, in this respect she was not entirely successful.

Chapter LXXXVIII / *A worthy pretext*

NO, THE IDEA OF GOING to the funeral did not come from remembering the chaise and its delights. Its origin lay elsewhere: by going to the funeral the following day, I could skip the seminary and pay another, somewhat more leisurely visit to Capitu. There you have it. The memory of the chaise may have followed as an accessory, but that was the immediate and principal reason. I would return to Rua dos Inválidos, under the pretext of inquiring after Miss Gurgel. I imagined that everything would unfold just as it had the previous day. Gurgel distraught, Capitu beside me on the settee, our hands clasped, her thick braids . . .

"I will ask Mama."

I opened the gate. Before entering, just as I had heard within me the words of the dead boy's father, I now heard those of his mother, and I repeated them softly:

"Poor Manduca!"

Chapter LXXXIX / *The refusal*

MY MOTHER WAS PUZZLED when I asked her permission to attend the funeral.

"Yes, but missing a day at the seminary . . ."

I reminded her of the friendship Manduca had shown me, and

they were such poor folk, too . . . I came up with every possible reason. Cousin Justina was resolutely opposed.

"So you think he shouldn't go?" my mother asked her.

"I think not. What friendship? I certainly never saw it."

Cousin Justina won. When I referred the matter to José Dias, he smiled and told me that Cousin Justina's hidden motive was probably that she did not want to lend the funeral "the luster of your presence." Whatever it was, I went into a sulk. The next day, thinking about her motive, I was slightly less offended; later on, I even took a certain liking to it.

Chapter XC / *The debate*

THE FOLLOWING DAY, I passed by the dead boy's house without going in or stopping. Or if I did stop, it was only for a moment, even briefer than this moment now. If I'm not mistaken, I may even have walked faster, fearing I might be summoned as I had been on the previous day. Since I was not going to the funeral, the farther away I could get, the better. I carried on walking and thinking about the poor boy.

We were not friends, nor had we known each other for long. As for any close friendship, what close friendship could there have been between his illness and my good health? Our encounters had been brief and distant. I began thinking about them, recalling some. What it came down to was a fierce debate that had arisen between us two years earlier, in relation to . . . Well, you'll find this hard to believe . . . it was all to do with the Crimean War.

Manduca lived at the back of the house, where he'd lie on his bed and read to pass the time. On Sundays, toward evening, his father would dress him in a dark nightshirt and bring him into the back of the shop, from where he could catch a glimpse of the street and passersby. This was his only entertainment. I saw him there once, and was more than a little shocked; the disease was eating away parts of his flesh and his fingers were growing stiff and clawlike; it was not an appealing sight, to be sure. I was thirteen or fourteen. The second time I saw him there, we talked about the Crimean War, which was raging at the time and all over the papers. Manduca said that the allies were certain to win, and I said they weren't.

"We'll see," he replied. "Only if justice does not prevail in this world, and that's impossible, and justice is on the side of the allies."

"No, sir, the Russians are in the right."

Naturally, we were only following what the city's newspapers told us, and they simply copied the foreign press, but it may also have been that each of us held the opinion that suited our respective temperaments. I was always somewhat Muscovite in my ideas. I defended the rights of Russia, Manduca did the same for the allies, and when I returned to the shop on the third Sunday, we broached the subject once again. Manduca proposed that we continue the debate in writing, and on the Tuesday or Wednesday of the following week I received two sheets of paper containing an exposition and defense of the rights of the allies, and of the integrity of Turkey, concluding with this prophetic sentence:

"The Russians will never enter Constantinople!"

I read what he wrote and set about refuting it. I do not recall a single one of the arguments I put forward, and now that this century is on its last legs, it is perhaps of no interest to know what they were; but the general impression that stays with me is that my arguments were incontrovertible. I personally delivered my treatise to Manduca. I was brought into the bedroom, where he lay on the bed, barely covered by a patchwork quilt. My enjoyment of the debate, or some other unfathomable reason, made me almost impervious to the repugnant state of both bed and occupant, and I handed him the piece of paper with genuine pleasure. As for Manduca, however loathsome the appearance of his face, the smile that lit it up disguised all his physical ailments. There are no words, in our own language or any other, that can completely and accurately describe the determination with which he took the piece of paper from me, telling me he would read it and respond; there was no zealotry, no fervor, no gesturing, nor would his illness allow that; it was simple, expansive, and profound, an infinite savoring of certain victory, before he even knew what my arguments would be. He had paper, pen, and ink ready by the bedside. A few days later I received his reply; I don't remember whether it contained anything new, but he was even more emphatic and the ending was the same:

"The Russians will never enter Constantinople!"

I replied, and for some time a fierce polemic raged, in which neither of us gave an inch, each defending his proxies with force and eloquence. Manduca's responses were longer and came faster than mine. Of course, I had a thousand other things to keep me busy: my studies, my hobbies, my family, and my own good health, which summoned me to other exertions. Apart from his glimpse of the street on Sunday afternoons, Manduca had only this war, which the whole city and world were talking about, but which no one came to discuss with him. Chance had given him me as a sparring partner and, as someone who enjoyed writing, he flung himself into the debate as if it were a new and radical cure. The long, gloomy hours now passed quickly and cheerfully; his eyes forgot how to weep, if indeed they had wept before. I sensed this change in him from his mother and father's behavior.

"You can't imagine, senhor, how much better he's been since you started writing those letters to him," his father once said to me, standing at the street door. "He talks and laughs all the time. As soon as I send the shop boy over to deliver his letters to you, he starts asking whether you've replied yet, and if you take too long, he keeps pestering the lad to go and check. While he's waiting, he rereads the newspapers and takes notes. Then, as soon as he receives your letter, he throws himself into reading it, and immediately starts writing his reply. There are times when he scarcely eats, so much so that I wanted to ask if you wouldn't mind not sending your replies when it's time for lunch or dinner . . ."

It was I who tired of it first. I began to delay my answers, and then stopped altogether; he persisted two or three times following my silence, but when he still received nothing in response, he, too, whether also from weariness or so as not to be a nuisance, called a halt to his treatises. The last one, like the first, like all of them, proclaimed the same eternal prediction:

"The Russians will never enter Constantinople!"

Nor indeed did they, either then, or later, or to this day. But will his prediction prove eternal? Might they not someday enter the city? A tricky problem. Manduca himself spent three years decomposing in order to enter his grave, for nature, like history, is no laughing matter. His life resisted, as did Turkey; if in the end he conceded defeat it was because he lacked an alliance like the Anglo-French one, for the unsophisticated pact between medicine and pharmacy cannot be considered to be of the same order. He died, as states will die; in our particular case, the question is not whether Turkey will die, because death spares no one, but whether the Russians will some day enter Constantinople; this was the big question for my leprous neighbor, beneath his wretched, tattered, fetid patchwork quilt . . .

Chapter XCI / *A comforting discovery*

CLEARLY THE IDEAS I have set out above were not formed then, on my way to the seminary, but now, in my study here in Engenho Novo. At the time, I formed no ideas, apart, that is, from this: that I had once provided some relief to my neighbor Manduca. Today, on further reflection, I think I gave him not merely some relief, but even happiness. And this discovery comforts me; I will certainly not now forget that I gave two or three months of happiness to a poor devil by making him forget his misfortune and everything else. This is something to be included in the balance sheet of my life. If, in the other world, there is some sort of reward for unintentional virtues, this will pay for one or two of my many sins. As for Manduca, I do not believe it was a sin to express an opinion against Russia, but if it was, then for the last forty years he has been expiating the happiness he felt during those few months— from which he will conclude (somewhat belatedly) that it would have been better just to lie on his bed and groan, without expressing any opinion at all.

Chapter XCII / *The devil is not so black as he is painted*

MANDUCA WAS BURIED without me. The same had happened to many other people without my feeling anything at all, but in this case I was particularly troubled for the reason just stated. I also felt a certain sense of melancholy on recalling that first polemic, and the pleasure with which he used to receive my letters and set about refuting them; not to mention the pleasure I would have felt to be riding in a carriage . . . But Father Time quickly erased all these nostalgias and resurrections. And not only Time; two people came to assist him: Capitu, whose image fell asleep with me that same night, and another person whom I will come to in the next chapter. The rest of this chapter serves simply to ask that, should someone happen to read my book and pay somewhat more attention to it than called for by its cover price, please draw the conclusion that the devil is not so black as he is painted. What I mean is . . .

What I mean is that my neighbor in Rua de Matacavalos, by tempering his illness with his anti-Russian views, gave his rotting flesh a consolingly intellectual veneer. There are, of course, greater consolations, and one of the greatest is not suffering from leprosy or any other illness, but Nature is so divine that she amuses herself with such contrasts, and waves a flower at those who are most wretched or most tormented. Perhaps that flower is thus rendered more beautiful; my gardener tells me that to give violets a superior scent, pig manure is essential. I have not investigated this claim, but it must be true.

== Chapter XCIII / *A friend instead of a corpse*

ANOTHER PERSON WHO POSSESSED that power of obliteration was my friend Escobar, who, on Sunday, before midday, paid a visit to Rua de Matacavalos. A friend thus took the place of a dead person, and so close a friend that he grasped my hand for almost five minutes, as if he had not seen me for many months.

"Will you have lunch with me, Escobar?"

"That is exactly why I came."

My mother thanked him for his friendship toward me, and he replied very courteously, albeit somewhat constrained, as if struggling to find the right words. You have already seen that this was not in his nature, that words came easily, but a man is not always the same at every given moment. What he said, in brief, was that he had the greatest respect for my good qualities and my careful upbringing; everyone was very fond of me at the seminary, and, he added, it could scarcely be otherwise. He emphasized the importance of upbringing, of good examples, of having "the sweet, incomparable mother" heaven had given me . . . All this was said in a choking, trembling voice.

They were all charmed by him. I was as pleased as if Escobar were my own invention. José Dias fired two superlatives in his direction, Uncle Cosme thrashed him twice at backgammon, and Cousin Justina could find no blemish to pin on him; only later, on the second or third Sunday, did she find something, declaring that my friend Escobar was a bit of a busybody and had the eyes of a policeman who missed nothing.

"They are *his* eyes," I pointed out.

"I didn't say they were anyone else's."

"They're thoughtful eyes," opined Uncle Cosme.

"They certainly are," agreed José Dias. "And yet my esteemed Senhora Justina may well be right. Indeed, one thing does not preclude the other, and thoughtfulness marries well with natural curiosity. He does seem to be on the inquisitive side, that much is true, but—"

"He strikes me as a very serious young man," said my mother.

"Precisely!" confirmed José Dias, so as not to disagree with her.

When I mentioned to Escobar what my mother had said about him (without mentioning the other opinions, of course), I could see that it gave him enormous pleasure. He thanked me, saying it was very kind, and also praising my mother's gravitas, elegance, and youth. "So very young . . . How old is she?"

"Over forty," I replied vaguely out of vanity.

"She can't be!" exclaimed Escobar. "Forty! She doesn't even look thirty; she's very youthful and pretty. And you must have taken after someone, with those fine eyes God gave you: they're just like hers. Is it many years since she was widowed?"

I told him what I knew about her life and my father's life. Escobar listened attentively, asking more questions and demanding explanations for anything I had skipped over or left unclear. When I told him that I remembered nothing about living in the countryside, because I was so young when we left, he told me about two or three memories he had from when he was three years old and which were still fresh in his mind. And were we not planning to return to the country?

"No, we've no intention of going back. Look! See that black man over there? He's from the plantation. Tomás!"

"Massa!"

We were in the vegetable garden of my house, and the man was busily working; he came toward us and waited.

"He's married," I said to Escobar. "Where's Maria?"

"She's pounding corn, senhor."

"Do you still remember the plantation, Tomás?"

"Remember it well, senhor."

"All right, then, off you go."

I showed him another one, and another, and another; first Pedro, then José, then, over there, Damião—

"All the letters of the alphabet," interrupted Escobar.

Indeed, the names did all begin with different letters, and I'd never noticed that until then; I pointed out yet more slaves, some with the same names, differentiated by a nickname describing either the person, like Crazy João or Big Maria, or the place they had come from, like Pedro Benguela, Antônio Mozambique . . .

"And they're all here at the house?" Escobar asked.

"No, some are earning their keep elsewhere, and others are hired out. It's not possible to have them all at the house. There were more of them on the plantation; most of them stayed there."

"What surprises me is that Dona Glória has adapted so quickly to living in the city, where everything is so cramped; the house you came from must have been much larger."

"I don't know, but I suppose so. Mama owns some other houses bigger than this one, but she says this is where she will die. The other houses are all rented out. Some are very large, like the one in Rua da Quitanda . . ."

"I know that one; it's very pretty."

"She also has one over in Rio Comprido, one in Cidade Nova, one in Catete . . ."

"Well, she'll never lack for a roof over her head," he concluded with a warm smile.

We walked around to the back of the house. We passed the washtubs; he paused there for a moment, staring at the stone used for beating the clothes and reflecting on the subject of cleanliness; then we walked on. What his reflections were I do not now recall; I remember only that I thought them very witty and laughed, and that he laughed too. My cheerful mood chimed with his, and the sky was so blue, the air so clear, that nature seemed also to be laughing with us. Such are the happy times of this world. Escobar gave expression to this harmony between the internal and the external in words so noble and exalted that I felt deeply moved. Then, regarding the matching of moral beauty to physical beauty, he spoke once again of my mother, "an angel twice over," he said.

Chapter XCIV / *Arithmetical ideas*

I WON'T REPEAT what else he said, for he said a great deal. Not only did he know how to praise and think, he could also calculate quickly and accurately. He had one of those arithmetical minds described by Holmes ($2 + 2 = 4$).* You can't imagine the ease with which he could add or multiply in his head. Division, which I had always found difficult, was for him a mere trifle: he would half shut his eyes, gaze at the ceiling, and softly call out the digits one by one; there was no delay, not even with seven, thirteen, or twenty digits. His vocation was such that he adored even the plus and minus signs, and was of the opinion that figures, being fewer, held much deeper meanings than the twenty-six letters of the alphabet.

"There are some letters that are utterly useless and others we can easily dispense with," he would say. "What is the point of the letters *d* and *t*? They have almost the same sound. I could say the same of *b* and *p*, of *s*, *c*, and *z*, and of *k* and *g*, etc. They're a complete calligraphic hodgepodge. Look at numbers, on the other hand: no two do the same job: 4 is 4, and 7 is 7. And admire the beauty with which a 4 and a 7 combine to form a thing that is expressed as 11. Now double 11 and you will get 22; multiply by the same number and it gives 484, and so on. But where the perfection is greatest is in its use of *zero*. The value of *zero* is, in itself, nothing; but the func-

* Oliver Wendell Holmes Sr. (1809–1894), in *The Autocrat of the Breakfast-Table*: "All economical and practical wisdom is an extension or variation of the following arithmetical formula: $2 + 2 = 4$. Every philosophical proposition has the more general character of the expression $a + b = c$. We are mere operatives, empirics, and egotists, until we learn to think in letters instead of figures."

tion of this non-sign is precisely to increase. A 5 on its own is a 5; put two os after it and it's 500. Thus something that is worthless makes another thing very worthwhile, which cannot be said for double letters, for I could just as well *aprove* with one *p* as with two.

Raised according to the spelling of my forefathers, it pained me to hear such blasphemies, but I dared not disagree with him.* One day, however, I proffered a few words of defense, to which he replied that this was mere prejudice, and added that arithmetical ideas could stretch to infinity, with the advantage that they were much easier to handle. This would explain why I was unable to resolve instantly a philosophical or linguistic problem, whereas he could add up any quantity of numbers in three minutes flat.

"For example . . . go on, give me an example, give me a list of numbers that I do not, and could not, already know . . . like the number of houses your mother owns and the monthly rents for each of them, and if I can't tell you the sum of all of them in two, no, one minute, you can hang me from the rafters!"

I accepted the wager, and the following week I brought him a piece of paper with the number of houses and their monthly rents. Escobar took the piece of paper, ran his eyes over it to memorize the numbers, and while I stared at my watch, he raised his eyes, closed his eyelids, and began murmuring to himself . . . Oh, but he was faster than the wind! It was no sooner said than done: in half a minute he cried out:

"Altogether, that gives 1,070 *mil-réis* a month."

I was utterly astonished. Bear in mind that there were no fewer than nine houses, and that the rents were all different, from 70 *mil-*

---

* Portuguese spelling reform, in particular concerning double letters and similar-sounding consonants, became a popular subject of controversy in the late nineteenth century. The reforms would eventually be adopted by Portugal in 1911, with Brazil following some years later.

réis up to 180 *mil-réis*. Something that would have taken me three or four minutes—and on paper—Escobar did in his head effortlessly. He looked at me triumphantly, and asked if he was right. To show him that he was, I pulled out the piece of paper from my pocket with the total amount, and showed him: it was exactly the same, not a digit out: 1,070 *mil-réis*.

"This proves that arithmetical ideas are simpler, and yet more natural. Nature is simple. Art is complicated."

I was so enthused by my friend's mental agility that I couldn't help clasping him in an embrace. We were in the courtyard; other seminarians noticed our effusive behavior, and a priest who was with them did not like it.

"Modesty," he told us, "does not permit such excessive gestures. You may show due regard for one another, but in moderation."

Escobar remarked to me that the other seminarian and the priest spoke out of envy, and suggested to me that we keep apart. I interrupted him, saying that no, if it was envy then so much the worse for them.

"Who cares what they think!"

"But . . ."

"Let's be even closer friends than before."

Escobar furtively shook my hand, but squeezed it so hard that my fingers still hurt even now. This is, of course, an illusion or perhaps the effect of the long hours I've been sitting here writing without a break. Let us put down the pen for a few moments . . .

⟹ Chapter XCV / *The pope*

MY FRIENDSHIP WITH ESCOBAR grew broad and fruitful; and my friendship with José Dias was determined to keep up. The following week José Dias said this to me:

"It's certain now that you will be leaving the seminary very soon."

"What?"

"Wait until tomorrow. I'm going to play cards with them now, since they've sent for me. Tomorrow, though, be it in your room, in the backyard, or in the street on the way to mass, I'll tell you what's what. The idea is so divine that it would not be out of place in the church itself. Tomorrow, Bentinho."

"But is it a sure thing?"

"The very surest!"

The next day he revealed the mystery to me. At first I confess I was dazzled. It possessed a spiritual grandeur that appealed to my seminarian's eyes. It was no less than this: In his view, my mother regretted having made her promise and wanted to see me out in the world, but felt that the moral strictures of that promise formed an irrevocable bond. It was now time to set her free, and that is where the Scriptures came in, with the power to dissolve such bonds conferred upon the apostles. Therefore, he and I would go to Rome to seek absolution from the pope . . . What did I think?

"It seems a reasonable idea," I replied after a few seconds' thought. "It could be a good solution."

"It's the *only* solution, Bentinho, the only one! I'll speak to Dona Glória today, explain everything to her, and we can leave in two months' time, or even earlier . . ."

"Best speak to her next Sunday; let me think about it first—"

"Oh, Bentinho!" he interrupted. "What is there to think about? What you really want . . . shall I tell you? You won't be cross with your old friend, will you? What you really want to do is consult a certain person."

Strictly speaking, there were two people, Capitu and Escobar, but I vehemently denied that I wanted to consult anyone. Who was he referring to? The rector? It was hardly appropriate for me to discuss something like that with him. Not the rector, nor the teachers, or anyone else; I just needed time to reflect, one week, I'd give him my answer on Sunday, and I'd already said I thought it wasn't a bad idea.

"You do?"

"I do."

"Then let's settle it today."

"A journey to Rome is not to be undertaken lightly."

"All roads lead to Rome, and in our case the road is paved with money. Look, you can spend all you like on yourself . . . Not a penny on me; a pair of trousers, three shirts, and my daily bread is all I need. I will be like Saint Paul, who lived on his earnings while preaching the word of God. But I go not to preach the word, but to seek it. We will take letters from the internuncio and the bishop, letters for our ambassador, letters from the Franciscans . . . I'm well aware of the objections that could be made to this idea; people will say that it's perfectly possible to request a papal dispensation from here; but, in addition to other reasons I won't mention, just consider how much more solemn and beautiful it would be for you yourself, the promised Levite, the very object of the request, to enter the Vatican and prostrate yourself at the feet of the Holy Father, begging God's dispensation for your sweetest and gentlest of mothers. Picture the scene, you kissing the feet of the Prince of Apostles; His Holiness, with his evangelical smile, leans forward, inquires, listens, absolves, and blesses. The angels gaze down upon him, the Virgin recommends to her Most Holy Son that all your wishes, Bentinho, be met, and that all whom you love on earth will be equally loved in heaven . . ."

I shall stop there, because I need to finish the chapter, and he had not finished his speech. He spoke to all of my sentiments as a Catholic and as a lover. I saw my mother's unburdened soul, I saw Capitu's joyous heart, both of them at home, and me with them, and him with us, all by means of a little trip to Rome. I knew where it lay geographically, and spiritually, too, but how far it lay from Capitu's wishes I had no idea. This was the crucial point. If Capitu thought it too far away, I wouldn't go; but I needed to hear what she had to say, and Escobar, too, for he would surely give me good advice.

≡ Chapter XCVI / *A substitute*

I EXPLAINED JOSÉ DIAS'S PLAN to Capitu. She listened attentively to what I had to say, and was very downcast by the end.

"When you go," she said, "you'll forget me completely."

"Never!"

"You will. People say Europe is so beautiful, especially Italy. Isn't that where all those pretty opera singers come from? You'll forget me, Bentinho. Isn't there another way? Dona Glória is desperate for you to leave the seminary."

"Yes, but she considers herself bound by her promise."

Capitu could not think of another plan, but couldn't bring herself to support this one. On the way, she asked me to swear that if I did end up going to Rome, I would be back within six months.

"I swear."

"By God?"

"By God, and by everything else. I swear that I will be back within six months."

"But what if the pope hasn't yet released you?"

"I'll send a message to let you know."

"And what if you lie to me?"

That word wounded me deeply, and at first I didn't know how to respond. Capitu made light of it, laughing and calling me a crafty fox. Then she said she believed I would fulfill my oath, but even so she couldn't agree to it straightaway; she would look into whether there was any alternative, and I should look too.

When I returned to the seminary, I told everything to my friend Escobar, who listened to me just as attentively and by the end was just as downcast as Capitu had been. His eyes, normally so restless, almost devoured me with their penetrating gaze. Suddenly I saw his face light up with the glimmer of an idea. And I heard him say loudly:

"No, Bentinho, it isn't necessary. There's a better way—I shouldn't say better, because the Holy Father is always the best of everything—but there is something that would produce the same effect."

"What's that?"

"Your mother promised God to give him a priest. Well, then, she should give him a priest, just not you. She could very easily take on some young orphan and have him ordained at her expense. The altar gets its priest, without you having to—"

"I understand, I understand. Yes, indeed."

"Don't you agree?" he continued. "Consult the protonotary on the subject; he'll tell you if it counts, or I can ask him, if you like. And if he hems and haws, we'll speak to the bishop."

I thought hard: "Yes, that seems right; in effect the promise is fulfilled, since the Church will still get its priest."

Escobar remarked that from an economic point of view the matter was clear-cut: my mother would spend the same amount of money as she would have spent on me, and an orphan would not need much in the way of home comforts. He cited the income from renting the houses, 1,070 *mil-réis*, not to mention the slaves . . .

"That's the only way," I said.

"And we'll leave the seminary together."

"You too?"

"Me too. I'll brush up on my Latin and then leave; I won't bother with theology. I don't even need Latin; what use is it in commerce?"

"*In hoc signo vinces*," I said laughing.*

I was in a jocular mood. Oh, but how hope cheers up everything! Escobar smiled; he seemed to like my answer. We spent a moment deep in our own thoughts, each of us doubtless staring into space. At least that's what he was doing when I looked back at him, and I thanked him again for the plan he had come up with; there couldn't be a better one. Escobar was delighted to hear this.

"Once again," he said gravely, "religion and liberty make good bedfellows."

---

* This Latin motto, meaning, "By this sign you will conquer," and associated with the Roman Emperor Constantine's conversion to Christianity, appeared on most nineteenth century Brazilian coins and banknotes.

≡ Chapter XCVII / *The departure*

EVERYTHING WENT ACCORDING to plan. My mother hesitated somewhat, but eventually gave in, after Father Cabral, having consulted the bishop, came back and told her that it was indeed acceptable. I left the seminary at the end of the year.

By then I was just over seventeen . . . I ought to be halfway through the book at this point, but my inexperience has let my pen run ahead of me, and I am almost out of paper, with the greater part of the tale still to tell. Now there's nothing for it but to proceed in great strides, chapter by chapter, keeping clarification, musings, and extraneous details to a minimum. This page itself represents many months, others will represent years, and so we will reach the end. One of the sacrifices I am making to this harsh necessity is the analysis of my emotions at seventeen. I don't know whether you were once seventeen. If you were, you must know that it is the age at which the half man and half boy form a curious whole. I was *most* curious, as José Dias would say, and he would not be wrong. What this superlative quality did for me I could never say here, without falling once again into the error I have just condemned; however, the analysis of my emotions at that time was always part of my plan. Although a true son of both the seminary and of my mother, I was already sensing beneath my chaste reserve some stirrings of impudence and boldness; they came from the blood, but also from the girls in the street or at their windows who would simply not leave me in peace. They thought I was handsome, and told me so; some of them wanted to gaze at my beauty from closer quarters, and vanity is the beginning of corruption.

≡ Chapter XCVIII / *Five years*

REASON SUCCEEDED; I went off to study in São Paulo.

I reached eighteen, nineteen, twenty, and twenty-one; by twenty-two I had my law degree.

Everything around me had changed. My mother had set her heart on aging; even so, her white hairs came grudgingly, one by one, here and there. Her bonnet, dresses, and flat leather shoes were the same as she had always worn. She no longer paced back and forth as much as she once did. Uncle Cosme developed a weak heart and had to rest. Cousin Justina was simply older. José Dias, too, although not so much as to prevent him from doing me the honor of attending my graduation and returning with me to Rio, sprightly and vigorous, as if he were the new law graduate, not me. Capitu's mother had died, her father had retired from the same job in which he had once considered retiring from life completely.

Escobar was starting his own coffee-trading business after working for four years at one of the leading merchant houses in Rio. Cousin Justina was of the opinion that he had harbored notions of proposing a second marriage to my mother; but, if such notions existed, one should not forget their great difference in age. Perhaps he was thinking merely of making her his partner in his initial commercial endeavors, and my mother did indeed, at my request, advance him some money, which he returned to her as soon as he could, but not without the following jibe: "Dona Glória is too timid and has no ambition."

Physical separation did not cool our friendship. He acted as go-between in the exchange of letters between Capitu and me. From the first time he saw her, he had encouraged me in my romantic endeavors. The relationship he had built with Sancha's father strengthened the one he had already forged with Capitu, and he served us both as a friend. Initially, Capitu was reluctant to accept him as intermediary, preferring José Dias, but I was reluctant to use José Dias because I still felt for him a certain respect, a remnant from childhood. Escobar won the day; overcoming her embarrassment, Capitu handed him the first of her letters, which would become mother and grandmother to all the others. His kindness did not cease even with his marriage . . . For he married—guess who?—none other than sweet little Sancha, Capitu's friend and almost-sister, so much so that he once wrote to me calling Capitu his "dear little sister-in-law." Of such things are family ties and affections made, likewise intrigues and books.

Chapter XCIX / *The son is the image of the father*

WHEN I RETURNED HOME a law graduate, my mother almost burst with happiness. I can still hear the voice of José Dias, who, upon seeing the two of us embrace, quoted from the Gospel of Saint John, saying:

"Woman, behold thy son! Son, behold thy mother!"

Through her tears, my mother said:

"Brother Cosme, isn't he the very image of his father?"

"Yes, there's certainly some resemblance in the eyes, and the general disposition of the face. Yes, he's just like his father, only a slightly more modern version," he concluded mischievously. "And now tell me, sister Glória, is it not better that he did not persist in becoming a priest? Can you imagine this young dandy making a decent priest?"

"How's my substitute coming along?"

"Oh, well enough; he'll be ordained next year," replied Uncle Cosme. "You must go to his ordination; I'll go, too, if this heart of mine allows. It would be good if you could feel that your souls were as one, as if you, too, were consecrating your life to God."

"Exactly!" exclaimed my mother. "But look closely, brother Cosme; isn't he the very image of my dear departed husband? Look, Bentinho, look straight at me. I've always thought you resembled him, and now the resemblance is even more marked. Apart, perhaps, from the mustache . . ."

"Indeed, sister Glória, the mustache does rather detract . . . but otherwise, the resemblance is very striking indeed."

And my mother kissed me with a tenderness I cannot begin to put into words. To please her, Uncle Cosme addressed me as "Doctor," as did José Dias, and everyone else in the house, Cousin Justina, the slaves, our guests, Pádua, his daughter, and my mother herself, repeated the title over and over.

Chapter C / *"You will be happy, Bentinho"*

IN MY ROOM, unpacking my trunk and taking my bachelor's degree from its scroll, I let my mind drift toward thoughts of happiness and glory. I imagined my marriage and the illustrious career that lay ahead, while José Dias helped silently and diligently. An invisible fairy appeared and said to me in a voice that was both gentle and wise: "You will be happy, Bentinho; you will be happy."

"And why would you not be happy?" asked José Dias, straightening up and staring at me.

"Did you hear that?" I asked in astonishment, as I, too, stood up.

"Hear what?"

"Did you hear a voice saying that I would be happy?"

"That's a good one! Why, you yourself said it . . ."

Even now I could swear it was the fairy's voice; of course, ever since fairies were expelled from stories and poems, they have slipped into people's hearts instead and speak from within. This one, for example, I often heard speaking loud and clear. She must be a cousin of the Scottish witches: "Thou shalt be king, Macbeth!"—"Thou shalt be happy, Bentinho!" It is, after all, the same prediction, set to the same eternal, universal tune. When I'd recovered from my astonishment, I heard the rest of José Dias's little speech:

"You will be happy, as you deserve to be, just as you deserved that degree you're holding, which wasn't a favor granted to you by someone else. The high grades you attained in every subject are proof of that; I've already told you that I heard from the lips of your teachers the very highest of praise being heaped upon you. Besides, happiness doesn't come from glory alone, there is something else as well . . . Ah! You haven't told old José Dias the whole story! Poor old José Dias is tossed aside like yesterday's newspaper, no use to anyone; now it's the new lot, the Escobars of this world . . . I don't deny he's a remarkable young man, and hardworking, and a first-rate husband; but even so, even old men know a thing or two about love . . ."

"What do you mean?"

"What do you think I mean? Everyone knows. That close neighborly friendship was always bound to end like this, and it truly is a blessing from heaven, because she is an angel, the *angelest* of angels . . . Forgive the solecism, Bentinho; it was simply a way of accentuating the perfection of that young lady. At one time, I thought quite the opposite; I mistook her childish ways for expressions of her real character, and I did not see that the same mischievous little girl, with those same pensive eyes, was the capricious flower from which would come a sweet, healthy fruit . . . Why did you not tell me what others already know, and about which everyone in the household knows and approves?"

"Does Mama really approve?"

"What do you think? She and I have talked about it, and she did me the honor of asking my opinion. Ask her what I said to her in clear, unambiguous terms; go on, ask her. I told her that she could not wish for a better daughter-in-law: good-natured, discreet, gifted, a close friend of the family . . . and, as I scarcely need tell you, a fine housewife. Since her mother's death, she has taken care of everything. Now that Pádua is retired, he simply draws his pension and hands it over to his daughter. She's the one who distributes the money, pays the bills, keeps the household ledger, takes care of everything, food, clothing, lighting; you saw it yourself last year. And as for her beauty, well, you know better than anyone . . ."

"But did Mama really consult you about our getting married?"

"Not expressly, no; she did me the honor of asking whether I thought Capitu would make a good wife, and it was I who, in my answer, used the word 'daughter-in-law.' Dona Glória did not object and even gave the tiniest hint of a smile."

"Mama always spoke about Capitu when she wrote to me."

"You know how close they are, which is why your cousin is becoming ever grumpier. Perhaps now she'll hurry up and get married herself."

"Cousin Justina?"

"Didn't you know? It's just a rumor, of course, but Senhor João da Costa was widowed a couple of months ago and I'm told (I can't vouch for it; it was the protonotary who told me), well, I'm told that the two of them are half-inclined to put an end to their respective widowhoods by getting together in matrimony. There's probably nothing to it, but it isn't inconceivable, even though she's always called him a bag of old bones . . . But then, since she herself is a cemetery . . ." he commented jovially, before adding seriously: "Just joking of course . . ."

I didn't hear the rest. I could only hear my inner fairy repeating to me, wordlessly now: "You will be happy, Bentinho!" And Capitu's voice telling me the same thing, in different terms, and Escobar's as well, both of them confirming José Dias's news from their own standpoints. And finally, some weeks later, when I went to ask my mother's permission to marry, she gave me not only her consent, but the same prophecy in appropriately maternal terms: "You will be happy, my son!"

Chapter CI / *In heaven*

SO, LET'S BE HAPPY straightaway, before you, dear reader, weary with waiting, gather up your things and wander off: We were married. It was in 1865, an afternoon in March, and it rained, which is always a good omen. When we reached the slopes of Tijuca, above the city, where we were to spend our honeymoon, the heavens rolled back the rain clouds and lit up the stars, not just the familiar ones, but even those that will only be discovered many centuries from now. It was a great courtesy, and not the only one. Saint Peter, who holds the keys to heaven, opened its doors to us, bade us enter, and after touching us with his crosier, recited several verses from his first epistle: "Ye wives, be in subjection to your own husbands . . . whose adorning let it not be that outward adorning of plaiting the hair, and or wearing of gold lace, but let it be the hidden man of the heart . . . Likewise, ye husbands, dwell with them, giving honor unto the wife, as unto the weaker vessel, and being heirs together of the grace of life . . ." He then signaled to the angels, and they chanted some verses from the Song of Songs, in such glorious harmony that, had the performance been on earth, they would have disproved the Italian tenor's theory; it was, however, in heaven. The music fit the words as if they had been born together, just like an opera by Wagner. Then we visited a part of that infinite space. Fear not, I will not attempt to describe it; no human language has the words to do so.

After all, it might have been a dream; nothing would be more natural for a former seminarian than to hear Latin and the Scriptures all around him. It is true that Capitu, who knew neither Scripture nor Latin, learned several words by heart, such as these, for example: "I sat down under his shadow with great delight, and his fruit was sweet to my taste." As for the words of Saint Peter, she told me the following day that she agreed entirely, and that I was the only lace and the only adornment she would ever wear. To which I replied that my wife would always wear the finest laces in the world.

Chapter CII / *Married*

IMAGINE A CLOCK that had only a pendulum but no face, so that the hourly markings could not be seen. The pendulum would swing from side to side, but no external manifestation would record the march of time. That is what that week in Tijuca was like.

From time to time, we would look to the past and amuse ourselves remembering our trials and tribulations, but this was itself a
means of keeping ourselves to ourselves. Thus we relived our long
courtship, our adolescence, the tittle-tattling I described in earlier chapters, and we laughed about how José Dias first plotted to
separate us and now celebrated our union. From time to time we
would talk about going back to the city, but the designated morning always turned out to be either rainy or sunny, and we wanted to
wait for an overcast day that obstinately refused to arrive.

Nevertheless, I found Capitu somewhat impatient to return.
She agreed that we should stay, but was always talking about this
or that, about her father and my mother, and how they would have
had no news from us, to the point that we had a little quarrel. I
asked if she was already bored with me.

"Me?"

"It seems like it."

"You're such a child," she said, cupping my face in her hands
and bringing her eyes very close to mine. "Do you think I've waited
all these years for you just to get bored with you in a week? No,
Bentinho; I only mentioned my father and your mother because I
think they really might be missing us or fearing we have fallen sick;
and I must confess that, for my part, I would like to see Papa."

"Then let's go tomorrow."

"No," she retorted with a laugh. "Only if the weather is cloudy."

I took her at her word (and at her laugh, if her laugh can be considered a word), but she remained impatient to go home, and we
returned to Rio with the sun still shining.

Her happiness at putting on her married woman's bonnet, and
the way she gave me her hand to mount and dismount from the carriage, or her arm when we walked down the street, all with the air
of a married woman, told me what lay behind Capitu's impatience
to return to Rio. It was not enough for her to be married between

four walls and a few trees; she needed the rest of the world as well. And when I found myself back in the city, walking through the streets with her, stopping, looking, talking, I felt the same. I would invent excuses to go for a stroll so that I could be seen, acknowledged, and envied. In the street, many men turned their heads in curiosity, others stopped, and others asked: "Who are they?" And someone in the know would explain: "That's Senhor Santiago the lawyer, who got married a few days ago to that young lady, Dona Capitolina, after a long childhood romance; they've set up house in Glória, and their families live in Rua de Matacavalos." And both men would say: "She's a real stunner!"

Chapter CIII / *Happiness is a generous soul*

"STUNNER" IS A RATHER VULGAR term; José Dias put it better. He was the only person from the city who visited us in Tijuca, bringing greetings from our families as well as his own words, words that were music itself; I won't set them down here so as to save paper, but they were delightful. One day, he compared us to birds raised in two adjoining attics. You can imagine the rest, the birds spreading their wings and soaring skyward, and the sky opening to embrace them. Neither of us laughed; we both listened starry-eyed and content, forgetting everything, ever since that afternoon in 1857 . . . Happiness is a generous soul.

⇒ Chapter CIV / *The pyramids*

JOSÉ DIAS NOW DIVIDED HIMSELF between my mother and me, alternating his dinners in Glória with lunches in Rua de Mata-cavalos. Everything was going well. After two years of marriage, apart from the disappointment of not yet having a child, every-thing was going well. I had lost my father-in-law, it's true, and Uncle Cosme was clearly not much longer for this world, but my mother's health was good, and ours was excellent.

I was now representing several wealthy merchants, and work was coming in regularly. Escobar had contributed a great deal to my debut at the bar. He had negotiated with a well-known lawyer to have me admitted to his chambers, and brought me several new clients, all without my asking.

In addition, our family connections were already established: Sancha's and Capitu's schoolgirl friendship continued into mar-riage, as did my friendship with Escobar from the seminary. They lived in Andaraí, up in the hills above the city, where they begged us to visit them frequently, and, not being able to go as often as we would have liked, we would sometimes go there for Sunday lunch, or they would come to us. "Lunch" scarcely does it justice. We would always go very early, shortly after breakfast, so as to make the most of the whole day, and would only leave them at nine, ten, or eleven o'clock, when we could stay no longer. Now that I think of those days in Andaraí and Glória, I feel sorry that life and every-thing else is not as constant as the pyramids.

Escobar and his wife seemed happy together; they had a little girl. At one time, I heard talk of him having an affair, a theatrical encounter with some actress or ballerina, but if it was true, it didn't cause any scandal. Sancha was modest, her husband hardworking. On confiding to Escobar one day how much I regretted not having a child, he retorted:

"Don't worry, Bento. God will give you one in his own good time, and if he doesn't, that's because he wants them for himself, and it's better for them to stay in heaven."

"A child, your own child, is the natural complement to life."

"It will come, if needed."

It did not come. Capitu asked for a child in her prayers, and more than once I found myself praying and begging for one. Prayers no longer worked as they had when I was a child; now I paid in advance, like the rent on the house.

<hr>

≡ Chapter CV / *Arms*

EVERYTHING ELSE WAS GOING WELL. Capitu liked to laugh and have fun, and, at first, when we went on outings or to the theater, she was like a bird freed from her cage. She would dress elegantly and modestly. Although, like other young women, she was fond of jewelry, she didn't want me to buy her lots of expensive pieces, and one day she got so upset with me that I promised not to buy her any more; but that didn't last long.

Our life was fairly tranquil. When we weren't with family or friends, or going to some play or soirée (and those were rare), we spent our evenings at our window in Glória, gazing out at the sea and the sky, at the shadows cast by mountains and ships, or at people walking along the beach. Sometimes I would tell Capitu the history of the city, sometimes I would give her some explanations of astronomy, amateur explanations to which she listened attentively and curiously, although sometimes she did doze off. Despite never having studied the piano, she learned to play shortly after our marriage; she was a quick learner and was soon playing in the homes of our friends. In Glória, it became one of our regular entertainments; she also sang, but not often and not for too long, since she did not have a good voice; eventually she came to the realization that it was better not to sing at all, and stuck to that decision. She did enjoy dancing, and would take a lot of care over what she wore when she went to a ball; her arms were . . . Well, her arms merit a paragraph of their own.

Her arms were beautiful, and the first time she went to a ball with her arms bare, I believe there were none to equal them in the whole of Rio, no, not even yours, madam reader, which at that time were those of a little girl if, that is, they had been born at all, for they were probably still in the block of marble they came from, or in the hands of the divine sculptor. Capitu's were the loveliest arms of the night, so much so that I was filled with pride. I could scarcely speak to anyone else, being so fixated on looking at them, even when they were entwined with other arms dressed in tailcoats. Things were different by the second ball; this time, when I saw that other men couldn't stop looking at her arms, seeking them out, almost begging for them, and brushing their black sleeves against them, I became irritated and annoyed. The third ball I did not attend, and here I had the support of Escobar, to whom I frankly confided my displeasure; he agreed with me at once.

"Sanchinha isn't going, either, or she'll go in long sleeves; anything else strikes me as indecent."

"It is, isn't it? But don't tell her your reason; they'll call us seminarians. Capitu already has."

I nevertheless told Capitu that Escobar agreed with me. She smiled and replied that Sanchinha's arms were most unshapely, but she was quick to agree and did not go to the ball; she did eventually go to others, but wore her arms half-sheathed in gauze or some such material, which neither covered nor uncovered, like Camões's "sheerest silk."*

Chapter CVI / *Ten pounds sterling*

I HAVE ALREADY SAID that she was thrifty (or if I haven't, I'm saying it now), and not only with money, but also with old things, the kind that we hold on to for reasons of tradition, as souvenirs, or for sentimental reasons. A pair of shoes, for example, flat slippers with black ribbons that crossed over the bridge of the foot and again at the ankle, her last pair before she began wearing proper grown-up footwear, and which she brought with her to our new house and from time to time would take out of the drawer, along with other old relics, telling me they were fragments of her childhood. My mother, who had the same inclinations, enjoyed hearing her say and do such things.

As for purely financial economies, I will give one example, and that will suffice. It took place during one of our astronomy lessons, on the beach at Glória. As you already know, she did at times doze off a little during these lessons. One night, though, she was so absorbed in staring out to sea, with such force and concentration, that I became jealous.

---

* In Luís de Camões's *The Lusiads*, Venus veils her modesty in such an enticing way as to "fire lust with redoubled ardor" (Canto II, Landeg White's translation).

"You're not listening, Capitu."

"Me? I can hear you perfectly."

"What was I saying?"

"You . . . you were talking about Sirius."

"Nonsense, Capitu. That was twenty minutes ago."

"You were talking about . . . you were talking about Mars," she said, hurriedly correcting herself.

I had indeed been talking about Mars, but it was clear she had only caught the sound of the word, not the meaning. I grew rather somber, and felt an impulse to leave the room; on realizing this, Capitu became the most affectionate of creatures, clasped my hand, and confessed to me that she had been counting, that is, adding up sums of money in order to identify one particular amount she couldn't put her finger on. It was all to do with converting some paper currency into gold. At first I assumed this was a ruse to pacify me, but soon I was doing my sums, too, with paper and pencil on my knee, until I finally identified the amount she was looking for.

"But where do these pounds come from?" I asked when I had finished.

Capitu looked at me and laughed, and replied that I was to blame for ruining her secret.

She stood up, went to our bedroom, and returned with ten pounds sterling in her hand; they were her savings from the money I gave her every month for household expenses.

"All that?"

"It isn't much, just ten pounds. It's what your stingy wife has managed to put away in a few months," she finished, tinkling the gold coins in her hand.

"Who did the conversion for you?"

"Your friend Escobar."

"How come he didn't say anything to me?"

"He only did it today."

"You mean, he was here?"

"Just before you came home. I didn't say anything so that you wouldn't suspect."

I felt like spending twice that on some celebratory present, but Capitu stopped me. On the contrary, she asked what we should do with the ten pounds.

"They're yours," I replied.

"No, they're ours," she said.

"Then you keep them."

The following day, I went to see Escobar at his warehouse, and laughed about their little secret. Escobar smiled and told me he was just about to come to my office and tell me all about it. His dear little sister-in-law (as he continued to call Capitu) had talked to him about it on our last visit to Andaraí, and told him the reason for keeping it a secret.

"When I told Sanchinha," he concluded, "she was shocked: 'How can Capitu manage to save money when everything is so expensive?'—'I don't know, my dear; all I know is that she put away ten pounds.'"

"Let's see if Sancha learns to do likewise."

"I very much doubt it. Sanchinha is no spendthrift, but nor is she thrifty; whatever I give her is enough, but only just."

And after several moments of reflection, I said:

"Capitu is such an angel!"

Escobar nodded in agreement, but without enthusiasm, like someone who felt unable to say the same thing about his own wife. You, too, would think the same, so surely do the virtues of those closest to us fill us with this or that vanity, pride, or consolation.

⟹ Chapter CVII / *Jealous of the sea*

IF IT HADN'T BEEN FOR ASTRONOMY, I would not have found out about Capitu's ten pounds sterling so quickly; but that is not the reason I'm returning to the subject; it is so that you do not think it was because of my vanity as a teacher that I suffered such pain from Capitu's lack of attention and ended up feeling jealous of the sea. No, my friend. I have just explained to you that I was jealous of what might be inside my wife's head, not outside or above it. It is a well-known fact that a person's inattentiveness can be entirely to blame, or half to blame, or a third, or a fifth, or a tenth to blame, for in matters of blame there is an infinite gradation. The memory of just one pair of eyes is enough for us to gaze at others that remind us of them and fire our imaginations. There is no need for actual mortal sin, or an exchange of letters, or a single word, a nod, a sigh, or some even more trivial sign. An anonymous man or woman passing in the street can lead us to confuse Sirius with Mars, and you, dear reader, are well aware of the difference between them in distance and size, but astronomy is full of such confusions. It was this that made me turn pale and speechless and want to flee the drawing room to return Lord knows when; probably ten minutes later. Ten minutes later would have found me back in the drawing room, standing at the piano or by the window, continuing my interrupted lesson:

"Mars lies at a distance of . . ."

Such a short time? Yes, such a short time: ten minutes. My jealousy was intense, but brief; I would bring everything crashing down in an instant, but in the same instant or even less I would reconstruct the sky, the earth, and the stars.

The truth is that I grew fonder of Capitu, if such a thing were possible, and she grew more affectionate, the air milder, the nights clearer, and the Divine more Divine. And it was not the ten pounds sterling itself that did this, nor the thriftiness that they revealed and which I was aware of, but the pains Capitu went to on one particular occasion for me to discover how scrupulous she was on all occasions. I became more attached to Escobar, too. Our visits became more frequent, and our conversations more intimate.

≡ Chapter CVIII / *A child*

WELL, NOT EVEN THAT quenched my thirst for a child, any little scrap of a thing, however pale and thin, but a child, a child of my own flesh. Whenever we went to Andaraí and saw Escobar and Sancha's daughter, familiarly known as Capituzinha so as to distinguish her from my wife (for they had baptized her with the same name), we would be filled with envy. The little girl was delightful and chubby, talkative and inquisitive. Her parents, like all parents, told stories about the clever things she said and did, and when we returned to Glória late in the evening, we would sigh with envy, and silently beseech heaven to put an end to our misery . . .

. . . Our envy died, our hopes were born, and it wasn't long before the fruit of those hopes came bursting into the world. He was neither frail nor ugly, as I had already requested, but a sturdy, handsome, bouncing baby boy.

I cannot describe my joy when he was born; I have never experienced anything like it, and I don't think there could ever be such joy again or even anything close. It was giddiness mixed with madness. I did not sing in the streets, due to a natural sense of propriety, nor in the house, so as not to torment the convalescing Capitu. Nor did I trip over my shoelaces, because there is a god who looks after new fathers. When I was out and about, the boy was always in my thoughts; at home, he was always in my sight, as I watched him, observed him, asked him where he came from, and why I was so utterly besotted with him, and other such sillinesses, not spoken out loud, but thought or imagined. I may even have lost some court cases through lack of attention.

Capitu was no less affectionate both toward him and toward me. We held hands, and, when we were not gazing at our son, we talked about us, our past and our future. The most charming and mysterious times were when she was feeding him. When I saw my son suckling his mother's milk, and when I considered how nature had come together to provide nourishment and life for a being that had been nothing at all, but which our destiny had decreed would be, and which our love and perseverance had brought into being, I entered a state I cannot and will not describe; for I don't precisely remember, and fear that anything I might say would just seem rather obscure.

Let me skip the details. I need not tell you how devoted my mother and Sancha were, for Sancha came to spend the first few days and nights with Capitu. I tried to refuse Sancha's kind offer, but she replied that it was not my affair; Capitu, before she married me, had gone to look after her in Rua dos Inválidos.

"Don't you remember going to see her there?"

"I do; but what about you, Escobar?"

"I'll come and have dinner with you, and at night I'll head back to Andaraí. One week and it'll all be over. It's pretty obvious you're a novice when it comes to babies."

"Look who's talking! Where's your second one?"

We used to tease each other like that. Now that I have withdrawn into my state of gloomy reclusiveness, I don't know if such banter still exists; I suppose it must. Escobar did as promised; he would dine with us and return home at night. In the evenings we would go down to the beach or to the Passeio Público, he engrossed in his sums and me in my dreams. I imagined my son as doctor, lawyer, businessman, I placed him at various universities and banks, and I even accepted the possibility of him becoming a poet. A career as a politician was also considered, and I was convinced he had the makings of an orator, indeed a great orator.

"He might well have those makings," reported Escobar. "No one anticipated what Demosthenes would become."

Escobar often went along with my childish notions; he too tried to peer into the future. He even raised the possibility of marrying the boy to his daughter. True friendship does exist; it was there in my hands when I grasped Escobar's on hearing him say this, and in the total absence of words with which I, there and then, signed our pact; the words followed later, tripping and tumbling, propelled by my wildly beating heart. I accepted his idea and proposed that we guide the two of them toward this goal by bringing them up in the same way and in each other's company, united in an irreproachable childhood.

It was my intention for Escobar to be the boy's godfather; his godmother would of course be my mother. But the first part of this plan was altered by the intervention of Uncle Cosme, who, upon seeing the child, said to him, among other endearments:

"Come here and get a blessing from your godfather, you little rascal."

And, turning to me, he added:

"I won't take no for an answer; and the christening will have to be quick, before my various ailments carry me off for good."

I quietly related the incident to Escobar, so that he would understand and forgive me; he laughed and was not in the least offended.

He went further, insisting that the christening breakfast take place at his house, which it did. Even so, I tried to delay the ceremony, just in case Uncle Cosme should succumb to his illness in the meantime, but it seems his ailments were more bothersome than fatal. There was nothing for it but to bring the child to the font, where he was given the name Ezequiel; it was Escobar's Christian name, which I intended as recompense for not making him godfather.

Chapter CIX / *An only child*

WHEN THE PREVIOUS CHAPTER began, Ezequiel had not yet been conceived; by the time it finished he was a Christian and a Catholic. This new chapter is destined to bring my Ezequiel to the age of five, a handsome young lad with his pale, restless eyes, as if eager to flirt with all, or nearly all, the young ladies in the neighborhood.

Now, if you take into account that he was an only child, that no others followed, confirmed or unconfirmed, living or stillborn, the one and only, you can easily imagine the worry he caused us, the sleep he stole from us, and the fright he gave us with his teething and so on, the very slightest of fevers, and all the other normal childhood events. We dealt with everything that came along, according to need and urgency—something which goes without saying, except that there are readers so obtuse that they understand nothing if you don't tell them everything, and then everything else besides. Let's turn now to that everything else.

—— Chapter CX / *Childhood traits*

THAT "EVERYTHING ELSE" will consume many more chapters; some lives require fewer chapters and even so are finished and complete.

At five and six years old, Ezequiel gave no sign of disappointing my dreams on Glória Beach; on the contrary, I could see in him every possible vocation, from idler to apostle. I say "idler" here in the good sense, meaning a man who thinks and says nothing; at times, he would withdraw into himself, and in this he reminded me of his mother when she was a little girl. Similarly, he would suddenly get all worked up and insist on going off to persuade the girls living nearby that the candy I gave him was real candy; he didn't do this, however, until he had first eaten his fill of it; but then the apostles did not spread the good word until they themselves had learned it all by heart. Escobar, ever the canny businessman, was of the opinion that the main reason for this latter inclination was to extend an implicit invitation to all the local girls to join in a similar apostolic mission whenever their parents gave them candy; and he would laugh at his own little joke, and tell me that he would make young Ezequiel his business partner.

Ezequiel liked music, no less than candy, and I told Capitu to play for him on the piano the tune the black man used to sing while hawking his coconut candy on Rua de Matacavalos . . .

"I don't remember it."

"You don't remember that black man who used to come around selling candy in the afternoon?"

"I remember a black man selling candy, but I don't remember the tune."

"Not even the words?"

"No, not even the words."

The lady reader, who *will* still remember the words, since she has been reading me very attentively, will be surprised at such forgetfulness, even more so given that they will remind her of similar voices from her own childhood and adolescence; a few will have slipped her mind, of course, for not everything stays in the memory. Such was Capitu's response, to which I had no answer. However, I did something she was not expecting: I went and rummaged through my old papers. When I was a student in São Paulo, I asked a music teacher to write down the tune of the street vendor's cry; he happily did so (I merely had to sing it to him from memory), and I had kept that piece of paper. I went to find it. Moments later, the scrap of paper in my hand, I interrupted a ballad she was playing. I explained what I had done, and she played the sixteen notes.

Capitu found the tune to have a peculiar, almost delicious flavor; she told our son the story of the tune, and then she played and sang it. Ezequiel seized the opportunity offered by the song's lyrics to ask me to give him some money.

He played at doctor, soldier, actor, and dancer. I never gave him shrines to pray before; wooden horses and a sword in his belt were more his style. I will say nothing of the way he would run off to watch the battalions marching down the street, for all the children did the same. They did not, however, do so with the same glint in their eyes. In none of the other boys did I see the joyous rapture with which he watched the troops pass by and listened to the beating of the drums.

"Look, Papa! Look!"

"I'm looking, son!"

"Look at the officer! Look at the officer's horse! Look at the soldiers!"

One day he woke up and pretended to play the bugle by blow-ing into his closed fist; I gave him a little tin cornet. I bought him lead soldiers, engravings of battles that he studied for long periods of time, wanting me to explain to him a certain piece of artillery, a soldier who had fallen, another with his sword raised; all his sympathy went out to the one with the raised sword. One day (ah, such an innocent age!) he asked me impatiently:

"But Papa, why does he not bring down his sword and be done with it?"

"Because he's only a drawing, my son."

"But then why did he draw himself?"

I laughed at this misunderstanding and explained to him that it wasn't the soldier who had drawn himself on the piece of paper, but the engraver, and then I also had to explain what an engraver and an engraving were: in short, he had Capitu's curiosity.

Such were his main childhood traits: I'll give just one more and then finish the chapter. One day, at Escobar's house, he came across a cat clutching a mouse in its mouth. The cat would not release its prey, nor did it have anywhere to run to. Without a word, Ezequiel stopped, crouched down, and remained there staring. On seeing him pay such close attention to something, we called out and asked him what it was; he motioned for us to be quiet. Escobar announced:

"I imagine it's the cat that's caught some mouse or other. This darned house is still infested with mice. Let's go see."

Capitu also wanted to see what her son was doing; I went with them. It was indeed a cat and a mouse, a trivial incident, neither amusing nor interesting. The only unusual circumstance was that the mouse was still alive and wriggling its legs, and my young son was entranced. Otherwise, the moment was brief. As soon as the cat sensed other people approaching, it prepared to run away; the boy, without taking his eyes off it, again signaled to us to remain silent; and the silence could not have been more intense. I was about to say "religious," then crossed out the word, but now I have written it again, not only to express the totality of that silence, but also because there was in the actions of cat and mouse something akin to a ritual. The only sounds were the final squeals of the mouse, and they were very faint; its legs flailed in all directions, to little effect. Somewhat repelled, I clapped my hands to chase the cat away, and it ran off. The others did not have time to stop me, and Ezequiel was crestfallen.

"Oh, Papa!"

"What's wrong? It'll have eaten the mouse by now."

"Exactly, but I wanted to watch."

The other two laughed; even I thought it was funny.

⟳ Chapter CXI / *Briefly told*

YES, I THOUGHT IT WAS FUNNY, and I still don't deny it; despite the passing of time, what happened later, and the sympathy I felt for the mouse, it was funny. It does not pain me to say so; those who love nature as it wants to be loved, with no partial exceptions or unfair exclusions, will find in it nothing that is inferior. I love the mouse, and I don't dislike the cat. I considered making them live together, but could see they were incompatible. As it happens, one of them gnaws my books and the other one gnaws my cheese; but it is not asking much for me to forgive them, since I have already forgiven a dog who robbed me of my sleep in far worse circumstances. I will tell the story briefly.

It happened when Ezequiel was born; Capitu had a fever, Sancha was constantly by her bedside, and three dogs in the street kept barking all night. I went looking for the local night watchman, which was about as useful as looking for you, dear reader, who have only now become aware of my predicament. So, I decided to kill them; I bought some poison, got the cook to prepare three meatballs, and I myself injected them with the poison. When night came, I ventured forth; it was one o'clock in the morning, and neither the patient nor her nurse could sleep with such a racket. When the dogs saw me, they ran off; two headed toward Flamengo Beach, and the other stopped a short distance away, as if waiting. I went toward it, whistling and snapping my fingers. The wretched animal was still barking at this point, but, trusting those signs of friendship, it began to quiet down, until finally it stopped barking altogether. As I continued whistling and snapping my fingers, it came slowly toward me, wagging its tail, which is a dog's way of smiling; I had the poisoned meatballs in my hand, and I was about to hold one out to it, when that special smile, that show of affection and trust or whatever it was, stopped me in my tracks. I just stood there, wracked with pity, and put the meatballs back in my pocket. The reader may well surmise that it was the scent of meat that had silenced the dog. I won't disagree; I suspect that the dog did not want to cast doubt on my gesture, and so surrendered to me. The result was that he escaped.

⸻ Chapter CXII / Ezequiel's impersonations

EZEQUIEL WOULD NOT have done the same. He would not, I suppose, have made those poisoned meatballs, but nor would he have rejected them. What he would certainly have done is run after the dogs, throwing stones at them, as far as his legs would take him. And if he'd had a stick, he would have used that too. Capitu was besotted with her future warrior.

"He's not like either of us; we like our peace and quiet," she told me one day. "But Papa was like that as a boy; Mama used to say so."

"Well, at least he won't turn out to be a sissy," I replied. "I can find only one small defect in him: he likes impersonating other people."

"In what way?"

"He imitates their gestures, their mannerisms, their behavior; he imitates Cousin Justina, he imitates José Dias. There's even something about the way he walks, about his eyes, that reminds me of Escobar . . ."

Capitu paused, looking at me, and finally said that we would need to fix that. She could see that it was indeed a bad habit of his, but she reckoned he was only imitating for the sake of it, as happens with many grown-ups, who mimic the mannerisms of others; and to make sure it didn't go any further . . .

"We shouldn't punish him. There's still time to correct it," I said.

"There is. I'll see how things go. Were you not like that, too, when you were angry with someone?"

"When I got angry, yes, as a form of childish revenge."

"Yes, but I don't like imitations within the family."

"And back then, were you fond of me?" I said, patting her cheek.

Capitu answered with a smile of gentle derision, one of those smiles that cannot be described, only painted. Then she stretched out her arms and threw them around my neck, so gracefully that they seemed (to use a rather old image!) like a garland of flowers. I did the same with mine, and my only regret was that there wasn't a sculptor on hand to transform the scene into a block of marble. Only the artist would dazzle, of course. When a person or a group of figures turn out well, no one wants to know about the model, only the work of art, and it is the work of art that endures. No matter; we would know that it was us.

Chapter CXIII / *Third-party injunctions*

SPEAKING OF WHICH, it's only natural that you should ask me whether, having previously been so jealously possessive of her, I continued to be so after the arrival of our son and with the passing years. Yes, sir, I did. I did, and to such an extent that the merest gesture tormented me, the slightest word, any kind of insistence on her part; often mere indifference was enough. I managed to be jealous of everything and everyone. A neighbor, a waltzing partner, any man whether young or old, would fill me with fear or distrust. Capitu certainly liked to be looked at, and the most appropriate means to that end (a lady once told me) is to look, and it's impossible to look without revealing that you are looking.

The lady who told me this had, I think, taken a fancy to me, and it was no doubt when she found her affections went unrequited that she chose to explain her persistent stare in that manner. Other eyes also sought me out; not many, and I will say nothing more about them, having moreover confessed at the outset to my future adventures, which still lay in the future. At that point, for all the pretty women I met, none received from me even the tiniest fraction of the love I felt for Capitu. I loved even my own mother only half as much. Capitu was my everything and more; in life and in work there was nothing I did without thinking of her. We went to the theater together; I can only recall two occasions when I went without her, one was a benefit performance for an actor, and the other was the first night of an opera, which she didn't go to because she was feeling unwell, but vehemently insisted that I should go anyway. It was too late to give Escobar the tickets for our box; I went, but came home at the end of the first act. I found Escobar at our front door.

"I was just coming to talk to you," he told me.

I explained to him that I'd gone to the theater but had come home because I was worried about Capitu, who wasn't feeling well.

"What's wrong with her?" asked Escobar.

"She was complaining about her head and her stomach."

"Well, then, I'd better be off. I was coming to see you about those injunctions . . ."

It was a handful of third-party injunctions; there had been an important development and, as he had been dining in the city, he hadn't wanted to go home without telling me about it. Under the circumstances, though, he'd tell me another time . . .

"No, let's talk now. Come inside; she may be feeling better. If she's feeling worse, you can leave."

Capitu was feeling better, even well. She assured me she had only had the slightest of headaches, but had exaggerated how bad it was so that I would go and enjoy myself. She didn't say this in a cheerful tone of voice, which made me fear she was lying so as not to worry me, but she swore it was the honest truth. Escobar smiled and said:

"My dear little sister-in-law is just as ill as you or I. Let's talk injunctions."

Chapter CXIV / *In which the explained is explained*

BEFORE COMING to the injunctions, let me explain a little further a point that has already been explained, but not very well. You saw (in Chapter CX) that I asked a music teacher in São Paulo to write down the tune of that street vendor's cry in Rua de Matacavalos. In itself, the subject is somewhat tedious and not worth the bother of a chapter, still less two, but there are subjects that bring with them lessons that are interesting, if not necessarily agreeable. So let us return to those explanations.

Capitu and I had sworn we would never forget that tune; it came at a moment of great affection between us, and the divine notary records any oaths sworn at such moments, and registers them in his eternal ledgers.

"You swear?"

"I swear," she said, holding out her arm in a tragic gesture.

I took advantage of the gesture to kiss her hand; I was still at the seminary. One day, after I went to São Paulo, I tried to recall the tune and realized I was beginning to forget it. I managed to dredge it up from my memory and rushed to see the music teacher, who was so kind as to write it down on that scrap of paper. I did this so as not to break my oath. But would you believe it if I told you that when I rushed to find the piece of paper that night in Glória, I, too, had forgotten the tune, and even the words? I made too much of a fuss about the oath; that was my sin. As for forgetting, well, anyone can forget.

The truth is, no one can know if they will keep an oath or not. Only time will tell! Our new constitution is, therefore, profoundly moral in switching from oaths to simple affirmations.* It has put an end to a terrible sin. Breaking one's word is always a breach of faith, but for someone who fears God more than men it is of little consequence to lie once in a while, since he will not thereby be placing his soul in purgatory. Do not confuse purgatory with hell, which is the eternal shipwreck. Purgatory is a pawnshop, which lends against all the virtues, at high interest and short maturity. But the loans are rolled over, until someday one or two middling virtues pay for all the sins, great and small.

⸺ Chapter CXV / *Doubts upon doubts*

NOW LET'S DEAL WITH those injunctions . . . And yet why should we? God knows how costly it is to draft them, let alone describe them. Regarding the new development that Escobar came to tell me about, I will merely tell you what I told him then, namely, that it was of no relevance.

"None?"

"Almost none."

"Then it might be worth something."

"In terms of strengthening the arguments we already have, it is worth less than the tea you and I are about to drink."

"It's a little late to be drinking tea."

---

* Brazil's new constitution of 1891 had abolished religious oaths, as well as, more substantively, establishing a republic, separating church and state, and confirming the abolition of slavery.

"We'll drink it quickly."

We drank it quickly. As we did so, Escobar eyed me warily, as if suspecting that I was rejecting the new development so as to spare myself any further drafting; but such suspicion was quite alien to our friendship.

When he left, I mentioned my doubts to Capitu; she unpicked them with her usual subtle art, a skill and grace that was all her own, capable of dispelling even the sorrows of Olympio.*

"It must be that business about the injunctions," she concluded. "And for him to come here at this hour means he must be worried about it."

"You're right."

One thing led to another, and I began giving voice to my other doubts. At the time, I was like a well brimming with doubts, and they croaked inside me like frogs, so loudly they sometimes kept me awake. I told Capitu that I was beginning to find my mother's attitude toward her somewhat cold and distant. Here Capitu's subtle art came into its own:

"I've already explained that to you: It's mother-in-law stuff. Your dearest Mama wants you all to herself; as soon as her jealousy passes and she begins to miss you, she'll be back to her old self. And she'll be missing her grandson . . ."

"But I've noticed that she's rather frosty with Ezequiel as well. When I take him with me, Mama doesn't dote on him as much as she used to."

"Perhaps she's not feeling well."

"Shall we go for dinner with her tomorrow?"

"Yes, let's . . . No . . . Yes, let's."

We went for dinner with my old mother. You could already call

---

* An allusion to Victor Hugo's poem *Tristesse d'Olympio* (1837), describing a man revisiting the scene of an old love affair.

her that, although her hair was not yet pure white or white all over, and her face was still comparatively youthful; it was a kind of quinquagenarian youth, or else a vigorous old age, the choice is yours. But enough of melancholy; I don't want to talk about her moist eyes, both when we arrived and when we left. She barely joined in the conversation, which revolved around the usual subjects. José Dias spoke about marriage and its delights, about politics, Europe, and homeopathy; Uncle Cosme talked about his ailments; and Cousin Justina talked about the neighbors, or about José Dias when he stepped out of the room.

When we returned home that night, we did so on foot, discussing my doubts. Once again, Capitu advised me to wait. All mothers-in-law were like that; then a day comes when they change. The more Capitu talked, the more tender she became. From then on, she grew ever more affectionate toward me. She stopped waiting for me at the window, so as not to arouse my jealousy, but as I came up the steps I would see, framed by the wrought-iron gate at the top of the steps, the delightful face of my dear friend and wife, smiling as cheerfully as she had throughout our childhood. Ezequiel would sometimes be there with her; he had grown used to seeing us give each other a kiss whenever I arrived home or left for the office, and he, in turn, would jump up and cover my face with kisses.

Chapter CXVI / *"Son of man"*

I SOUNDED OUT JOSÉ DIAS about my mother's recent behavior; he was greatly surprised. There was nothing in it, nor could there be, such was the endless praise he heard her heaping upon "the beautiful and virtuous Capitu."

"These days, I myself join in the chorus when I hear her say that; to begin with, though, I was *most* embarrassed. For anyone who, as I did, went so far as cursing this marriage, it was hard to admit that little Capitu has been a real blessing from heaven. What a dignified lady that naughty child has become! It was her father who came between us somewhat, before we got to know each other, but everything has turned out splendidly. So yes, senhor, when Dona Glória praises her daughter-in-law and mother of her godson—"

"So Mama doesn't . . . ?"

"Not at all!"

"So why hasn't she visited us in so long?"

"I think her rheumatism has been plaguing her. This year has been very chilly . . . Imagine how awful it must be for her: she used to go out walking all day long, and now she's obliged to stay in one place, beside her brother, who has his own ailments . . ."

I tried to point out to him that this would explain the interruption in her visits to our house, but not her coolness when we went to Rua de Matacavalos; however, I did not want to abuse my close relationship with José Dias. He then asked to see our "little prophet" (as he called Ezequiel) and fussed over him in his usual way. This time he addressed him in the biblical manner (I found out later that he had been leafing through the Book of Ezekiel the night before) and asked him: "How goes the son of man?" "Tell me, son of man, where are your toys?" "Would you like some candy, son of man?"

"What's this 'son of man' business?" asked Capitu irritably.

"It's a biblical expression."

"Well, I don't like it," she replied sharply.

"You're quite right, Capitu," agreed José Dias. "You cannot imagine how many crude and uncouth expressions one finds in the Bible. I used it just for a little variety . . . And you, my little angel, how are you? Come, my little angel, show me how I walk down the street."

"No," interrupted Capitu. "I'm trying to stop his habit of imitating other people."

"But it's very amusing; when he mimics my gestures, it's like seeing myself in miniature. The other day he even managed one of Dona Glória's waves, and he did it so well she rewarded him with a kiss. Come on, then, how do I walk?"

"No, Ezequiel," I said. "Mama doesn't want you to."

I also found this habit of his rather unappealing. Some of the gestures were already becoming more repetitive, such as Escobar's way of moving his hands and feet; recently, the boy had even picked up the way Escobar tilted his head when he was speaking and let it fall back when he was laughing. Capitu scolded him. But the boy was as mischievous as the very devil; we had no sooner started talking about something else than he ran into the middle of the room, saying to José Dias:

"This is how you walk."

We couldn't help laughing, I more than anyone. The first person to put on a stern look, reprimand him, and call him to order was Capitu.

"Enough of that, do you hear?"

Chapter CXVII / *Close friends*

BY THEN, Escobar had moved from Andaraí and bought a house in Flamengo; I went to see it only a few days ago, when I was seized by the urge to test out whether those feelings of old were dead or merely sleeping. I cannot say for sure, because sleep, when it's very deep, mixes up the living and the dead, except when it comes to the ability to breathe. I was wheezing somewhat, but it might have been because of the sea, which was rather choppy. Anyway, I walked past the house, lit a cigar, and found myself in Rua do Catete; I had gone up Rua da Princesa, an ancient street . . . O ancient streets! O ancient houses! O ancient legs! All of us were ancient, and (it goes without saying) in the bad sense, the sense of old and decrepit.

The house is old now, too, but the current inhabitants haven't changed anything. It may even have the same street number. I won't say what number so that you don't go looking and try to dig up the whole story. Not that Escobar still lives there, in fact, he's not even alive; he died shortly afterward in a manner I will describe. While he was alive, though, and since we were such close neighbors, we had what you might call a single home between us; I lived in his house, he in mine, and the short stretch of beach between Glória and Flamengo was like a private pathway for our own personal use. It made me think of the two houses in Rua de Matacavalos, with the wall in between.

A historian writing in our own language, I think it was João de Barros,* ascribes some wise words to a barbarian king, who, when the Portuguese proposed building a fortress nearby, told them that good friends should keep well apart, not close by, so as not to antagonize each other like the waves of the sea crashing against the rocky cliff visible from where they stood. May the author's ghost forgive me if I doubt that the king actually said those words or that they are true. It was probably the author himself who invented them to embellish his text, and he was quite right, because it's a fine thought, truly a fine thought. I believe that the sea did indeed beat

---

* João de Barros (1496–1570) chronicled the history of Portuguese expansion into Africa and Asia. The incident is reputed to have taken place in modern-day Senegal.

against the rocks, as has been its custom since the time of Ulysses and before. Now, as to whether the comparison is true, the answer is: Surely not. Certainly there are enemies who live side by side, but there are also sworn friends who do likewise. And the author was forgetting (unless of course it came after his time) the adage: "Out of sight, out of mind." Well, Escobar and I could not have been more in sight of each other. Our wives were constantly in and out of each other's houses, and we all spent our evenings in one place or the other, talking, playing cards, or looking out to sea. The two little ones spent their days together, sometimes in Flamengo, sometimes in Glória.

When I remarked to the others that the same thing might happen with our children as had happened between Capitu and me, they all agreed, and Sancha added that the two of them were even beginning to look alike.

"Ah, that's because Ezequiel is always imitating other people," I explained.

Escobar agreed, and suggested that sometimes children who spend a lot of time together can end up looking alike. I nodded, as I usually did concerning matters on which I had no particular views. Anything was possible. They were certainly very fond of each other, and might well have ended up married, but they did not.

Chapter CXVIII / *Sancha's hand*

EVERYTHING MUST COME TO AN END, dear reader; it is an old truism, to which one can add that not everything that lasts, lasts for very long. The second part of that truism does not find many followers; on the contrary, the idea that a castle in the air lasts longer than the air it is made of is hard to get out of your head, and so it should be, or else we might lose the habit of building such near-eternal structures.

Our castle was solid, but then one Sunday . . . The previous day, we had spent the evening together in Flamengo, not only the two inseparable couples, but José Dias and Cousin Justina as well. That was when Escobar, standing with me by the window, asked that we join them for dinner the following day; he said we needed to discuss a family project, a project that concerned all four of us.

"The four of us? A country dance?"

"No. You won't guess what it is, and I won't tell you. Come tomorrow."

Sancha did not take her eyes off us throughout that conversation by the open window. When her husband stepped outside, she came over to join me. She asked me what we had been discussing; I told her it was a project I knew nothing about; she asked me to keep a secret, and then revealed that it was a trip to Europe in two years' time. She said this with her back to the room, almost whispering. The waves were crashing on the beach; there was an undertow.

"Are we all going?" I asked finally.

"We are."

Sancha raised her head then and looked at me with such rapture that, given her close friendship with Capitu, I would not have thought it out of place to kiss her on the forehead. However, Sancha's eyes did not invite such displays of fraternal goodwill; they shone ardently and invitingly, saying something quite different, and she quickly moved away from the window, where I remained gazing pensively out to sea. It was a clear night.

From where I was standing, I sought out Sancha's eyes, over by the piano; I met them halfway. Our two pairs of eyes stopped in their tracks, waiting for the other pair to pass in front, but neither of them did so, as when two stubborn folk meet in the street. Caution disentangled us. Once again I turned around and gazed out to sea. I began rummaging through my memory as to whether I had ever looked at her with that same expression. I wasn't sure. I was sure of only one thing: I had once thought about her the way one might think about any pretty woman passing by; but what if she had noticed . . . Perhaps that simple thought had shone forth, and she had, back then, fled from me through shyness or annoyance, and now by some irresistible force . . . Irresistible: the word was like a priest's blessing at mass, which we each receive and repeat within ourselves.

"Tomorrow the sea will be quite a challenge for us," said Escobar's voice, right next to me.

"You're going swimming tomorrow?"

"I've been out in choppier seas, much choppier. You can't imagine what a good rough sea can be like. You need to be a strong swimmer, like me, and have lungs like these," he said, thumping his chest, "and arms like these: go on, feel them."

I squeezed his arms, imagining they were Sancha's. It pains me to confess this, but I cannot leave it out; I would be hamstringing the truth. It was not my only thought as I squeezed those arms; I also sensed something else: his arms felt bigger and stronger than mine, and I was envious of them. What's more, they could swim.

When we left, my eyes spoke once more with the lady of the house. Her hand gripped mine, and lingered longer than usual.

Modesty required then, as now, that I should see in Sancha's gesture nothing more than an acceptance of her husband's project, and an expression of gratitude. That is how it should have been, but a peculiar fluid coursing through my entire body robbed me of that conclusion. I could still feel Sancha's fingers between mine, fingers pressing against fingers. It was a moment of dizzying depravity. It passed quickly on the pocket watch of Time; when I put the watch to my ear, the only sounds of ticking were the minutes of virtue and reason.

"A *most* delightful lady," concluded José Dias, rounding off the little speech he had been giving.

"Most delightful!" I repeated enthusiastically, then, moderating my tone, added: "And a very lovely evening!"

"As must be every evening in that house of theirs," continued José. "Not out here, though; out here, the sea is furious: just listen!"

We could hear the raging sea—it had been audible even from the house—the undertow was strong and, out in the distance, we could see the waves building. Capitu and Cousin Justina, who had gone on ahead, paused where the beach turned, and the four of us walked on together chatting; but I was in no mood for chatter. I could not stop thinking about Sancha's hand, nor the looks we had exchanged. One minute I thought one thing, the next minute I thought the opposite. The Devil's moments interposed themselves between God's minutes, and the hands of the pocket watch alternately marked my perdition and my salvation. José Dias said good night at our front door. Cousin Justina slept at our house; she would leave the next morning, after breakfast and mass. I withdrew to my study, where I remained longer than usual.

Escobar's portrait, which I had hung there beside my mother's, spoke to me as if it were the man himself. I sincerely fought the impulses I had carried with me from Flamengo; I rejected the image of my friend's wife and branded myself unfaithful. In any case, who could say if there was any intention of that kind in her farewell gesture, or those that preceded it? It might have been merely her excitement at our trip. Sancha and Capitu were such good friends that it would be an added pleasure for them to go together. If there was any sexual intent, who could prove to me that it was anything more than a fleeting sensation, doomed to perish with a good night's sleep? Some pangs of remorse are born of no greater sin, and have no greater duration. I clung to this hypothesis that could be reconciled with the memory of Sancha's hand, which I could still feel in my own hand, warm and lingering, squeezed and squeezing . . .

I found myself in a truly awkward position, caught between a friend and temptation. Perhaps timidity was another cause of this crisis; it is not only heaven that gives us our virtues, but also timidity, not to mention chance, but then chance is mere accident; the best source of virtue is, therefore, heaven. However, since timidity also comes from heaven, which gives us our temperament, then virtue, the daughter of timidity, genealogically speaking, comes from the same celestial bloodline. This would have been my reasoning had I been capable of reasoning, but, from the outset, my thoughts drifted randomly. It was not passion, nor attraction. Was it a whim, or if not, then what? After twenty minutes it was nothing, absolutely nothing. Escobar's portrait seemed to speak to me; I saw his sincere, innocent expression, shook my head, and took myself off to bed.

Chapter CXIX / *Don't do it, my dear!*

THE LADY READER, who is my dear friend and has opened this book so as to rest a moment between last night's cavatina and this evening's waltz, now wishes to close it hastily, as she can see that we are walking along the edge of an abyss. Don't do it, my dear friend; I will change course.

Chapter CXX / *Legal documents*

I AWOKE THE FOLLOWING MORNING free of the previous evening's abominations; I decided they were hallucinations, drank my coffee, browsed the newspapers, and went off to peruse some legal documents. Capitu and Cousin Justina left for the nine o'clock mass at Lapa. Sancha's shapely figure disappeared entirely under the weight of the opposing party's allegations, which I was reading through in the documents; the allegations were false and inadmissible, unsupported by either law or precedent. I saw it would be easy to win the case; I consulted my volumes of Dalloz and Pereira & Sousa . . .

I glanced just once at the portrait of Escobar. It was a fine photograph taken a year earlier. He was standing in a buttoned-up frock coat, his left hand resting on the back of a chair, his right hand on his chest, and he was gazing into the distance just to the left of the viewer. He exuded ease and elegance. The frame I'd had made for it did not obscure the inscription, which was written at the bottom rather than on the back: "To my dear Bentinho from his dear Escobar, 4-20-70." These words reinforced my earlier thoughts, and drove away once and for all the memories from the previous night. Back then my eyesight was good; I could read the words from where I sat. I turned back to the documents.

== Chapter CXXI / *The catastrophe*

WHILE STILL IMMERSED in the documents, I heard hurried foot-steps outside, the bell clanging, hands clapping, fists banging on the gate, voices raised. Everyone ran to answer, myself included. It was a slave from Sancha's house calling for me:

"Come, sir, come . . . massa gone swimming . . . massa dying . . ."

He didn't say anything more, or else I did not hear the rest. I dressed, left a message for Capitu, and rushed over to Flamengo.

On the way, I pieced together what had happened. Escobar had gone swimming, as he often did, had ventured out a little farther than usual, despite the rough sea, had been caught by the swell, and drowned. The canoes sent out to rescue him served only to bring back his corpse.

== Chapter CXXII / *The funeral*

THE WIDOW . . . I will spare you the widow's tears, my own, and those of the others. I returned from Flamengo at around eleven o'clock; Capitu and Cousin Justina were waiting for me, one visibly stunned and weary, the other merely irritated.

"Go and keep poor Sanchinha company; I'll take care of the funeral."

And that is what we did. I wanted the funeral to be a grand affair, and indeed his friends were there in large numbers. All along the beach, the streets and the Praça da Glória, everywhere there were carriages, many of them belonging to private individuals. As the house was not big enough to hold everyone, many stood out on the beach, discussing the disaster, pointing to the place where Escobar had died, hearing how the body had been brought ashore. José Dias also heard talk of the deceased's business affairs; there were differing views as to the value of his assets, but the general consensus was that his debts were small. They praised Escobar's qualities; one or two of them discussed the recent appointment of Rio Branco's cabinet—this was March 1871.* I will never forget the month or the year.

As I had resolved to speak at the graveside, I wrote a few lines and showed them, at home, to José Dias, who found them truly worthy of the dead man and of me. He asked to see the piece of paper, read the speech slowly, weighing every word, and confirmed his initial opinion. In Flamengo, the news spread fast. Some acquaintances came and asked me:

"So are we going to hear something from you?"

"Just a few words."

It would not be much more than that. I had written it down, afraid that my emotions would prevent me from improvising. For an hour or two, while being driven around town making the arrangements, I had done little more than think about my time at the seminary, meeting Escobar, our fondness for each other, the friendship that had blossomed and continued unbroken until a blow from fortune separated forever two of God's creatures who seemed destined to be united for many years. From time to time, I dried my eyes. The coachman attempted two or three questions as to my state of mind; not getting anything out of me, though, he

---

* In March 1871 the emperor Pedro II appointed a new government led by the Visconde do Rio Branco. It was a watershed moment that began the slow process of abolishing slavery.

carried on with his job. When I arrived home, I put those emotions down on paper, and that would be my speech.

<hr>

≡ Chapter CXXIII / *Eyes with an undertow*

FINALLY, THE TIME CAME for the body to be removed for burial. Sancha wanted to say her last goodbyes to her husband, and the despair of that scene was upsetting to everyone. All the women were crying, and many men too. Only Capitu, at the widow's side, propping her up, seemed in full control of herself. She tried to console Sancha and pull her away from the coffin. Amid the general confusion, Capitu gazed at the body for several minutes with such a fixed gaze, such a passionately fixed gaze, that it was little wonder a few silent tears rolled down her cheek . . .

My own tears stopped immediately. I stood there watching hers; Capitu hurriedly wiped them away, glancing furtively at the others in the room. She redoubled her attentions toward her friend and tried again to draw her away; but the corpse seemed to be holding her back too. There was a moment when Capitu's eyes gazed at the deceased, just as his widow's did, only without the latter's weeping or wailing, but wide open like the swelling sea outside, as if she, too, wished to swallow up the early morning swimmer.

〰 Chapter CXXIV / *The speech*

"COME ALONG, it's time to go . . ."

It was José Dias, inviting me to close the coffin. We closed it, and I took one of the handles; a final burst of wailing broke out. I swear to you that when I reached the door, saw the bright sunshine, all those people and carriages, the bared heads, I had one of those impulses of mine that I never carry out: I wanted to throw out into the street the dead man, coffin and all. In the carriage I told José Dias to shut up. At the cemetery I had to repeat the same ritual as at the house, then untie the straps, and help carry the coffin to the graveside. You can imagine how difficult it all was. Once the corpse had been lowered into the grave, they brought the shovel and quicklime; all this you know, dear reader, as you yourself will have been to more than one funeral, but what you do not know, nor can any of your friends know, nor any other stranger, is the panic that gripped me when I saw all those eyes turn toward me, the motionless feet, the attentive ears, and, after several moments of total silence, a vague whisper, inquiring voices, gestures, and someone, José Dias, saying in my ear:

"Go on, speak."

It was the speech. They wanted the speech. They were entitled to the promised speech. Mechanically, I put my hand in my pocket, pulled out the piece of paper, and stumbled my way through it, stopping and starting, missing some words, mumbling; my voice seemed to disappear inside me rather than come out, and my hands trembled. It was not only my newfound emotion that caused this, it was the text itself, the memories of my friend, my fondness for him, praise for him and his many qualities; the occasion required me to say all of this and I said it badly. At the same time, fearing that people might guess the truth, I did my best to conceal it. I think only a few people heard me, but the general reaction was one of understanding and approval. The hands that reached out to shake mine did so in solidarity. Some said: "Very fine! Well done! Magnificent!" José Dias thought my eloquence matched the solemnity of the occasion. A man, who seemed to be a journalist, asked if he could take my handwritten notes and publish them. Only my seething inner turmoil could have refused so simple a request.

Chapter CXXV / *A comparison*

PRIAM CONSIDERED HIMSELF the most cursed of men because he had kissed the hand of the man who killed his son. It is Homer who relates this, and he is a good writer, despite telling the story in verse, for there are some good stories in verse, even in bad verse. Compare Priam's situation with my own: I had just been praising the virtues of the man who had, in death, received the loving gaze of those eyes . . . Another Homer would have described my situation to much better if not equally good effect. Do not say that we lack Homers for the reason given by Camões: no, sir, we do indeed lack them, but only because the Priams of this world seek obscurity and silence. Their tears, if they shed them, are wiped away before they come through the door, so that their faces appear clear and serene; their speeches are more about joy than melancholy, and everything carries on as if Achilles had not killed Hector.*

Chapter CXXVI / *Brooding*

SOON AFTER LEAVING the cemetery, I tore up the speech and threw the pieces out of the carriage window, despite José Dias's efforts to stop me.

"It's a terrible speech," I told him. "And since I might have been tempted to allow it to be published, it's best that I destroy it now, once and for all. It's no good, worthless."

José Dias remonstrated at length, then went on to praise the funeral service, and wound up delivering a panegyric for the dead man: a great soul, a quick mind, a loyal heart, a friend, a good friend, truly deserving of the superlatively devoted wife that God had given him . . .

At this point in his oration, I let him carry on talking to himself and began to brood. My brooding became so gloomy and confused that I lost my bearings. When we reached Rua do Catete I asked the driver to stop the carriage, and told José Dias to go and fetch the ladies from Flamengo and take them home; I would go on foot.

"But—"

"I am going to pay a visit."

---

* In book XXIV of Homer's *Iliad*, Priam, king of Troy, goes to Achilles to beg him to return the mutilated body of his son Hector, killed in battle and dragged around the walls of the besieged city. Camões blamed the lack of a contemporary Virgil or Homer on the Portuguese lack of appreciation of poetry (*The Lusiads*, canto V).

The real reason was so that I could finish my brooding, and reach some sort of resolution that suited the circumstance. The carriage would travel faster than my legs; the latter might pause, or not, they could slacken their pace, stop, turn back, and let the head brood as much as it liked. So I continued, walking and brooding. I had already compared Sancha's despair that day with her gesture of the previous evening: they were irreconcilable. She was truly the most devoted of widows. And so the illusion created by my vanity evaporated completely. Might it be the same with Capitu? I carefully reexamined what I had seen: her eyes, where she had been standing, the gathering of people around her that would naturally have forced her to conceal . . . if there was anything to conceal. What appears here in a logical, deductive order had initially been a mishmash of notions and sensations, thanks to the jolting of the carriage and José Dias's interruptions. Now, however, I was thinking clearly and remembering things as they really were. I concluded, to myself, that it was my old passion that continued to blind me, and, as always, to deceive me.

By the time I reached this final conclusion, I had reached the door of the house, but turned around and walked back up Rua do Catete. Was it my doubts that tormented me, or the need to torment Capitu by returning home so late? Let's say it was both; I walked for a long time, until I felt calmer, then turned for home. As I passed a bakery, the clock struck eight.

=== Chapter CXXVII / *The barber*

NEAR OUR HOUSE there was a barber who knew me by sight and who loved to play the fiddle and didn't play altogether badly. As I was passing, he was performing some piece or other. I stopped on the sidewalk to listen (any pretext will do for a tormented heart); he saw me and continued playing. He turned away two customers who, despite it being late and a Sunday, had gone there to entrust their faces to his razor. He sent them packing without skipping a single note, and carried on playing just for me. This token of consideration induced me to go right up to the shop door and stand facing him. Behind him, pulling aside the chintz curtain that divided the shop from the living quarters, I could make out a young woman with light brown skin, wearing a pale-colored dress and a flower in her hair. It was his wife; I think she had seen me from behind the curtain and was coming to thank me, with her presence, for the kindness I was showing her husband. If I'm not mistaken, she even said so with her eyes. As for her husband, he was now playing with more passion; seeing neither his wife nor the customers, he pressed his face to the instrument, put his soul into the bow, and played and played . . .

Divine art! A group was beginning to form, so I left the shop door and carried on walking homeward. I made my way silently up the front steps. I have never forgotten that incident at the barber's, perhaps because it coincided with such a somber moment in my life, or perhaps because of this maxim, which the compilers of maxims can copy from me and put into their school compendiums. The maxim is that people are slow to forget their good deeds, and indeed never forget them at all. Poor barber! He lost two beards that night, which would have been his daily bread the following day, just to be listened to by one passerby. Now suppose this passerby, rather than leaving as I had, had stayed at the doorway to listen to him and make eyes at his wife? Ah, that is when he would have bowed and fiddled in true desperation. Divine art indeed!

Chapter CXXVIII / *A cluster of events*

AS I WAS SAYING, I made my way silently up the steps, pushed open the wrought-iron gate, which was standing ajar, and came upon Cousin Justina and José Dias playing cards in the little sitting room. Capitu got up from the settee and came over to me. Her face was now serene and pure. The others paused in their game, and together we discussed the disaster and the widow it had left behind. Capitu blamed Escobar's recklessness, and did not hide her sadness at her friend's grief. I asked her why she hadn't stayed with Sancha for the night.

"There are lots of people there; I offered to stay, but she didn't want me to. I also told her it would be better for her to come here and stay a few days with us."

"She didn't want that either?"

"No."

"I suppose the view of the sea every morning would be painful for her," pondered José Dias, "and I don't know how she'll be able—"

"Oh, it'll pass. Doesn't everything?" interrupted Cousin Justina.

Since this comment provoked an exchange of words between us, Capitu went off to see if our son was sleeping. On passing the mirror, she primped and smoothed her hair so very carefully that it might have seemed like affectation, had we not already known how very fond she was of herself. When she returned, her eyes were red with crying; she told us that on seeing our son sleeping, she had thought about Sancha's little girl, and the widow's grief. And, without a glance at our visitors, or checking to see whether there were servants present, she embraced me and told me that if I cared about her, I must, first and foremost, take good care of my life. José Dias declared this a *"most* beautiful" statement, and asked Capitu why she didn't write poetry. I tried to make light of it, and thus the evening ended.

The next day, I regretted having ripped up my speech; not that I wanted to let anyone publish it, but it was something to remind me of Escobar. I considered rewriting it, but could only remember random phrases, which when I put them together made no sense at all. I also considered writing a new one, but by then that would be hard to do, and I might be caught out by those who had heard me speak at the cemetery. As for picking up the bits of paper scattered in the street, it was too late; they would have already been swept up.

I took stock of my mementos of Escobar: some books, a bronze inkwell, an ivory cane, a bird, Capitu's album, two landscapes of his native Paraná, and a few other knickknacks. He had also received things from me. We were always swapping keepsakes and gifts, sometimes on our birthdays, sometimes for no particular reason. All of this brought tears to my eyes . . . The morning papers arrived: they gave news of the disaster and of Escobar's death, describing his upbringing and his commercial ventures, his personal qualities, the condolences of the business community; they also spoke of the possessions he had left behind, and of his wife and daughter. All this was on Monday. On Tuesday it was the reading of his will, in which I was named alternate executor, the first executor being his wife. He did not leave anything to me, but the words he had written in an accompanying letter were sublime expressions of friendship and affection. This time Capitu wept copiously, but quickly regained her composure.

The will, the inventory of possessions, it all happened almost as quickly as it has taken to describe it here. Shortly afterward, Sancha went off to live with her in-laws in Paraná.

Chapter CXXIX / *To Dona Sancha*

DEAR DONA SANCHA, I beg you not to read this book; or, if you have read as far as this, then please abandon the rest. It is enough to close the book, although better to burn it so as not to give rise to any temptation to open it again. If, despite my warning, you decide to carry on to the end, you will have only yourself to blame; I cannot accept any responsibility for the harm it may cause you. Whatever I may already have done to you, in recounting our gestures of that Saturday evening long ago, is over and done with now that events, and I with them, have given the lie to my illusions. But what is about to come cannot be erased. No, my dear friend, read no further. Carry on growing old, with neither spouse nor child, for that is what I am doing, and it is the best that can be done once youth has gone. One day, we will go from here to the gates of heaven, where we will meet again renewed, like new plants,

> *come piante novelle,*
> *rinovellate di novelle fronde.*

The rest is in Dante.*

---

* "As new trees are renewed when they bring forth new boughs," from Dante's *Purgatorio*, canto XXXIII.

240 JOAQUIM MARIA MACHADO DE ASSIS

══ Chapter CXXX / *One day . . .*

ONE DAY, CAPITU ASKED ME what was making me so silent and
irritable. And she suggested trips to Europe, Minas Gerais, or
Petrópolis, or attending a season of dances, or a thousand other
such remedies commonly prescribed for melancholy. I did not
know what to say; I turned down all such amusements. When she
persisted, I replied that business was going badly. Capitu smiled
to cheer me up. So what if business was going badly? It would go
well again soon enough, and until then we could sell off jewels
and other valuables, and we would go and live in some backstreet.
We would live peacefully and quite forgotten, and then we would
rise again. She said this with a tenderness that would have moved
stones. But not even that worked. I replied brusquely that there was
no need to sell anything. I maintained my silent, irritable stance.
She suggested we play cards or checkers, take a stroll, or pay a visit
to Rua de Matacavalos. When I rejected all of these, she went to the
drawing room, sat at the piano, and began to play; I took advantage
of her absence, fetched my hat and left the house.

. . . Forgive me, but this chapter should have been preceded by
another one, describing an incident that took place a few weeks
earlier, two months after Sancha's departure. I will write it now; I
could insert it in front of this one before sending the proofs to the
printers, but changing page numbers is very tricky. So I'll send it
as it is; after this, the narrative will follow on straight to the end.
Besides, it's very short.

≡ Chapter CXXXI / *Previous to the previous*

ONCE AGAIN, my life was sweet and placid. I was earning enough as
a lawyer, Capitu was ever more beautiful, and Ezequiel was growing up. We were now at the beginning of 1872.

"Have you noticed that Ezequiel has an odd look about the
eyes?" Capitu asked me. "I've only ever seen two people like that,
a friend of Papa's and our dear departed Escobar. Look over here,
Ezequiel! Look straight at me, yes, that's it, now turn toward Papa,
no, don't roll your eyes, like this, no, like this . . ."

It was after dinner; we were still at the table, Capitu was playing with our son, or he with her, for they were indeed very fond
of each other, but it is also true that he was even fonder of me. I
peered more closely at Ezequiel and decided Capitu was right; he
had Escobar's eyes, but that didn't seem to me at all odd. After
all, there can't be more than half a dozen facial expressions in the
world, and many similarities occur naturally. Ezequiel understood
none of this, and, bemused, looked first at Capitu and then at me
before jumping into my lap:

"Shall we go for a walk, Papa?"

"In a moment, son."

Capitu, lost in her own world, was now gazing at the other side
of the table; but when I said to her that, in terms of beauty, Ezequiel's eyes came from his mother, she smiled, nodding her head in
a way I have never seen in a woman, probably because I have never
loved another woman nearly so much. People are worth the value
of the affection we place in them, and it is from this that popular
wisdom draws the old adage, "Beauty is in the eye of the beholder."
Capitu had half a dozen gestures that were utterly unique to her.

That smile of hers went straight to my very soul. Which would explain why I rushed over to my wife and friend and covered her face with kisses. But this second incident is not strictly necessary for an understanding of the previous chapter and those that follow; let's stay with Ezequiel's eyes.

Chapter CXXXII / *Outline and coloring*

NOT ONLY HIS EYES, but his other features, his face, body, entire person, were becoming clearer as time went on. It was like a rough outline that the artist gradually fills in with shading and color, and the face begins to see, to smile, to breathe, almost to speak, until the family hangs the picture on the wall, in memory of what once was and can no longer be. Here it could be and was. Habit helped to ward off the effects of change, but change was happening, not in a theatrical way, but like a slow dawn; at first you can scarcely read a letter at all, then, gradually, you find you are able to read the letter outdoors, then indoors, in your study, without opening the windows; eventually even daylight filtering through the blinds is enough to make out the words. I read the letter, at first with difficulty and only partially, and then I began to read it in full. Of course, I tried to put it off; I stuffed the letter in my pocket, ran home, shut myself in my study, refused to open the windows, even closed my eyes. When I finally reopened my eyes and reopened the letter, the words were clear and their message even clearer.

Thus did Escobar slowly rise from the grave, from the seminary, and from Flamengo Beach to sit at my table, greet me on the stairs, kiss me in my study every morning, and ask me for the customary blessing at bedtime. All these actions repelled me; I tolerated and performed them so as not to reveal my own secret to myself and to the world. But what I could hide from the world, I could not hide from myself, for I live closer to myself than to anyone. When mother and son were not with me my despair was overwhelming, and I would swear to kill them both, sometimes suddenly, sometimes slowly, so that the time it took them to die would contain all the long minutes of suffering and deceit. But when I arrived home in the evenings and saw the young child who loved me, waiting for me at the top of the steps, I would be completely disarmed and postpone their punishment from one day to the next.

What passed between Capitu and me during those dark days shall not be revealed here, for it was so nit-picking and repetitive, and so long ago, that it cannot be told without leaving things out or wearying the reader. But the main thing can be told. And the main thing is that our storms were by now continuous and terrible. Before discovering the accursèd land of truth, we had endured other storms of short duration, but it was never long before the sky turned blue, the sun brightened, and the seas abated, and once again we would unfurl our sails that would carry us onward to the fairest coastlines and islands in the universe, until another squall upset everything, and we would batten down the hatches waiting for another clear spell, whose arrival would never be in doubt or slow in coming, but speedy, reliable, and complete.

Forgive me these metaphors; they carry a whiff of the sea and of the tide that brought death to my friend and wife's lover Escobar. They also carry a whiff of the undertow in Capitu's eyes. This is how I, ever the landlubber, choose to tell that part of my life, like a sailor telling the tale of his shipwreck.

By now all that remained between us was to say the final word; we could read it clearly and decisively in each other's eyes, and each time Ezequiel came near us this served only to drive us further apart. Capitu suggested sending him to boarding school, so that he would only come home on Saturdays; the boy found this very hard to accept.

"I want to be with you, Papa! You must go with me!" he shouted.

It was I who took him one morning, a Monday. The school was on the old Largo da Lapa, close to where we lived. I walked him there, holding him by the hand, just as I had held the other Escobar's coffin. The boy was crying and asking questions at every step, whether he would be returning home, and when, and whether I would go to see him . . .

"I will."

"No, Papa, you won't!"

"Yes, I will."

"Swear, Papa!"

"Of course."

"You haven't said that you'll swear!"

"Well, then, I swear."

And there I took him and there I left him. His temporary absence did not lessen the harm done, and all of Capitu's artful attempts to alleviate it were to no avail; I felt worse and worse. The new situation in itself added to my torment. Ezequiel was now living farther from my sight, but every time he came home on the weekend, perhaps because I was less accustomed to seeing him, or because time was marching on and completing his transformation, it meant the return of an ever livelier and more boisterous Escobar. Soon it seemed to me that even his voice sounded like Escobar's. On Saturdays I would try not to have dinner at home, and return to the house only after his bedtime. But I couldn't escape on Sundays, in my study, deep in newspapers and legal documents. Ezequiel would burst into my study, full of life and laughter and affection, for the imp was becoming fonder and fonder of me. I, to tell the truth, now felt an aversion I could barely disguise, in front of either

Capitu or the others. Not being able to hide my inner thoughts completely, I took care to avoid any encounters, or at least to see him as little as possible; either I would make sure to have work that obliged me to lock the study door, or I would leave the house on Sundays to take my secret malaise on long walks around the city and surrounding neighborhoods.

Chapter CXXXIII / *A thought*

ONE DAY—IT WAS A FRIDAY—I could bear it no longer. A certain thought that was filling me with ever more gloom unfurled its wings and began flapping about from side to side, as happens with thoughts that want to escape. The fact that this happened on a Friday was, I believe, a coincidence, but perhaps not: I had been brought up to dread that day; at home I had listened to the slaves singing laments handed down from the plantation and from the old country across the ocean, places where Friday was a day of foreboding. However, since there are no almanacs in the brain, it is likely that the thought was only flapping its wings because it felt a need to escape into the open air, into life. Life is so beautiful that even the thought of death must first come to life before it can be fulfilled. You're beginning to catch my drift; now read another chapter.

Chapter CXXXIV / *Saturday*

THE THOUGHT finally emerged from my brain. It was nighttime and I couldn't sleep, no matter how hard I tried to shake off that thought. Then again, I've never known a night to pass so quickly. Dawn broke when it seemed to me that it could only be about one or two in the morning. I left the house, assuming I had also left that thought behind, but it came with me. Outside, it was the same dark color, had the same fluttering wings, and although it was flying, it seemed to hang there motionless; I carried it fixed on my retina, and while it did not conceal external objects from view, I saw everything through that lens, looking paler than usual, and always in a hurry to leave.

I don't have a clear memory of the rest of the day. I know I wrote some letters, and I bought a substance, which I won't name so as not to arouse in anyone else the desire to try it. The pharmacy later went bankrupt, it's true; the owner became a banker, and the bank is doing well. When I found I had death in my pocket I felt as happy as if I'd just won the lottery, or even happier, because lottery prizes get spent and death is never spent. I went to my mother's house on the pretext of paying her a visit, but really to say goodbye. Whether this was real or an illusion, somehow everything there seemed better that day: my mother appeared to be less sad, Uncle Cosme had forgotten about his heart condition, Cousin Justina had forgotten her tongue. I spent an hour there in peace. I even went so far as to abandon my project. What did I need to do in order to live? Never again leave that house, or simply clasp that precious hour to my bosom . . .

Chapter CXXXV / *Othello*

I DINED OUT. In the evening, I went to the theater. They were performing *Othello,* of all things, which I had never seen or read; I knew only the plot, and relished the coincidence. I watched the Moor's great rages, and all because of a handkerchief—a simple handkerchief!—and here I offer food for thought to the psychologists of this and other continents, for I could not help noticing that a handkerchief was enough to kindle Othello's jealousy and inspire the most sublime tragedy this world has ever seen. Mere handkerchiefs have disappeared, nowadays we need whole sheets; sometimes even sheets aren't enough, and only shirts will do. Such were the muddled, murky ideas wandering about in my head as the Moor was rolling about on the ground having a fit, and Iago was dripping calumny in his ear. During the intermissions I didn't leave my seat, not wanting to run the risk of meeting anyone I knew. Almost all the ladies stayed behind in their boxes, while the men went outside to smoke. I found myself wondering whether one of these ladies might have loved someone who now lay buried in the cemetery, and there were other incoherent thoughts, too, until the curtain rose and the play continued. The last act showed me that it was not I but Capitu who should die. I heard Desdemona's pleas, her pure, loving words, and the Moor's fury, and then the death he meted out to her as the audience frantically applauded.

"And she was innocent," I said as I walked down the street. "What would the audience have done if she'd actually been guilty, as guilty as Capitu? And how then would the Moor have killed her? A pillow would not suffice; it would need blood and fire, a vast, blazing fire that would consume her entirely, and reduce her to dust, with the dust then being thrown to the winds, condemning her to eternal extinction . . ."

I wandered the streets for the rest of the night. I did have supper, it's true, almost nothing, but enough to keep me going until morning. I saw the final hours of the night and the first hours of the day, I saw the last strollers and the first sweepers, the first carriages, the first stirrings, the first streaks of daylight, a day that followed another and would see me depart and not come back. The streets I walked seemed to flee from me of their own accord. I would never again gaze upon the sea at Glória, nor the mountain peaks of Orgãos, nor the fortress of Santa Cruz or other such places. There were not as many people in the streets as there would have been on a weekday, but there were still plenty heading off to work, as they would again the next day; whereas I would never do anything again.

When I arrived home, I slowly opened the door, tiptoed inside, and went into my study; it was almost six o'clock. I took the poison from my pocket, stripped to my shirtsleeves, and wrote one more letter, the very last, addressed to Capitu. None of the others were for her; I felt the need to write her a note that would fill her with remorse for my death. I wrote two versions. The first I burned because it was too long and rambling. The second contained only the bare minimum, clear and brief. It did not remind her of our past, nor the struggles we had endured, nor the joy; it spoke only of Escobar and of the need to die.

═ Chapter CXXXVI / *The cup of coffee*

MY PLAN WAS TO WAIT for coffee, dissolve the drug in it, then drink it down. Having not entirely forgotten my Roman history, I remembered that Cato, before killing himself, had read and reread a book by Plato. I didn't have any Plato at hand, but I did have an abridged volume of Plutarch describing the life of the celebrated Roman, which would suffice to occupy me during that brief period. In order to match Cato in every respect, I lay down on the sofa. I didn't do this just to imitate him; I also needed to instill myself with his courage, just as he had needed the philosopher's reflections in order to die so fearlessly. One of the drawbacks of ignorance is not having this remedy in one's final hour. There are many folk who kill themselves without it, and expire nobly; but I'm of the opinion that a lot more people would put an end to their days if they could get their hands on the sort of intellectual cocaine that comes from good books. Nevertheless, wishing to escape any suspicion of imitation, I clearly remember that to ensure Plutarch's book was not found beside me, or that such a juicy morsel should appear in newspaper reports along with the color of the trousers I was wearing that day, I resolved to put the book back in its place before drinking the poison.

The servant brought in the coffee. I stood up, replaced the book on its shelf, and went over to the table where he had left the cup. The house was already stirring; it was time to put an end to myself. My hand trembled as I unfolded the piece of paper in which the drug was wrapped. I nevertheless had the courage to tip the powder into the cup, and I began to stir the coffee, my eyes vacant, remembering innocent Desdemona; the play from the previous night was intruding into the reality of the morning. But the photograph of

Escobar gave me the courage I was lacking; there he was, his hand resting on the back of the chair, eyes gazing into the distance . . .

"Let's be done with it," I thought.

As I was about to drink the coffee, I wondered whether it wouldn't be better to wait until Capitu and the boy went out to mass. I'd drink it later; that would be better. Having decided this, I began to pace around the study. I heard Ezequiel's voice in the hallway, then watched him come in and rush over to me, shouting:

"Papa! Papa!"

There was at this point, reader, a gesture that I will not describe, having forgotten it completely, but rest assured that it was both beautiful and tragic. Specifically, the boy's appearance made me recoil and collide with the bookshelf. Ezequiel put his arms around my knees, then stood up on tiptoe, as if wanting to be lifted up to give me his customary kiss; and, tugging at me, he said again:

"Papa! Papa!"

Chapter CXXXVII / *Second impulse*

IF I HAD NOT LOOKED at Ezequiel, I would probably not be here writing this book, because my first impulse was to rush over to the cup of coffee and drink it down. I went as far as picking up the cup, but the boy was kissing my hand, as he usually did, and the sight of him, and his gesture, filled me with another impulse I find hard to describe, but here we go, since everything must be said. Call me a murderer if you wish—I will not contest or dispute it—my second impulse was purely criminal. I leaned over and asked Ezequiel if he had already had his morning coffee.

"Yes, Papa; now I'm going to mass with Mama."

"Have another cup, just half a cup."

"What about you, Papa?"

"I'll get them to bring some more; go on, drink it!"

Ezequiel opened his mouth. I reached toward him with the cup, trembling so much I nearly spilled it, but determined to get it down his throat, even if he found the taste repellent, or the temperature, because the coffee was cold . . . I don't know what it was that I felt and that made me step back. I put the cup down on the table, and the next thing I knew I was madly kissing the boy's head.

"Papa! Papa!" exclaimed Ezequiel.

"No, no, I am not your father!"

═══ Chapter CXXXVIII / *Enter Capitu*

WHEN I RAISED MY HEAD, I saw Capitu there before me. Another scene that will seem straight out of the theater, and yet it's just as natural as the first, given that both mother and son were going to mass, and Capitu would not normally leave the house without speaking to me first. By now we only exchanged a few terse words; most of the time I didn't even look at her. She, though, always looked at me, hoping.

This time, when I saw her, I don't know if it was my eyes playing tricks on me, but her face was positively ashen. There followed one of those silences that can, without exaggeration, be described as lasting a whole century, for that is how long time feels at moments of great crisis. Capitu regained her composure; she told the boy to step outside, and asked me to explain—

"There's nothing to explain," I said.

"There is everything to explain. I don't understand why you or Ezequiel are crying. What's happened between the two of you?"

"Didn't you hear what I said to him?"

Capitu replied that she had heard crying and the sound of voices. I believe she had heard every word, but by saying so she would have lost all hope of silence and of reconciliation; for this reason, she denied hearing anything and confirmed only what she had seen. Without saying anything about the coffee, I repeated to her my words from the end of the previous chapter.

"What?" she asked as if she had misheard me.

"He is not my son."

Such was Capitu's bewilderment, and her ensuing indignation, and both so natural that even the finest eyewitnesses in our court of law would have had reason to doubt. I've heard that such witnesses can be had for all kinds of cases, and that it's just a question of money; I don't myself believe it, not least since the person who told me this had just lost a case. But whether or not there are witnesses for hire, mine was genuine; Nature itself swore by it, and I had no wish to doubt it. And so without paying the slightest attention to Capitu's words, or gestures, or the pain tormenting her, or indeed anything at all, I repeated my words twice more with such resolve that she visibly wilted before me. After several moments, she said:

"Only someone who genuinely believed that was true could make such a slanderous remark; and yet you, who were so jealous of the smallest gesture, never revealed the slightest hint of suspicion. Whatever gave you such an idea? Tell me," she said when I didn't reply, "tell me everything. After what I've just heard, I can stand to hear the rest, for there can't be much more. What happened to make you believe this now? Come on, Bentinho, speak! Talk to me! Throw me out of the house if you will, but first tell me everything."

"There are some things that cannot be said."

"No, there are some things that cannot be half said, but now that you've said half, say it all."

She had sat down on a chair beside the table. She may have been somewhat confused, but her behavior was not that of a person accused of a crime. Again, I asked her not to insist.

"No, Bentinho. Either tell me the rest, so that I can defend myself, if you think I have a defense, otherwise I will ask for an immediate separation: I can't take this anymore!"

"Oh, we will definitely separate," I replied, taking her up on her offer. "It would be best if we did it tacitly and without a fuss, each of us going our own way nursing our own wounds. However, since you insist, here is what I can say to you, and it is all there is to say."

I did not say everything, but I could scarcely allude to Escobar's adventures without mentioning his name. Capitu couldn't help but laugh, a laugh I feel unable to describe here. Then, in a tone both ironic and melancholic, she said:

"So even the dead! Not even the dead can escape your jealousy!"

She adjusted her lace shawl and stood up. She sighed, at least I think she sighed, while I, who wanted nothing more than a full explanation from her, said words to that effect. Capitu regarded me with contempt, and murmured:

"I know what lies behind this. It's their chance resemblance . . . Only the will of God can explain that . . . You laugh? Of course you do; despite the seminary, you don't believe in God. I do . . . But let's not talk about it; there's really nothing more to say."

⇒ Chapter CXXXIX / *The photograph*

I WAS GENUINELY on the verge of believing that I was the victim of a grand illusion, a lunatic's phantasmagoria, but the sudden reappearance of Ezequiel, shouting, "Mama! Mama! It's time for mass!" brought me back to reality. Involuntarily, Capitu and I both looked up at the photograph of Escobar, and then at each other. This time her confusion became pure confession. They were one and the same; somewhere there must be a photograph of Escobar as a boy that matched our own little Ezequiel. Her lips, however, confessed nothing; she repeated her last words, drew her son to her, and off they went to mass.

⇒ Chapter CXL / *Returning from church*

NOW THAT I WAS ALONE AGAIN, the natural thing would have been to snatch up the cup of coffee and drink it. Well, no; I had lost the taste for death. Death was one solution; I had just found another that was all the better for not being definitive, and left the door open to some redress, if such a thing existed. I did not say "pardon," but "redress," that is, justice. However justified it might have been, I rejected death, and awaited Capitu's return. This took longer than usual; I began to fear she might have gone to my mother's house, but she hadn't.

"I have confided all my sorrows to God," said Capitu on returning from church. "I heard a voice within me saying that our separation is necessary, and I will therefore do as you wish."

Her eyes when she said this were veiled and wary, as if she were watching for a sign of denial or delay. She was counting on my weakness or perhaps a degree of uncertainty on my part as to the boy's paternity. To no avail. Perhaps there was in me a new man, one who was only now appearing, uncovered by all those strong, new impressions. If so, that new man was only just below the surface. I told Capitu that I would think about it, and that we would do whatever I decided. In fact, I can tell you now that everything had already been decided and acted upon.

In the meantime, I had recalled the words of the late Gurgel, when on that visit to his house he had shown me the portrait of his wife, saying how alike she and Capitu were. You must remember his words; if not, go back and reread the chapter. I won't tell you the number of the chapter since I can't remember it, but it won't take you long to find. Basically, what he said was that such inexplicable resemblances do indeed exist . . . For the rest of the day, and the days that followed, Ezequiel would come and see me in my study, and the boy's features reminded me ever more clearly of Escobar's, or perhaps I was simply paying more attention. Random memories began popping into my head, vague, remote episodes, words, encounters, and incidents, everything that I, in my blindness, had failed to perceive as mischief, and which my old jealousy had missed. The time I came across them sitting in silence and alone, a secret that made me laugh, a word she uttered in a dream, all those memories came flooding back to me now, in overwhelming profusion . . . And why did I not throttle the two of them that day when I turned my gaze back from the street where two swallows were perched on the telegraph wire? Inside, my other two swallows were perched on nothing at all, gazing into each other's eyes, but so cautious that they immediately drew apart and addressed some friendly, cheerful comment to me. I told them about the pair of mating swallows outside, and they thought it amusing; Escobar said that, as far as he was concerned, it would be better if the swallows were cooked and served up on the dinner table rather than perched outside on a wire. "I've never eaten their nests," he continued, "but they must be good if the Chinese invented them." And we carried on chatting about the Chinese and all the great authors of antiquity who have written about them, while Capitu, admitting that we were boring her, went off to attend to other matters. Now I was remembering everything that at the time seemed to be nothing at all.

≡ Chapter CXLI / *The solution*

HERE'S WHAT WE DID. We picked ourselves up and went off to Europe. Not on a tourist visit, and not to see any sights, either new or old. We stopped in Switzerland. A governess from Rio Grande do Sul came with us as a companion for Capitu, and to teach Ezequiel his mother tongue; everything else he could learn in Swiss schools. With our separate lives now in order, I returned to Brazil.

After a few months, Capitu began writing me letters, to which I responded coldly and succinctly. Hers were submissive, without bitterness, sometimes affectionate, and toward the end nostalgic; she asked me to come and see her. I embarked the following year, but did not go to meet her, and later, I repeated the same voyage with the same result. On my return, her old acquaintances asked after her, and I spoke as if I had just returned from living with her; naturally, the journeys were planned with the intention of pretending precisely that and deceiving public opinion. Then one day, finally . . .

≡ Chapter CXLII / *A saint*

YOU WILL UNDERSTAND that if José Dias did not go with me on my trips to Europe, it was not for lack of willingness on his part; he stayed behind to provide company for Uncle Cosme, now almost an invalid, and my mother, who had suddenly grown old. He, too, was old, although still robust. He would come on board to say goodbye, and the words he spoke, the way he dried his tears, yes, his very eyes, were enough to move me greatly. On my final trip, he did not come aboard.

"Come . . ."

"I can't."

"Are you afraid?"

"No. I simply can't. Farewell, Bentinho. I don't know if you will see me again; I think I will leave soon for the other Europe, the eternal Europe . . ."

He did not leave immediately; my mother was the first to embark. Go to the São João Batista cemetery and look for a tomb with no name, just these two words: *A Saint*. You'll find it. Getting this inscription was not without its problems. The sculptor thought it rather odd; the superintendent of the cemetery consulted the parish priest, who advised me that saints belong on the altar and in heaven.

"Forgive me," I said, "I'm not implying that within that tomb lies a canonized saint. My intention is to use that word to convey an earthly definition of all the virtues that the deceased possessed during her lifetime. So much so that, modesty being one of them, I wish to preserve that modesty by not writing her name."

"Nevertheless, the name, parentage, dates—"

"Who will pay any attention to her dates, parentage, or even names after I'm gone?"

"You mean to say that she was a saintly lady, isn't that it?"

"Precisely. Protonotary Cabral, if he were alive, would confirm what I'm telling you."

"Nor do I disagree; I only hesitate over the choice of words. So did you know the protonotary?"

"I did. He was an exemplary priest."

"A good canonist, a good Latinist, pious and charitable," the priest added.

"And a sociable fellow too," I said. "At home I always heard he made an exceptional partner at backgammon . . ."

"He was certainly very adept with the dice!" said the priest with a sigh. "A real master with the dice!"

"So then, do you think . . . ?"

"Since there is no other meaning intended, and nor could there be, then yes, we can allow it . . ."

José Dias attended these proceedings, steeped in melancholy. At the end, as we were leaving, he complained about the priest, calling him a persnickety old fussbudget. The only excuse he could find for him, and the others at the cemetery, was that they had not known my mother.

"They didn't know her; if they had known her, they'd have told the sculptor to carve *The Very Saintliest of Saints*."

Chapter CXLIII / *The last superlative*

THIS WAS NOT JOSÉ DIAS's last superlative. There were others that aren't worth recording here, except the last one, the best and sweetest of them all, and which made his death a part of life. By then he was living with me; although my mother had left him a small bequest to remember her by, he came to tell me that, with or without the legacy, he refused to be separated from me. Perhaps he hoped to see me buried. He was corresponding with Capitu, and asked her to send him a photograph of Ezequiel; but Capitu kept putting it off from one letter to the next until he stopped asking for anything at all, save for the affections of the young student. He also asked her to keep reminding young Ezequiel of his father's and grandfather's old friend, who was "destined by heaven to love the same blood." This was his way of ensuring his place with the third generation; but death reached him before Ezequiel did. It was a brief illness. I sent for a homeopath.

"No, Bentinho," he said. "An allopath will do; death comes whatever the school of thought. Besides, those were youthful ideas that time has dissolved; I am converting to the faith of my parents. Allopathy is the Catholicism of medicine . . ."

He died serenely, after a brief final struggle. Shortly before he died, he heard someone say there was a beautiful sky that day, and he asked us to open the window.

"No, the air might be bad for you."

"How can that be? Air is life."

We opened the window. There was indeed a bright blue sky. José Dias sat up and looked outside; after several moments he let his head fall back, murmuring: *"Most* beautiful!" They were the last words he uttered upon this earth. Poor José Dias! I won't deny that I wept for him.

Chapter CXLIV / *A belated question*

I CAN ONLY HOPE that the eyes of all my friends, male and female, that I leave behind in this world will weep for me likewise, but it's unlikely. I have made myself forgotten. I live far away and seldom go out. And there is little that really connects the two ends of my life. This house in Engenho Novo, although it reproduces the one in Rua de Matacavalos, serves only to remind me of it, and more by way of comparison and reflection than sentiment. But then I've already said as much.

You will ask me why, since I had inherited the old house itself, on the same old street, I didn't stop it from being demolished, but instead came here and made a copy of it. That question should have been asked at the beginning, but here is the answer. The reason is this: Shortly after my mother died, I went to stay in the house for several days in order to make a full inspection, with the intention of moving in. The entire house turned its back on me. In the yard, the aroeira and pitanga trees, the well, the old bucket and washtubs, knew nothing of me. The casuarina tree was the same one I had left at the bottom of the yard, but its trunk, no longer straight as it had once been, now had the look of a question mark; naturally, it was taken aback at my intrusion. I surveyed the scene, searching for some thought that I had left behind there, and I found not a single one. On the contrary, the foliage began to whisper something that at first I didn't understand, and it seems it was the song of new dawns.

Accompanying this melodious, cheerful music, I could also hear the pigs grunting in a sort of concentrated, philosophical derision.

Everything was strange and hostile toward me. I let the house be knocked down, and later, when I came to Engenho Novo, I had the idea of making this copy of it by giving detailed instructions to the architect, as I have already described at the appropriate juncture.

⸻ Chapter CXLV / *The return*

IT WAS IN THIS HOUSE that one day, as I was getting dressed for breakfast, I received a visiting card bearing this name:

EZEQUIEL A. DE SANTIAGO

"Is the person still here?" I asked the servant.

"Yes, senhor. He's waiting."

I did not go to greet him straightaway; I made him wait around ten or fifteen minutes in the drawing room. Only then did it occur to me that I should show a certain enthusiasm and rush in, embrace him, say something about his mother. His mother—I don't think I've yet mentioned that she was, by then, dead and buried. She was; there she rests in venerable old Switzerland. I hurriedly finished dressing. As I left my bedroom, I adopted a paternal demeanor; somewhere between kindly and severe, half Dom Casmurro. On entering the drawing room, I encountered a young man, his back to me, looking at the bust of Masinissa painted on the wall. I approached cautiously, and made no sound. He nevertheless heard my footsteps and turned around. He recognized me from photographs and rushed toward me. I did not move; it was, no more and no less, my former young companion at the São José seminary; a little shorter, not as well built, but, apart from his rosy complexion, his face was the face of my old friend. He was wearing modern clothes, of course, and his manners were different, but his overall appearance was a re-creation of the dead man. It was the same, precise, true Escobar. It was my wife's lover; he was the son of his father. He was dressed in mourning for his mother; I was also wearing black. We sat down.

"You look no different from the last photographs I saw, Papa," he said.

The voice was the same as Escobar's, with a slight French accent. I explained that I was very much the same as before, and began to ask him questions so that I would need to speak less and could thereby control my emotions. This, however, only enlivened his face still more, and my seminary friend rose ever more visibly from the grave. There he was before me, with the same laugh, although more deference; all in all, the same charm and the same wit. He had been looking forward to seeing me. His mother had often spoken about me, praising me to an extraordinary degree as the most virtuous man on earth, and the most worthy of being loved.

"She was still beautiful in death," he concluded.

"Let's have some breakfast."

If you imagine that the breakfast was disagreeable, you are mistaken. It had its awkward moments, it's true; initially it pained me that Ezequiel was not really my son, that he was not my completion and continuation. If he had taken after his mother, I would have believed everything, all the more easily because he seemed to have left my side only yesterday, recalling scenes and words from his childhood, him being sent off to boarding school . . .

"Do you still remember, Papa, when you took me to boarding school?" he asked laughing.

"How could I forget?"

"It was in Lapa; I was utterly heartbroken, and you wouldn't stop, dragging me along, and me with my little legs . . . Oh, yes, please, sir."

He reached out his glass for the wine I was offering him, took a sip, and carried on eating. Escobar used to eat like that, too, his face almost touching the plate. He told me about his life in Europe, his studies, particularly archaeology, which was his passion. He spoke of antiquity with great enthusiasm, describing Egypt and its countless centuries without getting lost in the numbers; he had his father's head for arithmetic. Although the question of his paternity was by now familiar to me, I still did not appreciate being reminded of it. At times, I closed my eyes so as not to see his gestures or anything else, but the young rascal talked and laughed, and the dead man talked and laughed through him.

Since there was no alternative but to take the fellow in, I made myself into a real father. The idea that he might have seen a photograph of Escobar, one that Capitu might have thoughtlessly taken with her, did not occur to me, and if it had, it would not have lingered. Ezequiel believed in me, as he believed in his mother. If José Dias had been alive, he would have found him to be the very image of me. Cousin Justina wanted to see him, but, being unwell, she asked me to bring him to her. I knew my relative well. I believe her desire to see Ezequiel had, as its objective, that of confirming the outline of the young man she may have seen in the child. It would be a final pleasure; I put a stop to it at once.

"She's very ill," I told Ezequiel, who was eager to see her. "Any sort of excitement might kill her. We'll visit her when she's feeling stronger."

We didn't go; death came to her a few days later. She is resting in the Lord or some such place. Ezequiel saw her face as she lay in her coffin and did not recognize her, how could he, so changed was she by death and the passing years. On our way to the cemetery, many things brought back memories of his childhood: a street here, a tower there, a stretch of beach, and all this made him very happy. The same thing happened when he returned home each day, and he would tell me about the memories that came back to him on seeing various streets and houses. He was astonished that many of these were the same as when he had left, as if houses died young.

After six months, Ezequiel told me about a trip to Greece, Egypt, and Palestine: a scientific expedition, a promise he had made to some friends.

"Of which sex?" I asked, laughing.

He gave an embarrassed smile and replied that women were such creatures of fashion and modernity that they would never be able to understand ruins from thirty centuries ago. He was joining two pals from university. I promised to provide him with funds and gave him the first installment. I told myself that one of the consequences of his father's furtive love affair was that I would pay for his son's archaeology; I would rather pay for him to catch leprosy . . . When this thought passed through my mind, I felt so cruel and wicked that I took hold of the young man and was about to clasp him to me, but I pulled back. Then I looked him square in the face, as you would a real son; the eyes that gazed back at me were tender and grateful.

Chapter CXLVI / *There was no leprosy*

THERE WAS NO LEPROSY, but there are fevers throughout all human lands, whether ancient or modern. Eleven months later, Ezequiel died of typhoid and was buried somewhere near Jerusalem, where his two university pals erected a tomb bearing this inscription, in

Greek, taken from the prophet Ezekiel: *You were perfect in your ways.*
They sent me both texts, Greek and Latin, a drawing of the tomb,
a list of expenses, and the rest of the money he had on him; I would
have paid the amount three times over never to have set eyes on it.

Wanting to check the quotation, I consulted my Vulgate, and
found that it was correct, but that it was missing the second part:
"You were perfect in your ways, *from the day you were created.*" I
stopped and asked silently: "When was the day that Ezequiel was
created?" No one replied. Here was one more mystery to add to this
world's many others. In spite of all this, I had a good dinner and
went to the theater.

≡ Chapter CXLVII / *The retrospective exhibition*

YOU KNOW ALREADY THAT MY SOUL, even though it had been torn
to shreds, did not stay sitting in a corner like a pale and solitary
flower. I did not give it that color or the lack thereof. I lived the
best I could, and not without female friends to console me for that
first friend. Fleeting affairs, of course. It was they who left me, like
people who attend a retrospective exhibition and either get bored,
or the light in the gallery begins to fade. Only one of those visitors
kept a carriage at her door and a liveried coachman. The others
lived modestly, *calcante pede*, as the Italians say, and, if it rained, I
would call for a hansom cab and put them inside it, with effusive
farewells and even more effusive recommendations:

"You've got the catalog?"

"Yes, I've got it. Until tomorrow, then."

"Until tomorrow."

They never returned. I would stand by the front door, waiting. I would go to the street corner, look around, consult my watch, and see nothing and no one. Then, if another visitor appeared, I would give her my arm and we would go inside, where I would show her the landscapes, the historical tableaux, scenes of everyday life, a watercolor, a pastel, a gouache, and she, too, would grow weary, and leave with the catalog in her hand . . .

Chapter CXLVIII / *So, what's left?*

NOW, WHY IS IT THAT NONE of those capricious ladies made me forget my heart's first love? Perhaps because none of them had those eyes with an undertow, nor those of a gypsy, oblique and sly. But that isn't all that's left to say in this book. What's left is to know whether the Capitu of Glória Beach was already present within the Capitu of Rua de Matacavalos, or whether one was turned into the other as a result of some intervening event. Had Jesus, son of Sirach, known of my first bouts of jealousy, he would have told me, as he says in his Chapter IX, verse I: "Be not jealous of your wife lest she sets herself to deceive you with malice learned from you." But I think not, and you will agree with me; if you think back to Capitu as a child, you will recognize that one was within the other, like a fruit inside its skin.

And anyway, whatever the answer, one thing remains, and that is the sum of sums, or the residue of residues, which is that my first love and my closest friend, both of them so loving and also so beloved by me, were destined to come together and to deceive me . . . May the earth weigh lightly upon them! Now let's get started on that *History of the Suburbs.*

Biographical Note

MUCH HAS BEEN MADE of Joaquim Maria Machado de Assis's humble beginnings, and yet he, apparently, thought his own life to be of little interest and insisted that what counted was his work. Of course, in general terms, he's right, but, given his evolution from poorly educated child of impoverished parents to Brazil's greatest writer and a pillar of the establishment, a brief biographical note would not seem out of place. His paternal grandparents were mulattoes and freed slaves. His father, also a mulatto, was a painter and decorator; his mother was a washerwoman, a white Portuguese immigrant from the Azores. Both parents could read and write, which was not common among working-class people at the time.

Machado was born in 1839 and brought up for the first ten years of his life on the remnants of an old country estate perched on one of Rio's many hills, and which was owned by the widow of a senator, Maria José de Mendonça Barroso Pereira, who became his godmother. He also had a sister, who passed away at four years old.

Although he did go to school, Machado was far from being a star pupil. It seems, however, that he helped during mass at the estate's chapel, and was befriended by the priest, Father Silveira Sarmento, who may also have taught him Latin.

When he was ten years old, Machado's mother died of tuberculosis. He then moved with his father to another part of Rio, and his father remarried. Some biographers say that his stepmother, Maria Inês da Silva, looked after him, and that Machado attended classes in the girls' school where she worked as a cook. Some say that he learned French in the evenings from a French immigrant baker. Others describe Machado as showing a precocious interest in books and languages. What is certain is that he published his first sonnet in 1854, when he was fifteen, in the *Periódico dos Pobres* (the *Newspaper of the Poor*). A year later, he became a regular visitor to a rather eccentric bookshop in central Rio owned by journalist and typographer Francisco de Paula Brito, which was a popular meeting place, especially for artists and writers.

At seventeen, Machado was taken on as an apprentice typographer and proofreader at the Imprensa Nacional, where the writer Manuel Antônio de Almeida encouraged him to pursue a career in literature. Only two years later, in 1858, the poet Francisco Otaviano invited him to work as writer and editor on the *Correio Mercantil*, an important newspaper of its day. Around this time, Machado also became closely involved in Rio's theater world, writing two operas and several plays, none of which, however, met with great success.

By the time he was twenty-one, Machado was already a well-known figure in intellectual circles. He worked as a journalist on other newspapers and founded a literary circle called Arcádia Fluminense. Machado read voraciously in numerous languages—it is said that, in addition to keeping up with modern literature, he set himself the lifetime goal of reading all of the universal classics in their original language, including ancient Greek. He built up an extensive library, which he bequeathed to the Brazilian Academy of Letters (of which he was cofounder and first president). Between the ages of fifteen and thirty, he wrote prolifically: poetry, plays, librettos, short stories, and newspaper columns, as well as translations from French and Spanish, and a translation of all or most of Dickens's *Oliver Twist*. It would appear that his reported ill health, notably the epilepsy described by several of his biographers, did not in any way hold him back.

In 1867 Machado was decorated by the Emperor with the Order of the Rose, and was subsequently appointed to a position in the Ministry of Agriculture, Commerce and Public Works. He went on to become head of section, serving in that same ministry for over thirty years, until just three months before his death.

The job, although demanding, left him ample time to write, and write he did: nine novels—of which the three most celebrated are *Posthumous Memoirs of Brás Cubas* (1881), *Quincas Borba* (1891), and *Dom Casmurro* (1899)—nine plays, over two hundred stories, five collections of poems, and more than six hundred *crônicas*, or newspaper columns. He also found time to marry, his wife proving crucial both to his happiness and to the expansion of his literary knowledge. Carolina Augusta Xavier de Novais, the sister of a close friend, was five years older than Machado; they fell in love almost instantly and were soon married, in 1868, despite her family disapproving of her marrying a mulatto. Carolina was extremely well educated and introduced him to the work of many English-language writers. They did not have children but remained happily married for thirty-five years.

When Carolina died in 1904, at the age of seventy, Machado fell into a deep depression. He wrote only one novel, *Memorial de Aires*, after her death, and died in 1908. A period of official mourning was declared, and he was given a state funeral. Yet his occupation on his death certificate was given as "Civil servant," and when his final work, *Memorial de Aires*, was published later that year, it went almost unnoticed. Since then, of course, Machado has come to be seen as Brazil's greatest and most original writer, and his novels, in particular, have brought him worldwide fame.

About the Translators

MARGARET JULL COSTA has worked as a translator for over thirty years, translating the works of many Spanish and Portuguese writers, among them novelists Javier Marías, José Saramago, and Eça de Queirós, and poets Fernando Pessoa, Sophia de Mello Breyner Andresen, Mário de Sá-Carneiro, and Ana Luísa Amaral.

ROBIN PATTERSON has translated novels by José Luandino Vieira and José Luís Peixoto. With Margaret Jull Costa he has co-translated works by Machado de Assis, Sophia de Mello Breyner Andresen, Clarice Lispector, and Lúcio Cardoso.